T̶H̶

Memoirs of a Bow Street Runner
nominated by the Crime Writers Association of Canada
for the Arthur Ellis Award for Best First Novel

"Set vividly in the squalor and urgency of its time. You
will never forget Lucy." —Anne Perry, author of *Death
of a Stranger*

"This lively re-creation of Regency London before
Scotland Yard fascinates." —*Chicago Sun-Times*

"Banks depicts a Regency London as grimly fascinating
as Dickens' Victorian London in this neatly plotted
historical.... Henry Morton shines in his debut."
—*Publishers Weekly*

"An energetic, authentic historical." —*Library Journal*

"This first entry in a new series is tightly knit and
capably written. And Henry Morton—nimble of wit,
ready of fist—makes an amiable guide through fog-
bound Regency London." —*Kirkus Reviews*

"Wonderful...the narration in the book is confident, the
suspense and climax are satisfying...[T. F. Banks doesn't]
strike a single false note." —*The Vancouver Sun*

"THE THIEF-TAKER...marks the thrilling debut of
Regency London police detective Morton. History
mysteries don't get any better than this."
—*Albemarle Review*

Also by T. F. Banks

The Thief-Taker

The Emperor's Assassin

Memoirs of a
Bow Street Runner

T. F. Banks

A DELL BOOK

THE EMPEROR'S ASSASSIN
A Dell Book / June 2003

Published by
Bantam Dell
A Division of Random House, Inc.
New York, New York

ISBN 0-440-24084-0

Manufactured in the United States of America
Published simultaneously in Canada

OPM   10   9   8   7   6   5   4   3   2   1

To:
Pat Dennis
and
Shirley Russell

Acknowledgments

Many people helped in the creation of the *Memoirs of a Bow Street Runner,* with their advice and their patient reading and re-reading of manuscripts in various stages of development. Thanks go in particular to Walter and Jill at Dead Write Books in Vancouver, Brian and Rose Klinkenberg, Marie-José Tienhooven, Karen Rei Nishio, Donna Jez, Valerie and Marylou MacIntosh, Catharine Jones, Vaughn Gillson, Andrew Bartlett, June Nishio, and Kathy Beliveau. And a special bow to John Burgoyne, for his invaluable data on the noble pedigrees and persnickety temperaments of Regency-era pistols.

The
Emperor's Assassin

July 1815

＊

*The turn of the century was a time of great import in the
history of England and, indeed, the world. Twenty years
of war with the French overshadowed almost all other
events, great and small. But the summer of 1815 brought
an end at last to that bloody conflict, as the fortunes of
Napoleon Bonaparte were dashed forever on the
battlefield of Waterloo. Little more than a month later
the fallen Emperor of the French surrendered to an
obscure English sea captain, was brought aboard one of
our ships of the line and carried to England. He did not
know then, nor did we, that it was to the remote Atlantic
isle of St. Helena that he was to be sent, never to return.*

*It has, even now, been forgotten just how uncertain
the whole matter was, as Bonaparte waited aboard
H.M.S. Bellerophon in Plymouth Sound. The Cabinet
debated long into the nights, and every kind of
speculation was heard on the streets and in the clubs and
coffeehouses of London. Newspapers printed the wildest
rumours, and folk rushed to the Devon coast hoping for a
glimpse of the infamous general. All the while esteemed
jurists debated the very legality of holding the man.
Then, on the evening of August 4, the Bellerophon
unexpectedly weighed anchor and sailed out into the
Channel, taking Napoleon Bonaparte into exile.*

*How close the fallen emperor came to never leaving
Plymouth Sound is a story known only to a few.*

Henry Morton, *Memoirs of a Bow Street Runner*

Chapter 1

A gust of wind combed up the grassy knoll and fluttered the women's shawls and dresses. A quick hand preserved Arabella's hat, and she stepped behind the small windbreak afforded by Arthur Darley and his friend. She took Lord Arthur's arm as she settled into his lee.

They had not been up on Plymouth Hoe a quarter of an hour before a charter member of Darley's vast acquaintance found them. This gentleman, a captain in His Majesty's navy, bent his head toward her, the wrinkles about his eyes suggesting a smile.

"Permit me to observe, madam, that your dress is luffing. I think you've sailed too close to the wind."

Arabella smiled in spite of herself. The cheek of the man! Would he have said the same to Arthur's wife? It was a lucky thing the man possessed considerable charm. Arabella had wounded bigger men without need of a pistol or second.

She remembered her rather unfamiliar duties, suddenly, and set her gaze scurrying amongst the crowd.

And there she found Lucy, in a lather of unselfconscious delight, chasing an escaped lapdog. Before Arabella could decide if this was an acceptable activity for a young lady (for she knew little of that particular species), a movement and murmur spread down the hoe like the gasp of an audience as, on the stage, a character is murdered.

"Well, there," said Captain Colgan, lifting a hand to point, as did so many others that afternoon. "Maitland arrives at last."

"The *Billy Ruffian*!" called a young man to some of his friends nearby, and Arabella could feel the excitement of the crowd.

Still holding her hat, she ventured out of Arthur's lee and into the full force of the wind. A ship of the line rounded the eastern headland, little ant men aloft taking in sail. It was not an uncommon sight here in Plymouth Sound.

"Well, there is a bit of living history," Arthur said. "Where is Lucy? She cannot miss this."

"But what is it, pray?" Arabella asked sweetly.

"H.M.S. *Bellerophon*," Captain Colgan explained. "And aboard her the deposed Emperor of the French— or as the Admiralty has ordered he be addressed, *General* Napoleon Bonaparte."

"But was he not luxuriating happily in Tor Bay?"

"I don't know how happily, but yes." The captain took off his hat a moment and combed a hand through his thinning hair—an unconscious gesture. The hat returned to its perch. "It is not widely known," he said quietly, "but they thought he'd slipped off the *Bellerophon* a few days ago. Did you hear, Darley?"

"Just a rumour. Was he not asleep, after all?"

"Yes. Asleep in his cabin. But Maitland did not quite

believe the general's followers, and rather than send someone into the great man's cabin, he had one of the topmen shinny out to the end of the spanker boom to peer in through the stern gallery. Astonishing! It got the Admiralty thinking that Tor Bay was rather an open anchorage and that Bonaparte still had numbers of supporters at large, even in the French navy. They might try to rescue him from seaward."

Some part of the crowd had begun to make their way hurriedly toward the paths leading down to the quayside.

"Or he might slip ashore," Darley said, "and avail himself of English law."

Captain Colgan made a snorting sound—as disgusting as it was disgusted. "What fools we are made of by our own laws! Bonaparte is not an Englishman. He is our enemy, perhaps the greatest enemy we have ever known. Shoot him, say I." He glanced over at Arabella and smiled sheepishly. "Do excuse—" But he did not finish. The general movement down toward the bay suddenly became a rush, the way orderly retreats turned of an instant into routs.

Arabella was suddenly aware of an absence.

"Lucy!" Arabella called. "Lu-cy!" She was jostled just then and grabbed Arthur's arm to balance. Her hat was torn free of her amber curls and thrown up into the sky, lost in an instant among the wind and clouds and forlornly crying gulls.

The boat reeked of fish. The two men who handled it did not smell much better. Arabella sat on a thwart, holding tightly to Lucy, as though she must keep her safe in case of calamity.

"Can you swim, Mrs. M.?" Lucy asked.

"Not a stroke. And you?"

"Less than that." Lucy clung a little more tightly to Arabella's hand, all the same.

"You needn't worry yourself, miss," said the older of the two watermen. "This crabber was built in Sennen Cove by men who knew their business. She'll keep the sea when more tender boats have all run for home. There not be another one like her round these parts, and a great deal of envy she causes as a result."

Arabella couldn't believe that this battered and stinking little boat caused any envy anywhere—not even in Sennen Cove, wherever that was. She looked about the harbour. Boats of every shape and size were putting out into the sound, all drawn in one direction like leaves on a running river. She shifted on the hard plank that made her seat.

Darley's largesse and Arabella's celebrity had secured them a place in a boat, for the demand to be taken out to see the *Bellerophon*—or rather the prisoner who waited aboard—was enormous, as were the fares being asked. They were loaded in like the fisherman's greatest catch, leaving just enough room for the two watermen to work the oars.

"There are rather a lot of boats setting out, aren't there?" Arabella said, trying not to sound too apprehensive.

"Oh, aye, ma'am. They've been coming here ever since the rumour spread that Bonaparte would be carried to Plymouth." He sat up a little and looked about. "Punts and dredgers and gigs. There be draggers and drivers and luggers. You know that the trade is rich when luggers have gone over to it."

This caught Darley's interest. "And why is that?"

The leather-faced little man looked suddenly down at his hands on the oars. "Well, your grace, their trade is usually found...elsewhere."

"They're smugglers, he means," said someone else aboard, and laughed.

"Well, I expect they'll need another trade," another man said, "now that the French ports have opened again."

This caused the waterman to smile. "Oh, I think there'll always be port duties, and governments in need of such revenue. Smugglers will have employment yet."

Darley reached over and patted Lucy on the shoulder. "Don't look so frightened, child," he said warmly. "We might catch a glimpse of the Corsican, if we are lucky. You can tell your grandchildren that!"

Arabella thought Lucy was looking a little pale and at that moment cared not a fig for what she might tell her grandchildren. The ways of adults, Arabella realised, must seem a strange, unfathomable mystery to her.

As the growing fleet made its way out into the greater sound, the waves began to lift the boat, dropping it down heavily into the trough after each green crest passed. The watermen strained at their oars, the tendons in their forearms bulging, their human catch as heavy as any they had known—though far more lucrative! A wave slapped the topsides and sprayed the occupants, scaring Lucy even more. Arabella put an arm about her, but the boat surged and rolled a little, throwing them to one side.

"The breakwater will do away with this slop," the older waterman managed. "I'll be glad when 'tis built."

"Wind's going light," his young partner offered. "Be calm by dark."

But it was not calm at the moment, or dry.

"I wish Mr. Morton were here," Lucy said.

"Yes, wouldn't he love to see this?"

"I'm sure he told me that he could swim," Lucy said, and both Arabella and Darley laughed.

Arabella tried to concentrate on the scene, to paint it into her memory. There were a good number of ships in the harbour: a few large three-deckers like the *Bellerophon* and many smaller craft—frigates and schooners and sloops, she guessed. There seemed to be a constant coming and going of small craft to the ships, but now even their boatmen forgot their business and slowed to watch.

Arabella could not believe the number of boats that had gathered about the *Bellerophon* in so short a time. The old warship looked like a great castle rising above the clutter of its dependent village.

As each wave passed, the throng of bobbing vessels seemed to undulate like a rope being snapped ever so slowly, and Arabella could hear them banging and thumping together and the watermen cursing and calling out for room. A pair of navy cutters circled the *Bellerophon*, trying to enforce a circle of clear water around the ship.

As the hired crabber made its way into the pack of boats, Arabella grabbed the gunwale.

"Oh, don't do that, ma'am!" the waterman said, dropping an oar to reach for her hand. She pulled it in herself. "You could lose a finger should we thump against one of these others."

He took up his oar again, looking anxiously over his shoulder. They came up between two other boats, one larger and the other about the same size as their own. As more and more boats began to crowd around the ship, the smaller boats were forced together, where they ground and thudded dully against one another. The watermen were busy trying to keep their sturdy craft from ruin, and Arabella was so unsettled, she barely remembered to look at the ship.

"Tide turned some while ago," the waterman said. "That'll make the difference. Wind against tide's the cause of this."

And then, as though he'd said some magic words, the sea did begin to calm and in the span of half an hour grew almost placid. People began to call out then, impatient, impolite.

After a time, however, a sailor came up from a hatch amidships and held aloft a hand-printed sign. Arabella saw Lucy scan it eagerly—the hunger for words was elemental in her. The sign read:

DINING WITH CAPTAIN MAITLAND

A murmur of interest and approbation ran through the watchers. After an interval the sailor turned the sign over.

BEEFSTEAK. PEAS. MADEIRA.

Heads nodded amongst the throng, and there were sounds of satisfaction. The sailor lowered his sign, made a brief bow, and went over to the other side to perform the same service for the people there.

"Do French people also drink tea?" Lucy wondered aloud.

"French people with no choice do," Darley answered.

A big lugger arrived from shore with some musicians in it, and they began to strike up, behind and to the left of where Arabella and Lucy's boat lay in the bobbing host. It was a small band, admittedly, and none too tuneful, but a band nonetheless. There was a fife, a fiddle, a cornet, and a snare drum. The players stood in their boat to perform—rather precariously, Arabella thought—and bowed after each of their ragged efforts. They were applauded. Coins were tossed, some of which were fumbled and fell into the sea.

Arabella imagined them drifting slowly down, down, among the fishes, as she would herself if this damnable boat overtipped.

At the end of each piece, all eyes turned to the decks of the *Bellerophon*, high above. But nothing stirred there. The sailors listened impassively. Then presently the cutter rounded beneath the jib boom, and the officer in the bow started shouting in a high, angry voice, calling for them to draw back, stand away. With a clumsy splashing and thumping of wood on wood, the closest boats attempted to comply but were hemmed in too tightly to move far. The rest of the watermen simply ignored the orders.

"Ho, there!" Someone in the next boat called over to the players. "Here's Mrs. Malibrant, of Drury Lane! Ask her to sing a song."

There was a general murmur in the nearby boats, heads turning, people shifting so that boats rolled precariously. There was even a bit of clapping, and the musicians swivelled in their own boat, and in Arabella's direction. Along the *Bellerophon*'s rail the sailors also languidly turned to look.

Inwardly, Arabella sighed, but she knew that the celebrated Mrs. Malibrant had not achieved her eminence by playing too coy. She gave her most brilliant smile and acknowledged her public with a small regal wave of one gloved hand. Voices began importuning her now from many quarters.

"An air, ma'am!"

"A song, Mrs. M.! He'll not be able to resist *you*!"

Arabella glanced down at Darley and made a face as if to say, *Do you see? My fame pursues me even here.*

"Give him a tune of the sort he'll like!" a young man suggested, which struck Arabella.

She let the demands mount just to the point she judged they might begin to falter and then, at that peak, put her shawl aside with a decisive movement and rose in her place. Cheers burst out from all sides, then settled quickly in expectation.

She did not immediately begin to sing, however. She arranged her pose with care, one foot forward in the bottom of the boat: an imposing figure, all in white silks. She raised one arm slightly in a dramatic gesture, though not too dramatic. The musicians likewise lifted their instruments, leaning forward in anticipation. She did not tell them what she would sing, not wanting to spoil the effect.

The famous melody announced itself, her rich, carrying contralto suddenly rising over the hushed audience.

> *"Allons enfants de la Patrie*
> *Le jour de gloire est arrivé!"*

"*La Marseillaise!*" someone realised.

"This is England!" a solitary voice shouted. "We'll not have their bloody anthem *here*!" But this voice of passion was ignored.

The ragtag band took up the tune uncertainly, and she waved her hand to encourage them and give them the proper beat.

"Ils viennent jusque dans vos bras!
Egorger vos fils, vos compagnes!"

Arabella cast back in her memory for an English
translation, and her voice rose in stirring fashion for the
chorus.

"Citizens! To arms!
Form battalions!
March on, march on!
Let their impure blood
Nourish our sacred ground!"

Whether it was the undeniable power of her performance or some other reason, now suddenly there was a
flurry of activity high up on deck of the man-of-war.
Then the sailors fore and aft all at once began taking
their hats off.

"He's coming up! That means he's coming up!" cried
a voice from one of the boats.

Arabella Malibrant turned toward the ship, even as
she continued to sing. She lowered her arm and let her
voice subside a little into the thumping of the band.
There were times, after all, when one allowed oneself to
be upstaged. Lucy, too, rose to stand on the thwart beside her. All around people were getting to their feet,
craning their heads and shading their eyes against the
afternoon sun, while some of the boats started making
convulsive efforts to get closer, causing the whole mass
to buckle and heave.

"Take care! Hold off, there!"

A woman's shriek. And then suddenly the loud report
of a ship's gun from above, trying to warn them back,
and near bedlam in the boats, more screams and cries,

startled people stumbling and falling. The music fal-
tered and stopped. The second cutter was coming
round, its crew bawling. There was a collision, and craft
on all sides rocked and bumped wildly, causing even
more people to topple. A woman's face rose from a tumble of her fellow passengers, her nose bloodied. Arabella
kept her feet, barely, lurching and steadying herself on
the shoulder of the man in front of her. Lucy tumbled
back into the bit of water slopping about the bottom of
the boat, then scrabbled desperately to get up again.

Just ahead of them people were shouting and struggling. Near the cutter a boat had capsized. There were
people in the water, thrashing desperately, and many
voices were calling out angrily for someone to do something.

"There! There! Reach an oar!"

The sailors above hollered and pointed. Spotting a
thrashing woman whose face was barely above the
rolling surface, Arabella added her voice to the cry.
"Seize hold of her! Seize hold of her dress! She's going
under!"

The cutter was trying to come round and return to
the place where it had struck the smaller boat, but it
could make no headway against the confused mass. A
man leapt into the sea, and a knotted rope splashed into
the water just beyond the woman's reach.

She gave a last frenzied flail to reach an oar someone
held out and went under as though pulled down from
below. There was a stunned silence, everyone staring as
though they expected her to reappear. And then a child
began to scream and cry and beat her fists upon the gunwale.

Lucy put her arms awkwardly about Arabella's
waist, and the actress reached out and pulled her close.

Darley looked back at her, his dignified manner fallen away, three fingers laid alongside his nose. Arabella thought he might offer the poor woman a tear. People murmured and cried.

Then, in quite different tones, someone else called out.

"*Look!* There he is!" All eyes turned upward again.

From the quarterdeck, gazing down at them imperturbably. The small, stout figure. The famous profile. The cockaded hat.

The genius of sixty battlefields. The man who'd had all Europe at his feet.

"*That* can't be him," someone nearby said.

But it was.

And then, from beyond the horrified circle that had witnessed the tragedy, a familiar sound. Slowly at first, uncertain, then with growing conviction, the English began to *applaud*. The sound seemed to course down the line of boats, like a rolling barrage.

Darley, however, had not even raised his eyes to the deck. His gaze was still fixed on the lapping waters, the unconsolable child. "May that be the last death to be laid at his feet," he said softly, as though it were a prayer.

Chapter 2

The dead woman lay draped in a sheet, once white, blemished now with faint smears of brown and sickly yellow. Henry Morton stood in the doorway of the dimly lighted surgery, gazing at the familiar shape beneath its blank covering.

As though beneath a fall of snow, he thought suddenly.

The place unsettled him, a man not unused to death. On a small table the surgeon's instruments lay: a darkly stained tourniquet, several knives of differing sizes, a bone saw with a fringe of pale pink flesh still caught in its teeth. The smell of the slaughterhouse could be detected here—faintly, but still there—and Morton was instinctively repelled by it. He cleared his throat.

"Death by misadventure, Presley told me," offered Morton. "Perhaps a self-murder."

The surgeon, Skelton, continued writing at his stand. His beadle had shown the Runner in a moment before, even announcing Morton's name, but the surgeon apparently had not heard.

"Is that what Mr. Presley said?" The man did not look up; the sound of his pen, scratching over the surface of the paper, continued.

Morton rocked back on his heels, trying to calm his impatience. Skelton was an eccentric man, but the Runner had deep respect for his skills and was willing to wait at least a short while to find out why he'd been summoned.

Around Bow Street Skelton had acquired the moniker "Skeleton," and one look at the ungainly surgeon was all the explanation this required. Morton had never seen a man of apparent good health so bony and angular. The surgeon removed a pair of spectacles, returned the pen to its stand, stared down at the paper on which he'd been writing, and sighed. He looked up at Morton and offered an unhappy smile.

"Let us look at the sad evidence of this act," he said.

He walked stiffly over the sawdust floor to the table upon which the body lay, and very softly set a hand upon the thigh, as though on familiar, indeed intimate terms with this cadaver. "Presley told you what he found?"

"Only that she was discovered in a little played-out sand pit, dead upon the rocks there, as though she had cast herself from the rim above."

"Yes, though whether she threw herself upon the rocks is difficult to say." Skelton put the curve of one spectacle arm between his lips, his gaze losing focus for an instant. "I wonder, in truth, if she cast herself upon those rocks at all. I wonder if she even met her end where she was found." He looked down at the covered form. "Certainly she might have died as a result of a fall—her injuries would not contradict it. But there is more, Mr. Morton." He pulled back the covering, revealing the unclothed corpse. Morton shut his eyes for a second. The skin had lost its plasticity, its life, and was dull, almost grey. The lips had pulled back, exposing the teeth. Upon her forehead was a wound, oddly concave. Only the hair still looked as Morton guessed it once had—honey coloured, fine, lustrous in the dull light.

"You see this contusion upon her skull? 'Twas this did her in. But look here." He pointed closely at the upper arm. "Do you see the bruising? And here on the other side..." He turned the arm a little, though it resisted stiffly. "Those are the marks of someone's fingers. She was restrained or held by someone—someone stronger than she."

"Well," Morton whispered.

"But there is more," Skelton said. "Upon her left arm you will find identical marks, or nearly so, suggesting that she was held from behind."

"Or held and then pushed."

The surgeon nodded.

"But look at this, Mr. Morton." He turned her hand. A dark welt encircled the narrow wrist.

"Her hand was bound."

"So I would say, though it was not when she was found." The surgeon bent down awkwardly and replaced his spectacles. "And look further. Here, upon her thumb."

Morton crouched down so that he might see. The smell of the cadaver repelled him, but he bent his head near and tried not to breathe. The thumb was dusky blue, as though terribly bruised.

"Did she put out her hands as she fell?" Morton wondered.

"You might expect that, but there is no other sign of

it." The two men crouched, their faces but a few inches apart. Morton could smell the man's sour breath.

Skelton continued his lecture. "Do you see the way the nail has come away and is deformed? And beneath it the quick is almost pitted?"

"And what caused this, pray?" Morton asked softly.

"I have only seen it once before, Mr. Morton, in the soldiers' hospital at Greenwich. What is particular is the rounded compression marks on the top and bottom of the digit. They are the signatures of the device that caused it. And the device that caused it, upon the testimony of the man who'd endured its ministrations whilst in the hands of our king's continental enemies, was the thumbscrew."

Morton stood up. "The thumbscrew! Are you certain? Without doubt?"

The surgeon too had straightened himself, and now he nodded solemnly. "I do not think Mr. Presley's verdict of self-murder will stand, unless she self-tortured, too."

"Tortured," Morton said, trying the word to see if it had weight, if it rang false in this room where certain matters were never in doubt—you were among the living or you were among the dead.

"Mr. Presley assured me that there was little or no blood found upon the stones where she was discovered, yet I believe she suffered substantial loss of blood from her nose, which was badly broken, the vessels ruptured."

Morton waved a hand at the body. "She was not found thus? Where are her clothes?"

Skelton crossed the room and from a shelf of shadowy bottles retrieved a mass of neatly folded clothing wrapped, but not tied, in brown paper. He presented this to the Runner, who began to go through the bundle carefully.

"Well, she did not live among the poor," Morton said.

"Nor did she die among them, it would seem. But who she might have been, among the living, is beyond my skills to tell."

"How old do you think she was?"

The surgeon looked thoughtfully over at the body of the dead woman. "Perhaps five and twenty. She had never borne children, I should guess."

"Is there anything more that you might tell me?"

"She stood five foot five inches, weighed eight and one half stone or thereabouts ... and was very beautiful when she was alive." He said this last wistfully.

Morton glanced first at the surgeon and then at the body. How the man would guess that, he did not know. Perhaps he had spent too much time among the dead.

"I will take these," Morton said, holding up the articles of clothing.

Skelton nodded. He crossed the few paces and covered the body, so again it looked like a sleeper adrift in snow.

Morton began to wrap the clothes in paper.

"You'll send your conclusions to Sir Nathaniel?"

"I will, yes," the surgeon answered.

Morton offered a perfunctory bow, but as he turned toward the door, the surgeon spoke.

"Mr. Morton? When, exactly, did the criminals of London begin torturing ladies of quality?"

Morton turned back to the man, who stood by the draped body, the light haloing his thinning hair.

"It is, Mr. Skelton, the strangest thing I have seen in my years as a Runner. I don't know what is worse: to think that someone might commit such a horror for ...

pleasure; or that another wanted something of this woman so desperately that they would buy it from her with agony. And if the latter is true—what was it that she knew or possessed, a woman so young and lovely as you imagine?"

The surgeon shook his head, his bony shoulders dropping.

"No, Mr. Skelton, we do not know," Morton agreed quietly. "But I assure you we will find it out."

It was but a short walk from the surgeon's rooms in Hart Street to the Drury Lane Theatre, where Arabella Malibrant was rehearsing her new play. Morton's man, Wilkes, had brought him an affectionate note from the actress that very morning saying she had returned from delivering her charge to Plymouth and was most anxious for a visit. His own note in answer had suggested they meet that evening, but he was about to look far more ardent than his note had suggested.

He was let into the back of the theatre and found his way through the flats and other props leaned here and there against the wall. Men were at work painting a backdrop, and actors lounged around gossiping, awaiting their scene.

Arabella he found in her rightful place—centre stage. She was there without makeup, of course, and the dim lamps made her fair complexion seem darker, almost exotic. She was dressing down a player in commanding style, and it took a moment for Morton to realise that she was not actually acting. Whatever this poor unfortunate had done, he looked as though he regretted it more than a little. Other actors stood about the stage, some embarrassed, others not hiding their great amusement.

The man whom Morton took to be the director stood in-effectually at the foot of the stage, attempting occasionally to interrupt the eloquent flow of Arabella's invective.

When she had finished—with a flourish, Morton thought—she swept up her skirts and exited the stage, as haughty as any queen.

"Morton!" she said as she came upon the Runner, and her manner changed of an instant. A light kiss she left on his cheek, and then she took his hand, leading him off to her dressing cabinet. And there, among her costumes and indifferently arranged powders and creams, she gave him a kiss that was more passionate and more joyful. She pulled back, a little breathless, her arms still about his neck.

"If you had come but a moment sooner, Henry, you could have challenged one of the company to a duel to defend my honour."

"I cannot believe you would need me to deal with such a matter," Morton said, as delighted to see her as she him.

"No, I suppose not. He will be gone when I return, anyway. The manager will not keep anyone who displeases me so."

"What did this poor cully do, pray?"

"Only was too free with his hands as we rehearsed our love scene." She sniffed, then wrinkled up her nose. "What is that dreadful odour, Morton?"

They disengaged.

"I have been visiting a poor woman who was no longer of this world. Her clothes, which I have with me, have retained a bit of the odour of—"

"And just what were you planning to do with a dead woman's clothes, if I dare ask?"

"Show them to you," Morton said, unwrapping the bundle.

Arabella made a face. "Well, I have seen them. Now take them away."

"I was hoping you might look a little more closely. These clothes are the only indication we have of who this poor woman might have been."

This piqued Arabella's interest, Morton could see. She brushed back an errant strand of luxurious red hair and took a step nearer.

"Are these not of some foreign fashion?" Morton asked.

"French," Arabella pronounced. She took up the pelisse and held it to the light. "And very finely made."

"And where would one purchase such clothing, I wonder?"

"Not from any woman's clothier. These were tailored for whomever wore them. I will find out," Arabella said confidently, and wrapped the clothes up tightly, tying the bundle with a bit of string. She turned back to Morton. "I might even be able to tell you something this evening. Arthur hopes that you will come by. And if you are terribly attentive and kind to me this evening, you might escort me home."

"I shall do all within my power to win your favour," Morton said seriously.

Arabella frowned. "But all men do that," she said. "You must do better than they."

Chapter 3

"Thumbscrews!"

Henry Morton nodded. He sat opposite Sir Nathaniel Conant, the Bow Street Chief Magistrate, in his book-lined office. He had really come here looking for Jimmy Presley, to ask him some questions about the nameless woman who now lay in Skelton's surgery, but he had been asked to attend the "Beak."

"Mr. Skelton is certain? Beyond doubt?"

"I believe he is, Sir Nathaniel."

The Magistrate gave a visible little shiver. Morton's respect for his superior had grown in last month's business about the corrupt Runner George Vaughan. Sir Nathaniel's moral compass was certain.

The Public Office's most celebrated police man, John Townsend, sat to Morton's right, listening quietly.

"And you don't know who this woman might be?" the old Runner asked, his deep, smoky voice echoing in the small chamber.

"I hope that I shall know soon. Her clothing was distinctive. It is very possible that it was French."

Sir Nathaniel stirred his bulky person uncomfortably in his chair. "Is she a citizen of France, do you think?"

"Many people have a partiality for things French, Sir Nathaniel."

"Of course." He splayed a large-knuckled hand across the blotter on his desk. "Why in the world would anyone apply a thumbscrew to this woman? What had she done?"

"What did she know, is the question I would ask," John Townsend said, and then continued, with that bland and oblivious pedantry of his that to Morton always sounded faintly ironic: "The thumbscrew is a small iron implement that compresses the digit for which it is named between two hard surfaces. Why the thumb? Because it is bigger and more convenient than the other fingers. The flesh below the protective nail on any digit is far and away the most sensitive part of a human body, so this is done for only one purpose—to cause pain of such intensity that one will tell all, betray a brother or even a lover. It is a terrible device, and the men who applied it are either desperate or monstrous. I do not know which I would hope for."

Sir Nathaniel continued to stare at his hand on the desk, then picked up a quill. "Didn't Presley fetch the body in? If you feel the need, Mr. Morton, employ young Presley. I should like some answers in this matter as soon as may be." He nodded to the Runners, who rose and left.

In the antechamber outside, Morton touched his old friend on the shoulder before he could take his leave.

"You had more to say, I think, Mr. Townsend," Morton ventured.

The venerable old Runner paused to think, rooting about in his frock coat for his snuff and examining his younger colleague as he did. "I will tell you this, Morton—you are beyond the realm of common crime now. Torture is imposed for reasons either of religion or of state. The Spanish Inquisition is a thing of the past. You have entered the world of politics, I would say."

Morton nodded slowly, trying to take it in. He respected Townsend immeasurably. The little man's mannerisms were impossibly eccentric, and some of their younger colleagues snickered behind his back. But Morton knew his worth and knew just how discreetly successful this odd old dandy had been. Townsend was an intimate of the highest circles in London, a friend and servant of the Prince Regent himself, and he had been quietly putting away his ample reward monies for more than five decades. He could probably buy up Sir Nathaniel and the whole lot of them, if he so chose. When he spoke in serious tones, as he did now, Morton listened.

"The world of politics is a different and more dangerous world altogether." Townsend paused and nodded, as if to himself. "Your common London malefactor will not give his life for a cause. No, he will preserve his life at all costs, and we Runners have come to depend on that. Knowing this tells us a great deal about what a criminal will do and what he will not. The world you enter now has different rules. Men who have been afflicted with the madness of politics might choose to take your life at the cost of their own, just to preserve their cause." He met Morton's eye. "Be wary, sir. I know I have cautioned you before in different circumstances, but mark what I say: none of those situations were as dangerous as this."

Chapter 4

Morton arrived at Portman House, Lord
Arthur Darley's elegant West End home, at
the hour of ten o'clock in the evening. It was
a house that Morton could never dream of possessing,
and one that he admired more than he cared to admit. In
truth, Lord Arthur was a man Morton envied, and envy,
he well knew, was not the healthiest of human emotions.
It was fortunate that Morton's envy was leavened by a
strong liking and respect. Darley was a man of such
enormous charm that Morton could hardly waste a moment resenting him. Even their peculiar understanding
about the lovely and broad-minded Mrs. Arabella
Malibrant did not spoil his liking of Darley.

A liveried servant let him in and took his top hat. It
was a warm, humid July night, and the coolness of the
house was welcome. A smiling Darley appeared before
Morton had been led across the entry. He was a pleasant, greying gentleman, impeccably dressed but somehow as relaxed as a man out for a country walk with his
gun and hounds.

"Morton! It is so good of you to come. Please"—he gestured toward a door—"Mrs. Malibrant awaits. She tells me that she is an acting Bow Street Runner and has all manner of news for you."

"I said no such thing," Arabella protested as they entered the small withdrawing room that looked out on the garden.

"Well, perhaps you can explain better than I," Darley said.

Morton kissed Arabella's hand, took an offered glass of port, and sank into one of Darley's comfortable chairs.

Darley raised his glass in silent salute. "We were, to be fair to Mrs. M., discussing the bit of history we witnessed whilst delivering Lucy to her new school."

Arabella's face, slightly flushed, lit like a candle. "You will not believe it, Henry," she said.

"You saw Bonaparte," Morton offered.

Arabella sat back in her chair, a bit deflated.

"It's in all the papers," Morton apologised.

"Surely even the London papers have not begun reporting *all* my activities," Arabella said. It was one of the charms of her particular humour that she could say anything without a hint of a smile. People who did not know her often couldn't decide if they were to laugh.

Morton smiled. "You really saw the scoundrel?"

"Indeed we did," Darley said. "Large as life, or small as life in the Corsican's case. He appeared on the deck of the *Bellerophon* in the company of Captain Maitland, I believe. There was a great row—"

"And a woman was drowned!" Arabella interjected.

Darley nodded, the quiet satisfaction that he habitually displayed dissolving into a look of utter desolation. "Yes, very sad. With her child looking on."

Morton found himself affected by Lord Arthur's sudden show of feeling for a woman he certainly did not know. But then Darley shook it off and smiled at his guests, his eyes glistening just noticeably.

"And what will they do with him, do you think— Bonaparte?" Morton asked softly, trying gently to steer the conversation away.

Darley shrugged. "It is the subject of intense debate, I can tell you, though little more."

"He knows more than he is saying," Arabella stage-whispered to Morton.

Darley's playful smile returned. "If I knew half as much as you believe, my dear, I would be the best-informed man in England."

"The papers say that Bonaparte wants to live quietly in England." Morton sipped his port.

Darley laughed. "Well, you can be sure that will not be allowed. No, he will be transported—somewhere remote, I think."

"But why not imprison him here?" Arabella asked. "Would that not be the safest course?"

Darley turned to her, shifting in his chair. "Undoubtedly, but there is a small matter of English common law. You see, according to our own laws, no man, no matter his nationality, can be imprisoned without first being convicted of a crime by a court of law. And it is very doubtful that Bonaparte could be so convicted under our present laws."

"Even though he has made war against us for twenty years?" Arabella said.

"Oddly, war is not a crime. Bonaparte was the head of a foreign state."

"Then we can do nothing to him?" Arabella looked a little disgusted by this foolishness.

Darley held up a finger. "Ah, but that is the very centre of the debate. Bonaparte is not on English soil. Not really in England, or so His Majesty's government claims. He is, at present, subject to the law of the Admiralty—which is very different from the laws that govern you and me, as Mr. Morton will no doubt tell you."

Morton leaned forward in his chair. "But I have read that some, even prominent men of law, say that the government's argument is fallacious. That I, for instance, could arrest a man on a ship in Plymouth harbour with every expectation that he would go to trial. Various authorities claim that the government considers Plymouth Sound part of England at their convenience, but at the moment it is not convenient, so they have excluded that bit of water from our borders."

"But the argument is even more specific than that." Darley was clearly fascinated by this debate. "The government claims that the *ships* of the Royal Navy are excluded from the laws of England, whether in an English harbour or not. And certainly Mr. Morton could not go aboard the *Bellerophon* and arrest a man, even a murderer. The navy have their own courts and due process. And upon this fact lies the government's case." Darley waved a hand in the general direction of Cornwall. "Bonaparte, of course, wants to be allowed ashore. He wants—I daresay, even expects—the protection of English law. But I do not think he shall have it. No, our deposed emperor shall be sent off to some remote place to live out his days under guard."

"But can we even do that?" Morton wondered aloud. "We return prisoners of war to their country of origin once the war is concluded. Should we not do the same with Bonaparte?"

"The French don't want him. Are afraid of having

him in the country, in fact. But it is an interesting argument. I should point out, however, that the war with France was already over when Bonaparte surrendered to Captain Maitland."

"Well, if he is not a prisoner of war," Arabella said, "then what is he?" She was clearly less interested than their host in the finer points of law.

"Exactly, my dear. What is he indeed, legally speaking? And do the Admiralty have the right to send him off to some outpost to spend the rest of his days? The security of the nation might so be served, though justice might not. Even so, I think Bonaparte will be sent off—it is only a matter of deciding where."

"Let his exile not be too comfortable, I say," Arabella offered with feeling.

"For a man such as Bonaparte," Darley said, and his smile disappeared again, "I think any place of exile would be a torture, were it as comfortable as man's ingenuity could make it."

Morton did see Arabella home, although until they had entered the hackney-coach, the issue had been far from certain, at least in the Runner's mind. Darley, of course, said good night to them as though not a thing were amiss, as though they were two of his dearest friends in the world—an actress and a Bow Street Runner. As though sending one's mistress home with another man were not at all unusual.

"He is a mystery to me, your friend Darley," Morton said.

Arabella had been lost in some other path of thought, but she glanced over at Morton now with her lovely green eyes, dark in the shadowy coach.

"He is not really such a mystery if you give up your expectations of a man in his position. Arthur cares nothing for the approval of others, and he is utterly discreet—you can tell him anything and it will go no farther—and so he is approved by everyone. Yes, his association is not what one might expect, too many writers, and even journalists and actresses, but for that he is admired for his independence of mind. Darley's genius is that he can take the measure of others—perfectly—and then reveal only what he wishes them to see.

"When first we met, he did not realise how carefully I observed human nature: a requirement of my calling. Darley thought he would confound me as he did all the others." Arabella laughed softly. She leaned her head against Morton's shoulder, as though suddenly tired from her long day of observing mankind. "He sees you, Henry Morton, for what you are—and do not think he is the least mistaken on that score. He sees that you are a man of great integrity and uncommon dedication to the concept of justice. That you are loyal to your friends and colleagues, yet sympathetic to the less fortunate. He also sees your great desire to be considered a gentleman. What you do fascinates him—solving great puzzles—and he is oddly attracted to the danger, and the base and disreputable world in which you walk, for in his life he has known only comfort and safety. Darley is not such a mystery. He is a little bored with his coddled existence. If he could accompany you as you prowl the flash houses looking for miscreants, he would do so in a second. You see, Henry, your life looks to him very . . . rich."

"Rich? I wish I could say it were so!"

"Well, it is rich, though not in silver." She sat up and met his eyes, a smile of triumph spreading over her face. "But I have not told you about the clothes! I have found the woman who made them, or at least have her name and instructions to find her. We might go see her tomorrow before I attend the theatre."

"Give her address to me, and I will go," Morton said.

"I will not hear of it. You will need a lady along to relieve the woman's apprehensions. And besides, she is French, and you know my French is so much better than yours."

In fact Arabella's French was not nearly as good as she believed—certainly not as good as his. But she was clearly so pleased with herself, and Morton so wanted to please her at that moment, that he smiled in acquiescence. Arabella leaned forward and kissed him, at once passionately and tenderly.

"You must come up, Henry. It has been too many days since I have had your company. I will feed you in the morning, and we may go off together to see the dressmaker. You shall have your mystery solved by noon, and then you may see me to the theatre and thank me as I deserve."

Morton encircled her in his arms and pulled her close. "My dear," he murmured, "that sounds like a perfect world."

Chapter 5

The dressmaker, Madame Madeleine De le Cœur, plied her trade from the back of a milliner's shop in Oxford Street. Morton wondered who her clientele might be: expatriate French noblewomen, most likely. But what would become of her now, Morton did not know. With the restoration of Louis XVIII, the French nobility were returning to France; many had already gone. Perhaps, like a camp follower, she too would soon be on her way.

They found Madame De le Cœur in a large workroom where high windows let the morning sun angle in, setting the dust motes to dancing. She was examining the work of her dozen seamstresses, holding spectacles in one hand. A handsome if severe-looking woman, she was thin, grey of hair, and surprisingly plainly dressed.

The young woman who had shown them into the workroom cleared her throat quietly and said, *"Maman?"*

"Oui?" Madame De le Cœur said, not raising her eyes from the stitching she examined.

"Madame Arabella Malibrant of Drury Lane to see you. And Monsieur Henry Morton...of Bow Street."

The woman turned and stared at Morton as though he were some urchin found thieving her wares. "Bow Street," she pronounced with little accent. "And to what do I owe this pleasure?"

Before Morton could answer, Arabella stepped forward.

"Madame Beliveau gave me your name," Arabella said.

The severity of Madame De le Cœur's countenance was erased by a smile. "Ah, *oui,* and how is my old friend?"

"She is well and sends her regards."

The woman dipped her head modestly as though receiving a compliment.

"And what is it that brings you here, Madame Malibran'? Shall I make you a gown so to meet the Prince Regent in style?"

"I should be pleased beyond measure to have one of your gowns, madame, but today we are on other business." Arabella set the package of clothes on a work table and unwrapped it. "We are trying to discover the identity of the woman who owned these beautiful clothes. Madame Beliveau said that only you could have made them."

Madame De le Cœur raised her spectacles but kept her other arm crossed over her bosom, as though unwilling to touch something so repugnant as another's clothing.

"And why you want to know this?" she asked, and Morton thought she looked suddenly shaken.

"A woman was found dressed in these clothes,

madame," Morton said, "and that woman was dead. We do not know her name."

Madame De le Cœur put out her hand to a table, her eyes closing. Her daughter was at her side almost immediately, and a member of her staff quickly brought forward a chair so that she might sit.

She wept softly, not sobbing or crying out. Just a silent stream of tears and a look of complete wretchedness upon her handsome face.

Morton stood silently by.

"Perhaps, monsieur—" the daughter began.

"Non," Madame De le Cœur said. " 'Ow did this 'appen?" she managed, her perfect English slipping away suddenly.

"We do not know, madame," Morton said. "Until we know the identity of the poor woman, we are at a loss to find the cause of her death."

"C'était" Angelique Desmarches," the woman said, mopping tears from her cheeks with a bit of linen she had been given. "It was her. She is dead? You are certain?"

"A woman was found dead wearing these clothes. Whether she is Angelique Desmarches, I cannot yet say. I need someone to view the body and tell me if this is so."

"Oh, I could not!" the woman moaned. She waved a hand at her daughter. "Amélie. *Allez.* Go with the Bow Street man and see if it is Angelique. I pray that it is not. I pray this very much."

But even in the city of London in the summer of 1815 prayers were not always answered. After accompanying Morton to view the body, young Amélie was certain beyond doubt that it was indeed the woman named

Angelique Desmarches. Arabella was too affected by the
sorrow of mother and daughter to be triumphant and
had gone off to the rehearsal very subdued.

Morton was as patient as he could be under the circumstances, but there was the matter of a likely murder—and murderers very often fled the vicinities of
their homicides as quickly as their ingenuity and finances would allow.

Back at the dress shop once again, Morton stood quietly by as Madame De le Cœur was given the bad news.
She surprised Morton by taking it calmly, as though she
had collected herself in his absence.

"I was so afraid this would be so," she whispered.

They were in a small office now, flanked by three
large oaken secretaries, all neatly organized, their papers weighted by small, ivory carvings of Oriental origin. The room was removed from the street, silent,
joyless, and grave.

"Who was Madame Desmarches?" Morton asked.

Madame De le Cœur looked up at him, patting her
eyes with a bit of linen. "And who are you, Mr. Morton,
when all is said and done?"

"I am just what your daughter told you I am,
madame. A constable in the employ of the Bow Street
Magistrate. And I am here to find the person or persons
who killed your friend, for I assume you knew her more
than a little. Where did she live?"

"Amélie? Find Madame Desmarches's address for
Monsieur Bow Street." She gestured to a chair, and
Morton sat down.

"I do not, in truth, know her well—or I did not, I
should say. She was a loyal customer, always paid her
bills on time—not a common thing among many of my
patrons, Monsieur Morton, despite their apparent

wealth. She was a very kind person, not too revealing of
her mind, if you know what I mean. She dressed well, if
I do say this myself. I don't know how long she was here
in England, but her English was less good than mine.
She was very beautiful and as young as one could ever
desire to be."

"And her husband, madame?"

She shook her head. "She was a widow. I know no
more than that. She did not speak of it. Many will not."

"What family did she have? Were many here in England?"

"I do not know, monsieur. She spoke nothing of family to me. I think she must have married well—above
her station, certainly—for she did not have the manner
of the French *noblesse*. That is really all I know."

"Were you aware of anyone who was her friend?
Anyone who knew her at all?"

The woman shook her head.

Morton sat back in his chair. A name and a dwelling
place were a start, but he had hoped, after seeing
Madame De le Cœur's reaction to the news, that she
knew much more. Ah, well, the French were more emotional than the English, which no doubt explained it—
or else losing a customer who paid on time was more
traumatic than Morton had at first guessed.

"And what of you, Madame De le Cœur? Will you return to France now that your king has been restored?"

The linen was applied again, as though there were
some new sorrow Morton had disturbed.

"I do not know what I shall do, monsieur. I have been
here so long now, here where my talents have hardly
been noticed. I once dressed the women at the court of
Versailles, but what kind of world will they make in
France now? Many hope that the hands of the clock will

be turned back, but it will not be so. I don't know what I shall do. I don't know. So many of us have been stranded here on your shores, like *la baleine* upon the beach. We belong nowhere now. We have only your English air to breathe, and we are smothering."

Chapter 6

Henry Morton and Jimmy Presley descended from a hackney-cab before a modest brick house in Hampstead Road, just past the turnpike. According to Madame De le Cœur, Angelique Desmarches had lived here, on the edge of town, her secluded little dwelling shadowed by oak trees and surrounded by a thick hedge. Opposite, but set back from the road, was the gleaming white expanse of Mornington Place, many of its houses so recently completed that they were still unoccupied. Behind on both sides stretched green fields, and as the two police men walked up the gravel path to her door they could hear the distant clanking of cowbells.

The housekeeper, a short, grey-haired woman with delicate features, opened the door.

"Sir?" she said, taking in Morton's appearance, making a quick assessment of how to treat these strangers—and then her eyes lit upon the gilt-topped batons that marked them as Bow Street Runners. A hand went to her mouth.

"What has happened?" she asked quickly.

"Is this the residence of Madame Angelique Desmarches?" Morton asked.

The woman nodded, a quick birdlike motion.

"Is there some member of her family here with whom I might speak?"

A shake of the head. "No one. She has no one."

Morton looked at the poor woman standing before him, so braced for bad news. He took a deep breath, feeling sadness settle over him like a grey winter day. "I regret to inform you, madame, that Madame Desmarches has been found dead."

For the briefest moment the woman leaned her forehead against the door, which she still held partially open. A moan escaped her, and she pressed her eyes tightly closed. With a visible effort she pulled herself upright, squaring her narrow shoulders and composing her face. It was a remarkable act of will, as though she had not a moment more to give over to grief.

"I was about to send John off for the local constables," she said, her voice deflated. "Madame has been gone now for more than a day."

"Why didn't you send for the constables earlier?"

The woman looked acutely embarrassed. "Madame has gone off unannounced before," she said, hardly seeming to move her lips, as though what she confessed should not be heard by others. "But mind my manners. Do come in."

Mrs. Johnson, for that was her name, led them into a small front parlour whose light, graceful appointments spoke of a French influence. On every side looking-glasses reflected their movements. Madame Desmarches apparently did not find her own appearance unseemly.

Tea was produced next, a stir audible in the other rooms as the arrival of the Runners became known.

Mrs. Johnson composed herself in a chair, crossed her arms, and said, "What has happened to my mistress?"

"At the moment we are not certain."

"We thought it might be self-murder—" Presley broke in but at a look from Morton fell silent.

"What might I do to help?" Mrs. Johnson asked, visibly shaken by the mention of suicide.

"Answer all my questions as honestly as you can. Leave out no detail, whether you think it relevant or not—I will be the judge of that, Mrs. Johnson, if you don't mind. Now tell me everything you can about Madame Desmarches, beginning with how long you have been in service here."

The woman thought a moment before she began. "Three years three months," she said. "I have the exact date written down somewhere."

"That is accurate enough for now. If you have served her so long, you will know much of her character."

The woman nodded, as though this were a compliment to her own judgement. "Madame was a good person, Mr. Morton, and a good mistress. Oh, she put on some continental airs, but for the main she was kindly, and never cold or haughty." She glanced at Presley. "I saw no sign that Madame was desponding, although 'tis certainly true she seemed very uneasy the last day I saw her."

"And which day was that?"

"Day before yesterday, Mr. Morton."

She glanced over at a chair set by a window, as though she expected to see her mistress there. "Even so, I would be very surprised if she would have committed the deeply dyed sin of self-murder."

"She was a papist—a Catholic?"

Mrs. Johnson shrugged. "I'm not sure, Mr. Morton, though her church certainly was not the Church of England and must therefore have been who knows what tottering pile of heathen or papist superstition, which would be no strong fortress against the cruel buffets of this world."

"She came from France. Do you know where?"

Mrs. Johnson shook her head, as though ashamed to admit such ignorance.

"Do you know anything of her family?"

"Not a thing, sir. She never spoke of them. I thought the memories might be ... painful to her."

"Perhaps they were. What became of Monsieur Desmarches?" Morton wondered. "Madame Beliveau told us that Madame was a widow."

"As for him, Madame said only that he'd vanished in the French wars. The Corsican had swallowed him up into his armies, and she had never heard more of him. If he died on campaign, she had not been informed, as she herself had chosen to flee France and stay true to her anointed king. For that sentiment, at least, sir, I honoured her. It showed a good and faithful heart, even if deprived of the succour of true religion."

"The last day you saw her, you say she was uneasy. In what way? What led you to believe this?"

"She were distracted, sir. Not unhappy, or not deeply so, but twice I spoke to her, and she did not notice, which was very unlike her."

"Was there anything more? Anything at all unusual?"

"No, sir. Not that I can think ..."

"How did she pass that day?"

"She spent some time sitting in the garden. She cut and arranged some flowers before the supper hour. She read for some time in the garden—a French book, sir. Gave me instructions for supper." She shook her head. "A most common day it was, Mr. Morton."

"No visitors?"

"None."

"And the next morning, what happened then?"

"Madame was not here, Mr. Morton. Nothing else was amiss."

"Not a thing? Think very carefully, Mrs. Johnson. This might be terribly important."

"I'm sorry, Mr. Morton, but the house was in perfect order." A gnarled finger shot up. "No, that is not true. The vase containing the flowers had been broken and cast away. I found it and the flowers behind the kitchen, which, now that you mention it, is odd."

"Why so?"

"Well, it is not where we would normally dispose of broken glass, Mr. Morton. I thought Florrie, the scullery maid, had done it, for she is a thoughtless little thing, but I asked, and she claimed to know nothing of it."

"What did you think had happened to it?"

"That Madame had somehow knocked it over and broken it, Mr. Morton. Such accidents happen."

"Indeed they do. When you realised your mistress was not here, what did you think?"

"That she had gone to visit friends. It has happened before, though she would always leave a note saying when to expect her back and giving any other instructions she might have."

"And whom did she visit?" Morton wondered.

"I don't know, sir. Madame never said."

"But certainly her friends came to visit her?"

"Only Madame De le Cœur or her daughter. They came most often to fit her for garments—she dressed very well, Mr. Morton, and was a beautiful young woman. Madame De le Cœur or her daughter visited occasionally when there appeared to be no business. No one else."

Morton glanced over at his young companion.

"Who was in the house two nights past, when last you saw Madame?" asked Jimmy Presley.

"Just Florrie, who I've mentioned. She sleeps in the pantry. The rest of us live out. I'll grant you 'tis not a common arrangement, but this is how Madame wished it. Perhaps 'tis done this way in foreign parts."

It was done this way in parts of England, too, Morton reflected, when discretion was desired.

"John, the footman, and the cook Françoise and I generally arrive just about six o'clock each morn and leave after our supper at nine of an evening. If Madame wants—wanted . . . anything in the night, she could ring for Florrie. We were given thirty shillings extra, in place of lodgings, and we had our board. Madame was generous, as any of us will tell you. We have our wages now till the end of the month. After that"—she sighed—"we will be put to sore shifts to find positions as good again. But the Lord will provide."

Morton tried to phrase his next question delicately.

"Did Madame ever mention if . . . she owned this house outright?"

A look of indignation flared in Mrs. Johnson's eyes. "I should never have spoken to Madame about such things, nor she to me."

"No, certainly not. Well, we would have a word with Florrie, if she be here."

Mrs. Johnson led them back through the servants' door, along a covered walkway, and around into the kitchen, which was in a brick annex at the back and to the side of the main house. The cook Françoise was here, a gaunt middle-aged woman, whose awkward grin revealed very bad teeth as she nervously curtsied to the two visitors. It seemed Florrie was in the herb garden, and Françoise went for her. While Morton and Presley waited, they looked about. As kitchens went, Morton thought, it must be a reasonably pleasant place to spend the long hours of drudgery that were the lot of women like these—and of his own mother in years past. A fairly clean and spacious room, cool even in July, and well enough lit by the long row of windows set in one wall, even if the view was just of the tall green wall of privet. The only disadvantage would be the distance to the main house and thus the extra steps, many times a day, as trays and teacups and a thousand other things were carried into and out of the presence of the mistress.

Florrie, when produced, proved to be a thirteen-year-old slip of a girl in a very grubby smock. The Runners seemed to be her deepest terror.

"Were you in the house two nights past?" demanded Jimmy Presley. Florrie gaped up at him in horrified silence.

"You were, Florrie, weren't you?" prompted Mrs. Johnson. "The way you always are?" Florrie managed a small, uncertain nod.

"Where does she sleep?"

"Show the men where you sleep," Mrs. Johnson told her. The girl led them to a windowless alcove behind the oven, adjoining the coal scuttle, where a pathetic pallet, the stump of a candle, and a single alternate dress hanging on a nail in the wooden crossbeam indicated the abode of the most menial member of the household.

"Did your mistress have any callers that night?" Morton wanted to know.

For a moment Mrs. Johnson stayed mute, giving
Florrie a chance to respond independently. This was beyond her, however. In a convulsive movement she hid
her face in her apron. The housekeeper reached and
briskly pulled her hands down again.

"Foolish girl! Now, attend to the gentlemen. Madame
had no visitors that night, did she?" Mrs. Johnson's tone
was firm but not harsh. "She never did have visitors of a
night, did she? She was a most proper lady, wasn't she?"

Florrie looked quite helpless until, unexpectedly,
Françoise came to her aid. "*Alors, ma petite*, tell the
shentlemens, joost, did Madame 'ave no visitor two
night ago?"

"She didn't!" squeaked out Florrie now, and looked
profusely relieved.

"There, *bon*, good, you see." Françoise smiled apolo-
getically to Henry Morton. "Really, sir, she is a good *fille*,
but not accustom'..." She trailed away, glancing uneasily at Mrs. Johnson, who now wore a deep frown.
Jimmy Presley, however, had picked up the same notion
the housekeeper had.

"You mean there *were* visitors on other nights?" he
bluntly demanded. This, however, produced total silence—shocked, alarmed, or indignant—on the part of
all three domestics. Henry Morton took another approach.

"Well, it matters little enough who was or wasn't
here, except on the night in question. Now, Florrie, on
that night, did you hear any noises? Did you hear anything unusual, especially coming from the upstairs part
of the house, from your mistress's room?"

Florrie looked almost desperate now but could be induced to say nothing.

"Caterwauling, or screechinglike?" prompted Jimmy

Presley. Morton's young colleague had shown real potential as a Runner since his promotion from the Worship Street Patrole a couple of months earlier. Morton already owed much to his courage and resolution, in the recent business with George Vaughan and his confederates. But there were some things Jimmy had yet to learn about questioning and patience.

"Would Florrie remember if Madame rang for anything that night?" Morton asked, generally. Florrie looked nervously at Françoise, who repeated the question in slightly different words, which induced the maid to close her eyes and vigourously shake her head.

"But she usually does, doesn't she?" Morton smiled encouragingly. "Florrie usually takes her something or other during an evening?"

"Aye!" piped Florrie, without assistance. "Tay, or biscuits!"

"But not that night."

A shake of the head so forceful that Florrie's stringy blond locks flung about her thin shoulders.

Morton had Mrs. Johnson call John the footman as well and instructed them all to come with the Runners as they made their way back into the house. They went through each room, asking Mrs. Johnson to look carefully at each and tell them if there was anything out of place or unusual. Morton and Presley also ran their practised eyes over each finely appointed room, but they saw nothing. Certainly no signs of anyone being tortured.

They finished their inspection with Madame's bedroom. Morton kept them waiting in the hall, as questions might occur to him.

The room was in perfect order, the windows open on the summer afternoon for airing, the counterpane on the four-poster smooth and neat, and the furniture dusted and polished. He called in the housekeeper.

"Who makes up the bed?" Morton asked.

"That is my task, sir," said Mrs. Johnson stiffly. No matter what was being investigated, clearly from her perspective it was most improper for any man to enquire into even the most prosaic secrets of the female preserve. But Morton was not to be put off. And there were worse things to be asked.

"On the morning after Madame Desmarches's disappearance, what was the condition of this bed?"

"I do not take your meaning, sir. 'Condition'?"

"I mean, firstly, did it appear to have been slept in?"

A hesitation. "No."

Mrs. Johnson's face reddened. As Morton watched her, he wondered if certain possibilities about the life her beneficent mistress led were only now occurring to the devout mind of the housekeeper. Or was she merely trying to hold fast in some unfathomable female solidarity?

"Have they been laundered since Madame disappeared?"

Mrs. Johnson wrung her hands in agitation at such vulgar questioning. "They have," she muttered.

Morton suppressed his irritation. "Were they stained? Did they have any traces of blood? Or other stains?"

Now, finally, Mrs. Johnson rebelled. "Mr. Morton, sir! Where is your decency!"

"I am doing my duty, Mrs. Johnson. Were there stains? I am perfectly aware that their causes might be ... diverse."

Mrs. Johnson's face was an undescribable hue. "They were that morning, *sir,* in the state one would expect of a gentlewoman of Madame Desmarches's standing."

"That morning..."

Morton surveyed the room silently a moment with folded arms. What had gone on here? Surely if thumb-screws had been applied in this genteel little world, there would be some signs of struggle. A broken vase hardly seemed enough—just as likely an accident after all.

"Where is Madame's writing-desk?" Morton asked. He was led by the silently disapproving Mrs. Johnson into the next room, a sunny, cheerfully furnished lady's boudoir. The walls were ornamented with prints of peasant life, something in the manner of Chardin, he thought—more earnest than licentious.

The little roll-top secretaire was not locked: the key sat casually on the ledge on top. Morton slid back the veneered cover. Everything was orderly: neat, but not obsessively so. Blank paper, ink, quills, a sharpening knife, wax. He opened the drawers, one after the other. Empty, or half-filled with other casual piles of blank pa-per, nibs, blotters, the usual paraphernalia. And that was odd.

"Has this room been tidied since Madame's death?" he asked. "Has the desk been put in order?"

"There was no need," replied Mrs. Johnson. "Every-thing was proper, as you see it. I only dusted."

"Where are Madame's letters?"

Mrs. Johnson blinked at him a moment. "Which let-ters do you mean, Mr. Morton?"

"There is pen and ink, a quire of blank paper, but no letters, written or received. Where does Madame keep her letters and papers?"

Mrs. Johnson stared, apparently baffled. "Well, here, sir—the few that there were."

"But they are not there." Morton considered. The pen

nibs were sharpened, the blotter stained. "Was it her habit to lock this desk?" he asked.

"She trusted her servants, sir!"

"I've no doubt of that. But did she lock the desk? Do you recollect?"

Mrs. Johnson hesitated, in apparently genuine uncertainty. "I do not remember, sir. Or I never noticed. It was not my habit to try her drawers! But perhaps...she did."

"A foreign practise, perhaps." Morton allowed himself a slight smile. "Picked up in France, where domestics are less reliable." And where, he silently added, servants had been known on occasion to betray their masters and mistresses to Madame Guillotine.

Jimmy Presley had opened the window and was looking down.

"Morton?" The tone of the young Runner's voice alerted Morton.

He went and stood beside Presley and looked down into the courtyard below. There, on the paving stones, one could see, as clear as clear, an almost-round area that was of a different colour, free of dust—as though it had been washed clean.

The two Runners went quickly down the stairs. It took them a moment to find the spot, for close up it was not obvious, which no doubt explained why no one had noticed it before.

Morton crouched over the paving stones, searching, cursing the fashionable tightness of his breeches. There was nothing to be seen. Morton looked up at the window above. Certainly anyone falling from Madame Desmarches's window could have landed here.

"Who washed this spot clean?" Morton asked.

Mrs. Johnson, who stood by clutching her hands

tightly together, shook her head. "I don't know, Mr. Morton. John might have done so, but I don't know why."

Morton stood up. "Jimmy, find a spade or a bar of some kind and pry these stones up."

A quick tour of the outside of the house revealed a third door, the back entrance, partly screened by a rose trellis. Private, discreet. And in the meadow beyond a small gate in the hedge, plenty of room to leave a hobbled horse to graze, even for hours, and not have it seen from the road.

"And the broken vase?" he said to the hovering Mrs. Johnson.

"Back here, sir." Morton followed the slight woman to the back of the kitchen, where they found the shattered ceramic vessel and wilted flowers. Morton turned the shards carefully. There was some brown substance dried on the sharp edge of one, but even if it was blood, it proved nothing. The wilted flowers and what had clearly been a beautiful vase made Morton suddenly very sad. He stood for a moment staring.

"No one disliked your mistress," Morton said, still staring at the cast-away blooms. "Be absolutely truthful, now."

"No, sir. She was kindness itself."

"And she had no paramours that you know of? Do not be shocked—it is the most likely scenario. I have seen it before."

"None, sir. I swear."

Morton felt at a complete loss. No door or window had been forced. Whoever had done Angelique Desmarches to death had gained access to her house without the use of force.

"Are windows habitually left open on the lower floors?"

"Oh no, sir. Not with Madame here alone."

Morton did not even know what to ask next. Had the harm done to Angelique Desmarches been inflicted here, in this house? Wouldn't someone have heard?

Morton went around to the courtyard and found Jimmy hard at work, his coat laid over a shrub.

"Anything there at all, Jimmy?"

"Just this." The young man reached down and retrieved a small clump of matted hair.

Certainly it was of the same color as he had seen on the corpse in Skelton's surgery. Morton showed it to the housekeeper.

"That is Madame's," she confirmed.

Morton looked up at the windows again.

"I think she fell here, Morton."

"There is little to prove you right, but I agree," Morton said.

He sent Jimmy Presley up again to the bedchamber, with instructions to close the window and shutters. He was then to recite the oath he had learned when he was sworn as an officer of the king's peace, first in a normal voice, then somewhat louder, then louder still, till he reached as great a bellow as he could manage. Morton himself crossed the lawn and reentered the kitchen, then bent down to wedge himself into Florrie's little sleeping space. Only when Jimmy was shouting his loudest—and Morton knew the power of that voice from experience—could he be heard from behind the coal scuttle.

"And one is to consider that Florrie was asleep, and it was a woman's voice, not yours."

Presley, downstairs again, nodded. "Maybe they muffled her, too, to keep her quiet."

"Aye, perhaps. Go round to the neighbouring houses, Jimmy, and ask the folk there if they heard or remarked anything out of the ordinary. I shall have some words with the footman and the cook."

Morton asked Mrs. Johnson for a private room, that he might speak to her, and then to each of the servants, alone. He could see well enough that the housekeeper's understanding of the establishment she had charge of was imperfect. He didn't want her influencing the others as she attempted to protect the good name of her mistress and by extension her own.

In the dining room, with the doors closed, he and the housekeeper sat down across the polished satinwood table.

"You said your mistress looked troubled the day she died, Mrs. Johnson. Is there nothing at all that might have caused this? Did she receive a letter?"

"I only know, sir, that she seemed quite herself in the morning, but that her spirits seemed to fall later in the day. In fact, I went out about midmorning to do some errands, some marketing for the house, and when I came back, she had retired to her room, and she seemed poorly when she came out finally for dinner. She ate but little."

"Then I shall speak with the footman, if you please, Mrs. Johnson."

The footman was sent in and took a seat as Morton indicated.

"What is your true name, John?" he asked.

The other man raised his head in surprise. Like most servants, he had been given—and accepted—a traditional appellation. Half the footmen in London were "John," and most of the rest were "Thomas." Doubtless the case with "Florrie" was the same. "Oh well, sir," he replied with a modest smile, "I be Archibald Gedge, since ye ask me. I am a Lambeth man originally, but 'ave been in St. Marylebone Parish and hereabouts some seventeen years now."

They talked awhile of his life and of the occupation he had entered as a boy.

"I had a turn in the glassworks, sir, afore I went into service. I knowed then as what my chances would be if I stayed *there*. I'd be in my grave now, sure, like others I could tell you of. To catch on in private service was the luckiest chance as ever befell me. You'll not hear a hard word for my masters and mistresses of *me,* sir."

"Nor would I ask one. Your housekeeper feels the same way, I'd warrant."

"Oh aye, Mrs. Johnson's a good woman. She sees no evil, nor hears it, nor speaks of it." Morton could sense a certain, slightly unusual loyalty here. If most servants were unwilling to criticise their employers, they usually had less reticence about their overseers or superiors of the servant class.

"But I think you're not quite so blind, Archibald, be your heart ever so much in the right place. Madame had a gentleman visitor of a night, didn't she? And this cove had a key to the back entrance, didn't he?"

Now the footman fell silent, lowering his eyes and frowning in discomfort.

"Now, Archibald," Morton went on, turning his voice slightly harder, "this is a matter of a capital crime. Your mistress was murdered, I'm quite sure."

"Truly?" asked the man in surprise.

"Aye, there was foul play, and you are obliged to help me find it out. You owe it to your king. And perhaps you owe it to your poor mistress, too."

The other man swallowed and said, " 'Tis true that Madame, at the beginning, asked me to have another key made up for the garden door, and give it her."

"And you did?"

The footman nodded unhappily.

"You've been here going on four years. Did you ever see the gent as used this key?"

After another long pause, Archibald Gedge cleared his throat and began to speak, low. "Once or twice, of a morning, I catched a view of 'im going out just as I was coming in. He even bade me a good morning once, very politelike, as if it were no great matter. He were a gentlemanlike toff, sure, well dressed, and old enough to be young Madame's father. But he were a likely looking cove, for all that."

"What was his name?"

"Oh, I knowed nothing of that."

"What do you remember of him?"

Archibald thought a moment. "Oh, well, when he saluted me that one time, his voice were Frenchy-like, same as the young mistress. He's one of them Frenchies, sure."

"Did he come the day she died?"

"Not as I saw, sir."

"Did anyone else?"

Archibald Gedge rubbed his jaw.

"One cove did, I think. That day, unless t'were the day before. Another of those Frenchies, I should guess."

"Who was this man? What was his name?"

"Oh, he gave me his card, and I took it up to her, I think. He stayed p'raps half an hour, is all. If it were the same day. Short, dapper cove. Ask Françoise, constable. She took them in some tay, as Mrs. Johnson were out just then."

He knew nothing more, and Morton let him go, asking for the cook. He drew out a chair for her, before seating himself.

"How long have you been in this house, madame?" he began politely.

"A year, monsieur, a little longer. I am recommend by my employer who went back to France when Bonaparte first fell and went to Elba."

"And you did not wish to go with your former employer?" Morton asked, curious.

"Ah, *monsieur le constable,* you see," she nervously explained, "we 'ave been living here so long, many of us. We 'ave, how do you say, *les connexions.* Our friends, our homes. Many of us, we joost decide to stay. Me, I 'ave been in Angleterre since twenty-five year. The English milords, they treat me vary well, they like *ma cuisine.*" She again revealed her excruciating teeth, in the slightly apologetic smile that seemed her most natural expression.

Morton nodded. And besides, one might want to wait, just to see who really ended on top of the heap in France. Bonaparte had come back once. Who could say that he wouldn't come back again?

"Now, madame, I know you wish to protect the honour of your mistress. But it is very clear to me that she had *un ami,* a gentleman, who visited her. I expect also he provided this house for her. Now, were it for any other reason, I would not think of asking about such things. An *affaire de coeur* is no concern of mine. But Madame Desmarches did not do herself to death. Someone came here and did her harm. I must have the name of her... protector."

"*Vous dîtes*—you say... she was murdered? It was not some accident?" Françoise gazed at him in distress.

"It was no accident, madame. She was murdered, so young and so beautiful."

"Ah oui, elle était belle," murmured the cook. *"C'est tragique."*

"I am sure you knew the name of her gentleman," said Morton flatly.

She looked up at him, brushing at a tear with the heel of her palm, and sighed. "Ah, *oui*—yes, I did. It was *le comte* d'Auvraye. He live...not too far, near Square Manchester. But, monsieur. He did love her, I think, yes, he did. I do not understand why he would have cast her off! I do not understand that, *pas de tout.* But *non, non,* he would not 'ave killed her. This I can*not* believe."

"He cast her off, you say? When?"

"Oh, the very day, monsieur. That very day. A man came, from him, in the morning. None of the other servants ever knew, because she said nothing to us, but I heard her and him talking, in her parlour, behind the door. She is crying *pourquoi, pourquoi,* very angry. And he speaking back, low. And when I went in with the tea, he is saying that she might stay tonight, but no longer. Then she must be gone. And we *domestiques,* too. He asked her about us, how many of us there were, and for how long had we been paid, and such things. She was angry, *furieuse,* but he said it was so, and *le comte* d'Auvraye had decided it, and it could not be changed."

Morton's face must have shown his surprise.

"Alors, oui, monsieur, so it was," she said with a shrug. "She was going to have to leave this 'ouse. And us, too. I did not want to tell the others, because...*alors,* because that was for her to do. I thought she would announce it the next morning. But of course...poor lady!"

"What was the name of this man?"

"I do not know, but he came from *le comte.*"

"Do you know *why* the count was dismissing her? Did she have...some other lover?"

Françoise shrugged and sighed. "Ah, monsieur. *Mais* you must understand, I could not know that. But I never saw 'im, if there would be."

"And yet you think that the count could not have killed her, or had her killed?"

"*Non, non,* I do not think ever he could do this!"

"But how do you know?"

She wrung her hands a little in discomfort. "From time to time, because we spoke together the language, Madame say things to me, little things, things a woman says to a woman, about how he treat her, about how he love her.... She say...*adoré*...that he...adore her."

Morton frowned.

"Then who do you think could have killed her?"

The cook looked anguished and shrugged in eloquent helplessness.

Chapter 7

They could not get in the door of the London
home of Count Gerrard d'Auvraye. It was a
white stuccoed town house in the new Nash
style, just around the corner from the austere bulk of
Manchester House on as eminently respectable a little
street as the West End could offer. The liveried footman
who answered insisted—in exquisitely accented English—that the count was not home, and nor was his
secretary. Morton left a calling card and instructions to
inform the count that he would return in the morning at
ten o'clock and would expect to speak with him regard-
ing a matter of the most serious nature.

The Count d'Auvraye was clearly a man of some
fashion—his address and his home announced this
clearly—but Morton could bring the force of the law
against him if required and was fully prepared to do so.
He made a great effort to impress this fact upon the servant.

The two Runners retreated into the street, but
Morton brought them up there.

Jimmy Presley had an ingrained distrust of the French of any stripe. "If he's guilty, as I dem well guess he is," he said, "then he'll likely light out for France as soon as he hears that Bow Street has come calling."

The young Runner stared back defiantly at the imposing home. A clatter of traffic passed—tradesmen's carts, delivery wagons, and elegant private carriages. The street life of London varied starkly from neighbourhood to neighbourhood but never ceased. The greatest city in the world, Morton was certain, alive with flash men and princes, foreigners and kings. And two Bow Street Runners, staring with some envy and even greater puzzlement at this grand home off Manchester Square.

"I'm not quite so ready to convict him," Morton said, "but I think it wise that we keep this house under our eye. Can you stay until I find Farke or some other to come take your place?"

Presley nodded grimly, looking around for a spot where he might loiter inconspicuously. "I can and I will. But why would a man with so much to lose do something so foolish as murder his mistress?"

"It is a good question, Jimmy, and one worth asking. But even more important, why would such a man use thumbscrews on his mistress? Now that does make one wonder."

Morton left Presley to his vigil and was about to set out for Bow Street when he had another thought. It was late afternoon, but there was a chance that Arthur Darley might be home, and he lived only a short walk away, barely the other side of Baker Street.

Morton was standing on the step of Portman House in a few moments and was immediately let in to speak with the amiable master of the house.

"Morton," Darley said, rising from a chair and setting aside a newspaper. "What an unlooked-for pleasure. I am having a late tea—would you join me?"

"I would, and gladly, though I must say that I am on police business and have come only to beg a little information."

"Begging shall not be necessary." He gestured to the servant. "Mr. Morton will sit down to tea."

They were immediately alone, seated by a large window that looked out over the green park in the centre of Portman Square.

"I was wondering if you had seen this," Darley said. He held up his folded newspaper.

"What is it?"

"The *Times*, of a few days past." Darley opened the paper. "A letter addressed to the Prince Regent from Bonaparte himself. 'Your Royal Highness; A victim of the factions which distract my country,' et cetera, et cetera, 'I come, like Themistocles—'"

"Ah," Morton interjected, "I like that."

"'—to throw myself upon the hospitality of the British people...to put myself under the protection of their laws, which I claim from your Royal Highness, as the most powerful, the most constant, and the most generous of my enemies.'"

"Well, he has given us the acknowledgement we are due, and recognised us for what we are," Morton said.

"He has recognised man's susceptibility to flattery and rhetoric. I don't think it will work here as it once did in France, but he has no army at his back now, so he must resort to other tricks." Darley looked up from the paper and recognised something in Morton's manner. "But you have not come here to listen to fallen emperors rant."

"I do apologise ... ," Morton began, but Darley swept this aside with a wave and a smile.

"Do you know anything of your near neighbour, the Count d'Auvraye?"

"Gerrard d'Auvraye over in Spanish Place off Manchester Square? Well, I have met him a few times. He is a ... *favourite* would be too strong a word. Let us say that d'Auvraye is a supporter, well known to the present French king. Do I dare ask why you are interested?"

"The count's mistress has been murdered."

Darley sat back in his chair, wincing a little. Tea arrived.

"But that is not the strangest thing," Morton continued as the servant left. "This young woman had upon her person the marks of a thumbscrew."

Darley's cup stopped on its path to his mouth.

"My reaction was much the same," Morton said. "*Thumbscrews!* The poor woman was subjected to an unspeakable agony before she died."

Darley's cup rattled down into its saucer, contents untested. "You can't think d'Auvraye would do such a thing?"

"I have accused no one, Lord Arthur. Nor have I yet had the chance to speak with the count."

"Well, I know where he is—or was, earlier this day. He was at Whitehall, as I was myself."

Morton's interest was piqued. "And what business would take him there, I wonder?"

"I'm told he is acting as the unofficial ambassador of the French court, of our good friend Louis the Gouty, whose throne has been restored to him by the Duke of Wellington's prowess on the field of battle. I don't know specifically why d'Auvraye was at Whitehall, but it was assumed to have had something to do with our dilemma over Bonaparte—though of course, it could have been anything, really. Louis has great need of our continuing support. There is still an army wandering round in the south of France, ostensibly loyal to the deposed emperor." Darley raised his cup again, suddenly very thoughtful. "What else might I tell you?"

"Anything would help. I know nothing of d'Auvraye."

Darley turned and looked out the window in the direction of Spanish Place and Manchester Square. "D'Auvraye is a few years older than I, though a great deal stouter. He is of a good family, though his wife's, I think, was even better. I can't claim to know him well. He is a bit progressive for a French aristocrat: I suspect all his years living in exile in London have led to that— he's been here since the Revolution itself, some twenty-five years now. Oh, certainly he is a monarchist, but he once privately professed great admiration for our form of government and even suggested that France might benefit from such a system. He is no fool, I would say, though his manner belies this a little." Darley paused as he considered this last remark, as though wondering himself what he meant. "He is a ponderous thinker. That is my opinion. Not quick of mind—say, like Fox— but that does not mean he will not arrive at the correct answer if given enough time. He needs to contemplate matters before committing himself.

"I will tell you one peculiar story. I had dinner with the count at his house in Barnes Terrace, really the only prolonged social contact we have had. The conversation was not contemptible, not at all. I have never been in his town house, but I'm told he has good marbles and, of course, a superior cellar."

"There is a countess?" asked Morton.

"Oh yes, there is a countess." Darley's tone suggested this was a fact of limited interest. There was a Lady Darley, too, if one cared to ask, although in her case her husband "retreated" to town. Lord Arthur passed on smoothly. "D'Auvraye has weaned himself of much of the pomp and conservative thinking that most of the French royalists brought to England, but this is not true of everyone in his family or in his circle. It is really quite extraordinary, the manners some of them have preserved, even after twenty-five years: the toasts, the order of precedence, the rituals.

"At any rate, there was a visitor, the evening I was there, a most eminent man by the name of Bayarde, a monarchist who fought against Bonaparte. Now, Monsieur Bayarde was a soldier and a philosopher, and he had done much for their cause, both in his actions and in his writings. But he was a commoner, you see, and a Huguenot, to boot. It wasn't clear who had invited him, but he was the only untitled person in the party. When the count's son Eustache got wind of his being there, he refused point-blank to allow him to be seated at table, and made a great fuss, quarrelling with his father and insisting that if Bayarde were seated, *he* could not be. 'This is what we are fighting against!' he argued. 'This dissolution of all distinctions, this levelling!' Can you credit that?"

"With difficulty," admitted Morton.

"But so it was. In the end the countess supported her son, and he had his way. Monsieur Bayarde pretended not to take offence and had his dinner separately, but I do believe he left that house an embittered man. It is very much as Talleyrand said, you know, *they have forgotten nothing and learned nothing.*"

"But you say that the count does seem, at least in degree, an exception."

"In some small degree, yes," Darley agreed.

"Do you know enough of him to pass judgement on his character?"

Darley poured tea for both of them. "He is rather kindly and inoffensive. The French will replace him here with someone...who will care less if he is well liked, if you know what I mean."

Morton looked out over the sunny park, leaves ashiver in the fresh breeze. Nursemaids watched over children at play. "Can you think of any way that his position would lead to his mistress being tortured?"

Darley rubbed a finger into the corner of his eye as though he had a stray lash. Morton had seen this before and recognised a habit that allowed the man time to collect his thoughts. "Well, I can't really think how d'Auvraye's rather nominal position would lead to such an act. One might imagine that someone could believe the poor woman had enough of the count's confidence that she would know certain things—but I can hardly imagine d'Auvraye knows anything worth torturing a person to learn. The King of France has only just crossed the Channel. It just isn't feasible that he is planning to, say, make war against...anyone. France is a shambles and will remain so for some time. It is the most damnably strange thing I have ever heard."

"I agree entirely. Who, though, might be considered the enemies of this restored French regime?"

"Well, the governments of the continent welcome King Louis. He is not Bonaparte, and this makes him, at least for the moment, a considerable improvement. Though of course they have set him on the throne themselves, with our help. Enemies? Any crowned head has

his rivals, I suppose, even if no one is sure yet that he
will hold France. If I were he, I'd be watching my own
family and my own supporters closely, I think. They've
fought long and hard against Bonaparte all these years,
the royalist opposition, but even longer and harder for
position amongst themselves. Even so, I can't imagine
any of them are quite so foolish as to attack their own
man just yet."

"What about Bonaparte himself? He has a few supporters still, surely."

"More than a few—English, French, of every nation.
Political radicals, old soldiers, camp followers ... anyone
but aristocrats. But without their great leader they are a
rabble, a serpent without a head. The body might twitch
and thrash about for a while, but that is all—they need
Bonaparte himself. At the moment I suspect his followers are scattering, seeking places to hide or trying to in-
gratiate themselves with the new regime."

"I'm sure you're right, though I notice our government is not treating the deposed emperor as a spent
force quite yet."

Darley looked reflective.

"Indeed, no. That would be folly, wouldn't it?"

Chapter 8

A letter awaited Morton upon his arrival at number 4 Bow Street. He broke the seal and opened it, to find only a few lines in a graceful hand.

My dear Mr. Morton:

Excuse the brevity of this note, but I do hope we will have an opportunity to speak at length. An art object of some value has been stolen from my family, and I hope to engage your services for its recovery. The Viscount is traveling so this duty has fallen to me. I will be at home this day until the supper hour, if it is possible for you to call; 17 Lincoln's Inn Fields.

It was signed Miss Caroline Richardson.

Morton stared at the note in disbelief. His first reaction was anger, but this was quickly followed by an almost overwhelming feeling of powerlessness. He read the note again and almost threw it into the waste.

Caroline Richardson was his half-sister. That is to say, Morton was the offspring of Miss Richardson's father and a servant—Morton's mother. He had spoken to Miss Richardson once, when they were children—she had been but a small girl at the time, for she was at least half a dozen years younger than he was himself.

Looking around, he realised that he'd wandered into the Runners' ready room. Tucked away in the rear of the building behind the hearing room and Sir Nathaniel's chambers, this was where the Bow Street men took their ease, awaiting commissions, sharing information, and biding their time before giving witness.

"Good day, Morton," a voice said, and Morton looked up to find Vickery, a fellow Runner, perched on one of the hard-backed chairs, with his booted feet propped up against the grate of the unlit hearth.

"Ah, Vickery," Morton said, trying to smile, "just the gentleman I was looking for. Have you time for a bit of private work?"

The older man shook his head of grey hair, as he lowered his feet to the floor. "With difficulty. I was just about to set off to see some of my favorite peachers." And then: "Is it private work worth doing, do you think?"

Morton had almost begun to hand the man the note but drew it back. "Perhaps not. Let me look into it a little further."

Vickery smiled and rose, reaching for his hat from its peg. Tipping it to Morton, he walked purposefully out.

Morton stood a moment, wondering why he'd not given the job away. He took out his watch and assured himself of the time. It was but a short stroll to the house where his mother had once toiled as a servant—until she was set out on the street for the crime of being young and falling victim to the desires of the master of the house.

Outside the Magistrate's Court he was met by a pleasant, warm London day. Towering white clouds, tattered and torn, scattered across the pale summer blue. The streets streamed with traffic of every sort. At the entrance to Great Wild Street a barrel dray lay at an odd angle, half its cargo spilled onto the cobbles. Hackney-coach drivers cursed, horses struggled, and men milled about, trying to right the situation. At the turmoil's centre a Charlie ostentatiously diverted carriages and carts, making the most of his position.

The street life of Morton's native city had little appeal to him that afternoon. His attentions were drawn inward, into a confusion of resentment and desire, anger and hurt. Though he walked toward the house of his half-sister, he was not at all sure why.

In a few moments Morton entered the comparative quiet of Lincoln's Inn Fields. It was a square of large mansions surrounding a green park on three sides. The prominent architect and art collector Sir John Soane dwelt at number 13, and other notable Londoners lived their privileged lives behind other doors in the same street. At the door of number 17 Morton hesitated. "Viscount Richardson is away," he assured himself, having no desire to meet the man who'd put his mother out in the street.

A footman answered, and Morton proffered a calling card.

"Ah yes, Mr. Morton. Miss Richardson is expecting you."

A surprised Morton was led into a sun-drenched drawing room, the sounds of London retreating into the vague distance. It was very unlike the home of Arthur

Darley, at once both more opulent and less tasteful—at least less currently tasteful, for it was done up in an older style. Morton stood by the window a moment, watching the people pass, wondering what it would have been like to have this view from childhood, this room in which to contemplate one's future.

A light footfall behind him, and Morton turned to find the little girl of memory banished by a young woman. She did not look unlike him: that was his first thought. Oh, a feminine rendering, to be sure. But she had the same dark hair and eyes—his "poet's eyes," as Arabella called them. She was of good height for a woman, erect in her carriage, her dress hinting at a lovely feminine shape beneath. A smile, nervous and hesitant, but more disarming for all that.

She was looking at him, too, and Morton was certain he knew her thoughts—he had heard often enough from his mother that he looked like the Viscount Richardson.

"It is so very kind of you to come, Mr. Morton," she said in a pure, refined voice. "I feared you would not."

"I very nearly didn't."

"And you would have had every reason to make that decision—but I'm glad you are here. I have wanted to meet you again for some time. Do you remember ... ?"

Morton nodded. "Yes. I got quite a smack from old Mrs. Collicott for talking to you when I was told never to."

She shook her head. "I didn't know about that."

"A lifetime ago," Morton said, and smiled. "You wrote of an art object."

"A painting, yes. A Vernet—one of his sea storms. A ... a very powerful canvas, really. I—we all thought it quite sublime. It was taken from our house sometime in the last few days."

"You don't know when, exactly?"

A slight look of embarrassment. "No, it was hanging in the viscount's study. No one had been in there since he departed, four days ago." She met his eye and smiled charmingly. "But let me offer you some refreshment, Mr. Morton. Certainly a Runner must need to rest his feet occasionally."

Morton was as susceptible to charm as the next man, when his mood allowed it—but his mood was very low this afternoon. "Why have you called on me, Miss Richardson, if you don't mind me asking?"

The young lady struggled with a look of distress, then said in a slightly trembling voice, "Your recent legal triumph has proven you to be a man of unimpeachable integrity, Mr. Morton. And I was being entirely honest when I said I had long wanted to make your acquaintance."

"Curiosity?"

"Perhaps. Was it not something like that that drew you here?"

Morton shrugged. "Something like."

"Well, here we are, curious. The only way to satisfy our curiosity would be to have speech, I believe."

Morton fought off the temptation. "I mean no offence, Miss Richardson, but I'm engaged in another matter of some importance, and my time is very short."

"Ah," she said. "And what foul crime calls the formidable Mr. Henry Morton today?"

"The murder of a lovely young woman, I regret to say."

"Oh," she said, "I'm sorry to hear it."

"May I ask some questions?"

She nodded her assent.

"How many servants do you employ?"

"A good number. I will have a list drawn up."

"And who else lives in the house?"

"Myself, the viscount, of course, my brother Lord Robert, and my aunt, Mrs. Eugenie Childers. I rather suspect Aunt Eugenie myself, though she is more than a little infirm and can't get around of her own—but she has an eye for a good painting."

Morton smiled in spite of himself. "Might I see the room from which it was stolen?"

The viscount's study was shadowed by oak panelling and books. Morton was a bit abashed to find how widely his father read. The scent of pipe smoke emanated from carpet and furniture. Upon the desk were some neatly stacked papers beneath weights and an almost new blotter. All was perfectly ordered. Nothing was out of place but the missing painting, which was marked by a light rectangle upon one wall.

"Nothing else is missing?" Morton wondered.

"Not that we know of. The viscount would have to say, but the painting seems to be the only thing that was taken." She stood tentatively by the door, as though this room were forbidden to her. She looked somewhat younger, hovering there so hesitantly.

Morton took a last look around the study. "I wonder how they got access to the house."

"Through a service door that opens onto Whetstone Park, the street that runs behind. They broke a small window and managed to unlatch the door from there."

"Would you have a servant show me?"

"I'll show you myself."

They wound downstairs to the servants' domain, a world familiar to Morton. This was where his mother had been employed—perhaps where she had been seduced.

"Anyone new belowstairs?" Morton asked.

"No. Most have been with us forever. Charles, the footman who answered the door, joined us a little more than a year ago, I think. He would be the most recent addition."

The glazier had already been by to repair the shattered pane, and all signs of the breakage had been swept away. Morton sighed. He looked briefly outside but found that the glazier's efforts had erased or muddied any signs of the burglary.

An hour was spent talking to servants, taking names and histories. None of them seemed the type, to Morton's practised eye, though he had been initially mistaken before. When done with the servants, he sat a moment alone. The afternoon was wearing on to early evening.

Caroline Richardson let herself into the room and took a seat on a divan.

"You look troubled," she said.

Morton let his gaze wander over the opulent surroundings. He was troubled. What did this rather too perfect young woman want of him? "As you know, Miss Richardson, I am a Bow Street Runner in the employ of the Magistrate, Sir Nathaniel Conant. My livelihood is derived from rewards I receive for the conviction of criminals I have caught. I live alone in rooms I let—not uncomfortable, but not so lovely as this. I read, I attend the theatre, a small circle of friends takes up much of my time. I don't shoot—not at game, at any rate—nor do I spend summers in the country. I am a member of no clubs other than Gentleman John Jackson's Boxing Club, and I've only travelled abroad on one occasion, and I was, at the time, pursuing a murderer." He looked at her, raising his hands a little. "That, in brief, Miss Richardson, is my life."

"And you do a great deal of good within the city of London," she said after a moment. "I'm told you are a friend of Lord Arthur Darley's."

"We are acquainted."

"He is a man well respected within prominent circles." As she paused to consider, the look of trouble or distress passed over her face again, wrinkling her fine brow. But she took up his challenge, all the same. "I wish I could reveal something that would distinguish me from all the other young ladies of my station, but the truth is I cannot. I'm told that my conversation is adequate, my social graces barely so—I laugh at all the wrong things. My dancing is better, but I find it rather tedious. I play the piano with some artistry, though it is immodest of me to say so. My father despairs that I am not married, but I detest Almack's and the conniving seven dragons. Oh, and I paint—as does every other young lady of my acquaintance." She looked at him rather directly. "I hope I have not imposed upon you overly, Mr. Morton. It is just that, since my mother passed away... well, I wanted to know who you were, and when I read in the *Times* of the recent events..." She shrugged.

"You read the papers?"

"Shh," she said theatrically. "Of course not. What proper young lady would subject herself to the vulgar goings-on of the nation?"

Morton smiled. "It is most likely that the thief will advertise in the *Morning Chronicle,* describing the painting in some cryptic way that only someone who knows it well would recognise. This will allow him to deny possession should he be found. He will ask for a reward for the painting's return. I will look in recent editions of the *Chronicle*. Perhaps the thief has advertised his wares already."

"Do you think there is any chance we will get it back?" she asked.

"There are some things that you can never get back, Miss Richardson," Morton said. "But the painting? I think there is a good chance. Let me look into the matter a little more. I shall send you a note if I learn anything at all."

They both rose of the same instant, then stood awkwardly. Their gazes kept sliding around the room, touching lightly on each other, then slipping quickly away.

"I'll see you to the door," Miss Richardson said, so softly that Morton could barely hear. They went in silence to the entry hall.

Morton bowed as he left, then found himself out on the street. Behind him the lock ticked closed.

Arabella lounged on Morton's divan, her head propped upon a hand, the exquisite petals of her mouth hinting at dissatisfaction. Night spread over the city of London, a warm summer's night, close and dark and starless.

"If Madame Desmarches had merely been murdered, well then, I would suspect her lover, the Count d'Auvraye. But the thumbscrews—" She paused. "You know, Henry, there are men who gain pleasure from hurting women."

"Yes, and if the count has this predilection, we will quickly uncover it. There are certain places in the city frequented by such men."

"I suppose one must consider the countess: she might have found this woman a threat."

"According to one of Madame Desmarches's domestics, the count had just cast off his mistress. She would not have been much of a threat."

"But that could have been a ruse. Perhaps the count and his beautiful young mistress planned to return to France together and leave the countess and her children behind to suffer forever in . . . *England*."

Morton reached for his wine goblet. Arabella had arrived with a fine, dark Bordeaux—the first of the legal wines to cross the Channel. It was from an admirer, she'd told him, making Morton only slightly uncomfortable. But when a woman had as many admirers as the acclaimed Arabella Malibrant, one must make peace with it. Morton sipped his wine and tried not to think of its source.

"I suppose anything is possible." Beyond a certain point he found that this kind of speculation offered little return. He needed to speak with the Count d'Auvraye, find out where the man had been during the night of the murder, discover why he had cast Angelique Desmarches aside. Morton needed to take the measure of the man and watch him as he answered questions. There were many things Morton would need to learn before he could begin to speculate.

"Do you know what I do find odd?" Morton said suddenly. "The dressmaker, Madame De le Cœur; she claimed not to know Angelique Desmarches well, though her grief at the news belied this."

"We both noted that." Arabella plucked her wine goblet from the small side table that Morton had moved within her reach. He often felt like a creature utterly without grace beside her.

"Indeed we did. But Angelique Desmarches's servants told me that Madame De le Cœur or her daughter came to visit often—at times when they had no business to transact."

"They might have been collecting bills, or trying to."

"But Madame De le Cœur said specifically that Madame Desmarches paid her bills on time. Do you remember?"

"I don't, but I would never doubt your memory, Henry."

Arabella returned her glass to the table in a rustle of silk, enticing Morton's mind for a moment to things more romantic.

"If she was a friend of the poor woman who was murdered, why did she not say so?" Arabella asked.

"I have wondered the same thing."

"Fear of Bow Street?"

"She did not seem afraid. When first we arrived, I believe she was a little disdainful, as though vexed that a mere Runner would dare disturb *her*." Morton closed his eyes and tried to recall the conversation to its smallest detail. After a moment he opened his eyes. "There is something odd there. I believe I shall speak to Madame De le Cœur again."

"I will do it for you, if you like," Arabella said. "Perhaps she was less than truthful with you, Henry, but you are more intimidating than you realise."

"I was a perfect gentleman."

"Indeed you were—a perfect gentleman of six foot three inches height, twelve plus stone. Not to mention that you represent the law of a foreign land." She smiled. "Leave Madame De le Cœur to me. I think her daughter was rather pleased to have me appear in their establishment. Do you remember she paid me a very fine compliment?"

"Did she indeed? Odd that you would remember that."

" 'Man can be cured of every folly but vanity.' "

It was a quote, clearly, but not one Morton recognised. He took a guess. "Dr. Johnson?"

"Rousseau!"

Morton nodded and took up his glass again.

"You are in low spirits this evening, my love," Arabella said.

"Am I? It is this murder, I suppose," Morton said, knowing it was a lie. The visit to his half-sister was at the heart of his mood, and he knew it. How bold she had been to write him! They had more in common than just appearance—he felt that. Yet they were separated by barriers as invisible as borders, and as real.

He opened his mouth to tell Arabella of the letter he had received and the subsequent meeting with his half-sister. But for some reason he could say nothing.

Chapter 9

Before knocking at the door of the Count d'Auvraye's house in Spanish Place, Henry Morton
and Jimmy Presley had words with their
watcher. Harold Farke had spent the dark hours in the
shadows of an elm tree a discreet distance up the way, in
Manchester Square. The shutters of most of the houses
were closed, their inhabitants gone to the country for the
summer, and there was little chance of him being observed or troubled. And Farke was a man who made a
fine art of seeming a nondescript but somehow natural
prop to almost any scene.

"An old cove came in p'raps an hour after Mr. Presley
left me. I figure him to be your count. Came in his coach
and didn't go out again. He ought still to be there."

"Good. Were there others?"

Farke hardly moved as he spoke, lounging against his
tree, eyes still coolly fixed on the house across the way.
He merely shifted the splinter of wood he was chewing
from one side of his mouth to the other.

"Oh, aye. Several folk came, and a few went again.

Gennl'men mostly, and two young ladies. They stayed, and a couple of the other gennl'men stayed, too. Lights on till nigh on one o'clock in the morn."

Morton dropped a couple of shillings into the man's jacket pocket and murmured, "Commendable, thorough work, Harold. Off you go, now."

"Ye know where to come at me, if ye need me."

"How many *young ladies* does the fellow need?" grunted Jimmy Presley, as Farke drifted away and the two Runners turned to contemplate the count's house.

Morton laughed. "I wouldn't expect they're mistresses, Jimmy. Not openly, here, in his town dwelling. After all, there are other explanations. Besides, I'm reliably informed he has his daughters living here as well as his countess."

"Bloody French hareem."

"Nay, that's the Turks you're thinking of. All foreigners are not the same, whatever they may have told you in Cheapside. Let's go have a word."

Morton had half-expected the Comte d'Auvraye to treat the Bow Street Runners as a kind of tradesmen, to be let in at the servants' entrance, then ushered discreetly through to his office, the way the squire of an English country manor did his tenants. But apparently the police had a different kind of status in the France that d'Auvraye wanted to keep alive. If gentlemen of the police came to call, on the king's business, a certain formality was in order, and the household was expected to present itself.

And they did. After a brief interval waiting in a small gilt-and-white retiring room off the front hall, Morton and Presley were ushered into a salon—red-carpeted,

richly furnished—in which the count stood amidst his
family, as if posing for a group portrait. He bowed, and
the two Runners responded in kind, awkwardly enough.
There were no handshakes. Morton's quick glance took
in some large bright paintings in what looked to be the
style of Watteau, and a couple of small marble statues
on wooden stands.

"Monsieur Morton, Monsieur Presley, I am Gerrard
d'Auvraye. Permit me to introduce my intimates." His
voice was gravely polite, slow, and only slightly accented. The man himself was above fifty years of age
and dressed with subtle splendour in a costume in which
silver predominated and that would not have looked out
of place in a royal court. He wore a full powdered wig
and a short goatee. "May I present Madame *la comtesse*
d'Auvraye."

Morton bowed in the direction of a small, black-eyed
lady, also sumptuously dressed in blue silks. She barely
raised an eyebrow in response, her face a rigid, powdered mask. If *le comte* felt that he must present his
family to the men from Bow Street, Morton had the dis-
tinct impression that his countess felt differently.

"My daughters, Mademoiselle Honoria and Mademoiselle Celestine."

Two rather fine-looking young ladies, both taller than
their mother and dressed in English fashion, performed
curtsies.

"I believe you have a box at the theatre, Mr. Morton,"
the dark-haired one offered.

"I regret to say that I do not, Mademoiselle Honoria,
but I attend often."

The young woman glanced at her sister, as if to say,
An odd pastime for a police constable.

"My son and heir, Monsieur Eustache d'Auvraye."

A slim, thin-faced, mustachioed young man, he looked much like his mother but had an even more impenetrable air of lofty reserve. His bow was so formal as almost to be a parody, Morton thought. But then, he was not the best judge of such things.

"My cousin, Monsieur Henri Pellerin, of La Rochelle, who is doing us the honour of an extended visit."

A pale, rather flabby middle-aged gentleman, less well dressed, all deference.

"And finally, my private secretary, Monsieur Rolles."

A short man, clad more in the English fashion, with a sharp face and a few long strands of hair combed over his almost completely bald pate. His bow was quick and efficient.

"Monsieur Rolles and I will receive you in my own cabinet, if you will be so good as to follow."

He led them through another door, leaving the assembled family without further ado. As they proceeded sedately down the carpeted hallway, Morton tried to imagine the people in the room they had just left. Were they relaxing now? Dispersing to their several pursuits? Or did they merely sit down in those uncomfortable-looking chairs and grimly await the next summons of paternal authority?

Morton let the count enter his room, then turned to murmur confidentially to the secretary: "Monsieur Rolles?"

"Monsieur?"

Morton indicated Presley with a brief gesture of his head. "My...man," he said quietly in French, "is not normally...present at my interviews. I wonder if he mightn't be entertained in the kitchen, till we are done?"

Rolles bowed and beckoned for a footman. Jimmy

Presley, as he and Morton had planned, was led off to see what he might glean from the servants.

The count's private study was dark, formal, and ornamented more with statues and tapestries than with bookshelves. Rolles closed the door gently behind them, and the three men took straight-backed library chairs in a circle in the midst of the room. Morton had a chance now to study the Count d'Auvraye's face more closely. It was a fine face, with a noble brow and well-proportioned mouth, complemented by the exceedingly closely groomed white goatee. He shone, somehow, with the glow of self-conscious dignity and old prestige, like a Van Dyke portrait. But there was, even so, something slightly static and heavy about him, some absence of lively apprehension, as if all his breeding and education had been unable to prevent a certain obtuseness. Morton recalled Darley's assessment of the man—a ponderous thinker. Morton wondered if Lord Arthur was being overly kind.

Rolles spoke first.

"Monsieur, *le comte* d'Auvraye has condescended to see you on such short notice out of his profound respect for the king whom you serve and for the nation that has rendered our beloved France such signal services of late, at so great a cost of her best blood. However, the calls upon *monsieur le comte*'s attention are many and pressing just now. His time is very short. I am sure you can appreciate the need for brevity today."

Morton smiled perfunctorily. "I shall try to oblige *monsieur le comte*." This, however, was not entirely candid. Whenever Henry Morton heard that someone's time was short—and he heard it often enough in the course of his duties—he in fact tended to find himself settling more comfortably into his seat, in readiness for a prolonged stay.

Rolles bowed his head in polite gratitude, while the count, very erect in his chair, continued to gaze at them with a fixed and wordless solemnity. "In what manner can we be of assistance to you?" asked the secretary. Morton wondered if the absence of expression on the faces of the two men before him was so complete because it was studied.

"Comte d'Auvraye," Morton began, "you are acquainted with a young woman of your own nation, Madame Angelique Desmarches."

"You assume," began Rolles, "an acquaintance that—"

"Thank you, Monsieur Rolles," the count interrupted, "but I believe we may speak in all frankness. I know Madame Desmarches, yes."

For the moment Morton kept his tone scrupulously civil.

"May I presume, then, to ask the nature of your acquaintance with her?"

This question, which might have produced bluster in an English house, seemed not outwardly to trouble the two Frenchmen.

"Madame Desmarches at one time enjoyed my protection." The count shifted slightly as he spoke, clasping his hands upon his knee. The phrase was stiff enough, of course, but Morton heard a measure of pride in d'Auvraye's voice. Pride, and perhaps... affection? But there was something else, too, that he was not quite able to conceal as he made this admission. Something different. Undercurrents of grief, perhaps disappointment, some still-raw anger.

"You are the owner, then, of the house at number 3, the Hampstead Road?"

A slight pause. This was cutting rather closer. "I am."

"And a frequent visitor at this dwelling?"

Now, however, Monsieur Rolles interposed, with delicacy. "Monsieur Morton, I am sure you can appreciate that one does not ask a gentleman to speak of such matters in any specific detail."

Morton had no intention of listening for long to this sort of cant. But he was still interested in the ambiguity in the count's attitude toward his onetime mistress.

The count sat up suddenly, as though he had just wakened. "Monsieur Morton," he said a bit breathlessly, "why are you asking about Madame Desmarches?"

"She was found dead two mornings ago, *monsieur le comte.*"

The man's hauteur fell away like a shroud slipping off a body. He turned to his secretary, eyes glittering with tears. He opened his mouth but could produce no sound but a rasping breath.

Rolles stood immediately and reached out to support his employer.

"Our interview is at an end," the secretary said.

But the count held up a hand, and Morton did not move. It was a long moment before the count could collect himself, and then he turned to Morton. "How did this happen?"

"That is what I wish to learn, Count d'Auvraye. She was found dead a little distance from her home—"

"Could it have been . . . a suicide?" now Rolles quietly asked.

The count crossed himself. "May God forgive her."

"It is true that she looked troubled that day—and I believe you know why. But I do not think that self-murder explains her death, messieurs. Nor do I think it was an accident."

The count shook off his secretary and rose from his chair, unable suddenly to be still. He walked a few paces, restlessly clasping and unclasping his hands. Then he turned back to Morton, blinking quickly.

"Then what, monsieur, was the cause of Madame's death, if I may ask?"

"It seems likely that she died of a fall, but from the window of her home. Her body was then moved to a small sand pit and placed so that it appeared she had thrown herself or fallen onto some rocks." Morton paused to let these words sink in. The count considered this information, the look of sadness on his face unchanging. Morton glanced at Rolles, who sat on the edge of his chair, eyes fixed on his employer, like a little dog who feared being left behind.

"Monsieur le comte," Morton said, "I am informed that a man of yours visited Madame Desmarches's house on the day of her death, to evict her." He turned to the secretary, his voice still polite, but his eye a little harder. "This, I presume, was you, Monsieur Rolles?"

Rolles dipped his head. The count turned to face Morton.

"You ordered Madame Desmarches from her house with but a single day's notice, *monsieur le comte*? It is my duty to ask why."

The count raised his eyes again. "It was not kind of me, monsieur. It was not just. I acted in anger. In fact, I commanded that she be dismissed upon the very hour, but Monsieur Rolles, who has the truest instincts of a Christian gentleman, took it upon himself to offer her the shelter of that house for another night, so that she might properly arrange for her departure. When my choler had passed, I respected this decision."

"I salute Monsieur Rolles's humanity—"

"Monsieur Morton," Rolles interrupted, "I can assure you that the count has not been to the house of Madame Desmarches in several days. He has not seen her at all." He glanced at the count, as though wondering if he were overstepping himself. "Only I have been to see Madame Desmarches, and that is why immediately I suggested self-murder...because I saw Madame when she received the count's decree." Again a glance at the count as though in apology. "She was disconsolate."

"I see. And you, Monsieur Rolles? Where were you, the night of the twenty-eighth, twenty-ninth of July, this two nights past?"

The man looked more than surprised that Morton would even consider asking him. "Why, I was here, in my chamber, preparing *monsieur le comte*'s correspondence."

"And who can confirm this?"

The man looked utterly confused. "I—I don't know. I shall have to ask the servants. I was alone, as I often am."

Morton turned to the count, but Rolles answered for his master, as though having to account for his presence were too great an indignity.

"*Monsieur le comte* was with your sovereign, monsieur, attending the *fête* at Carleton House, upon the express invitation of His Royal Highness the Prince Regent. Men of the highest standing will be able to vouch for his presence there. At some hour near upon midnight he returned here and retired."

Morton looked to the count.

"That is correct," d'Auvraye said softly.

Well, Morton thought, John Townsend knew the Prince Regent personally. The old Runner would be able to verify the count's claim.

"Who would have wished to harm Madame Desmarches, Count d'Auvraye?"

The count shook his head, his gaze rising to the ceiling for a few seconds. "I cannot say, monsieur. She—she was a woman of great beauty and charm." The man put a hand to his brow, hiding his eyes a moment.

Long ago John Townsend had impressed upon Morton that it was not his duty to be respectful and considerate in such situations. It was his duty to find out the truth.

"Why did you cast her off, sir?"

It took d'Auvraye a long moment to answer, but finally he looked up. "She betrayed me, monsieur. She betrayed me."

Morton was about to ask with whom, but the count spoke again, his tone flat and filled with sadness.

"I have answered your questions, Monsieur Morton. Now perhaps you can answer one of mine. You say you believe she was murdered. How do you know this?"

In such situations Morton liked to direct the course of the interview, but he intended to tell the count this, anyway—perhaps now was the right time. "The pit where she was found, *monsieur le comte*, was small and shallow. The height she would have fallen from was not great—likely not great enough to inflict the injuries that killed her—and there was very little blood where she was found. The surgeon who examined her remains was certain there should have been more. But these are not the only reasons I doubt she fell or self-murdered." Morton paused a second. "You see, upon Madame's person were the unmistakable signs of a most infernal instrument." Morton glanced again at Rolles, then back to the count. "She had been tortured with a thumbscrew, Comte d'Auvraye. Tortured and then murdered."

The count gave a small, sobbing cry. His powdered wig fell to the floor, a little storm of snow spreading over the red carpet. D'Auvraye spun and pushed awkwardly through a small door before Morton could even begin to protest.

The Runner was immediately on his feet, but Rolles interposed his small person between Morton and the door.

"This interview is at an end," the secretary said.

Morton looked down at the small man, who appeared more than a little frightened.

"I have more questions to ask."

"Tonight *monsieur le comte* will go to his house at Barnes Terrace. You may find him there, or in three days when he returns. For the moment he needs... to consider all that you have revealed."

"Then I shall ask questions of you."

The secretary looked around quickly as though seeking his own method of escape. "I—I shall try to answer them."

"Indeed you will." Morton returned to his seat and gestured for the secretary to do the same.

"Tell me, Monsieur Rolles, who would have done such a thing? Was Madame Desmarches in the count's confidence enough that someone would torture her to gain information?"

Rolles looked utterly miserable and kept glancing toward the small door through which his master had retreated. "It is possible, monsieur. Upon the pillow much is said.... *Le comte* d'Auvraye is an intimate of the King of France. He is acting as the French ambassador to the

Court of St. James's until they send another, allowing *monsieur le comte* to return, finally, to the country he loves."

"But you have not told me who might have performed this terrible act. *Torture,* Monsieur Rolles. Who would do this, and to learn what?"

"To learn what, I cannot say, but..." Rolles leaned closer. "The Bonapartists, monsieur. Who else hates us so? Poor Madame Desmarches. I'm sure she could tell them little, and yet she paid with her life." He crossed himself.

"But Bonaparte is a prisoner of my government. He will spend the rest of his life in some kind of confinement. Bonaparte's day is done, Monsieur Rolles. *Finis.*"

Rolles shook his head, his dark eyes staring earnestly into Morton's. "Bonaparte is a phoenix, Monsieur Morton. He can rise from the ashes. You English do not understand this. There is no safe place to confine him. No place distant enough. He is a phoenix. You will see."

Chapter 10

There must be twenty of them here," said Sir Nathaniel Conant, gazing down at the paper on his table. It was a list of the names Rolles had given to Morton.

"Twenty-two," said Morton.

"And he would say no more? He gave no specific reason for suspecting these people?"

"They are partisans of Bonaparte. Or were. At least that was his claim."

The Chief Magistrate scowled. "He gives every impression of a man trying to protect his master by diverting suspicion to others."

Morton, standing, gave a shrug of agreement. It was certainly possible. Young Jimmy Presley and the eminent John Townsend nodded from their position in the back of the room.

"Well, I did look into this matter, as Mr. Morton asked," Townsend said. "D'Auvraye was at Carleton House, just as he claimed."

"But not for the entire night." Morton took back his

list from Sir Nathaniel's desk. "The secretary, Rolles, cannot account for his time either, except to say he was in his own chamber at Spanish Place."

"I found one of the serving men as was English," Presley told them, "and he says the count came in late, around midnight, just as he claimed. But he could have killed her before he came home, couldn't he? Or he could have gone out again to do it. This fellow, Henshawe, an underbutler, had something else to say, too. He was shylike, mind, and just whispered me to wait about a bit and see him round the back in the coach-house."

The other three men listened closely now.

"Aye, well, this sounded good, didn't it?" Presley was pleased with himself. "So I waited, tried to get the coachman to blow the gab, but he didn't understand a word except his own parlee-voo. Finally Henshawe comes and says that all the servants are supposed to keep quiet about the family, as anybody might be a spy. The count has serious business to do for the French king, and even Bow Street officers might be spies, or might squeak to them as are."

"Who gave them orders not to speak to Bow Street?" demanded Sir Nathaniel. "The count?"

Jimmy Presley's face went blank for a moment, but then he recovered. "Henshawe didn't say, sir. But I assumed as much, head of the house and all that. At any rate, he was bothered about it, and as a true loyal Englishman he wanted to serve his king and country."

The venerable Townsend laughed. "How much did ye tip him, Jimmy boy? A shilling? Two?"

Presley again looked disconcerted. "Three, actually."

"That's steep! I hope the goods were worth it!"

"Proceed, proceed," the Chief Magistrate demanded impatiently.

"Well, Henshawe tells me, the day before Madame Desmarches died, a man comes and visits the count and his son. He's a Frenchy, seems, but not one Henshawe has ever seen before. Something of a down-at-the-heel Frenchy, with a balding pate with one of those raspberry stains just on the top of it. Not the kind of folk as the count usually entertains, not one of those perfumey aristocrats. He comes to the door claiming to be an importer of French goods. But then he stays with the count an hour or so in his cabinet, and as soon as he leaves, the count storms out in a passion and sends Monsoor Rolly to give his mistress the boot, chuck her right out of the house he gave her, without so much as a fare-thee-well! The servants never saw him in such a rage."

The young Runner folded his arms now and gave the little group a look of satisfaction, as if he had come close to resolving the whole matter.

"The name of this man with the raspberry?"

"Nay, Henshawe didn't have it. Oh, but he did say the cove told the footman to announce the gent from"—Presley tried to get it right—"from . . . *Mal-mace-on*. Or maybe *mason,* or some such. But Henshawe's warranted to call for me if he sees anything more."

There was a thoughtful pause all round.

"Should we have brought Count d'Auvraye before you?" Morton asked Sir Nathaniel Conant.

The Magistrate shook his head. "We've not enough cause. Not yet. Why, if he intended to murder her, would he first of all send his man to evict her? And you say he wouldn't have expected her still to be in the house that night."

"I don't know when Rolles admitted to him that he

had not tossed her out on the street immediately, as he'd been ordered. If not for the thumbscrews, I could imagine the count riding out to the home of Madame Desmarches that night. Men who have been betrayed have been known to act out of passion, to do things completely against their character. But why would he torture her? It seems too barbarous a revenge for the man I met, no matter how he'd been wronged. And I was fairly convinced by his reaction that he did not know of her death. He would have to be a masterful actor to have managed that."

"I trust your judgement in such things, Mr. Morton. But if not the count, then whom?" Sir Nathaniel turned in his chair to look a moment out the window. "What do we know of this woman?" he asked, turning back to his Runners. "Was she the sort to play the count false? Where did he meet her? Had she been a whore, or a demi-rep?"

"We were told she came over here to stay loyal to the Bourbons," said Morton. "Her husband was a soldier in Bonaparte's armies, but what happened to him is apparently unknown. It seems to me that if Desmarches had been an officer of any rank, his death or other fate would have been announced in the Bonapartist equivalent of a gazette, or found out otherwise. This suggests the man was a private soldier, even a conscript. His wife was most likely of the same class."

"Bonapartist camp follower turned royalist mistress? An odd progression."

"She was a beautiful woman," said Morton quietly.

The Chief Magistrate frowned a moment longer, then seemed to summon himself.

"Well, you will certainly have to have another talk with the Count d'Auvraye. But let us first see what else we can turn up. I have reported the business of the thumbscrew marks to the Foreign Office, and they want you to speak to someone, a Captain Westcott over at the Admiralty."

"The navy? Why are they concerned?"

The Magistrate shrugged. "You'd think they'd have enough to worry about, with Bonaparte himself slinging a hammock in one of their ships. But I suppose they have their own people who look into this sort of thing." He nodded at the paper Morton still held. "Give your list to him. He's asked that you wait on him at his chambers at three, and I said you would. Let us see what light he might be able to throw on the business. Mr. Townsend? Your views?"

The celebrated old Runner had out his snuffbox and did not respond at once. Those in the room, of course, were familiar with his eccentricities. They were also familiar with his unsurpassed skill in their profession and were prepared to wait.

"I'm sure you all have noticed the oddity in this business," he remarked, then sneezed loudly. Wiping his nose and putting away his handkerchief as if nothing had happened, he went on. "Betrayal and rejection, yes. Even betrayal, rejection, and then murder. Yes, that still has a certain logic to it. The man's wounded pride festers as he reflects on the enormity of what she has done to him, and then passion erupts and he pursues her for further vengeance—just as Mr. Morton has said. Or if the woman had been subjected to torture and then murdered *without* ever being rejected by the count, I hardly think we would be sitting here having this discussion. We would all assume, rightly, that she had been tortured by one of his enemies, who hoped to learn some vital piece of intelligence." He raised his silvery eyebrows waiting for anyone to gainsay this. No one did. "But she was put to the torment immediately *after* the count had rejected her. If she had already betrayed his secrets, for example, why did they need to torture her? Betrayal, rejection... *torture*... *murder*. How do these things sort with each other?"

They all waited for Townsend to answer his own question, but the old man grinned and slowly eased himself up from his chair. He straightened stiffly, and then to no one in particular said, "It is in this odd conjunction of matters that the mystery abides, gentlemen. It is in this peculiarity of timing. I believe we are obliged to reject any *obvious* suspect or conclusion. We need to look further, reflect more deeply."

Chapter 11

Morton called on Captain Geoffrey Westcott at the Admiralty and, after being left to ponder in the waiting room for a quarter of an hour, was greeted by an officer of perhaps thirty years. Morton's first impression was of the man's height, for the captain was the precise height of Morton himself: six feet and three inches. A longish face, a beaked nose in the style of Wellington, and a disarming smile—these impressed one next. And last, a firm handshake, and a clear eye, blue as the sea itself on a summer day. Westcott was dressed in a uniform so well tailored and spotless that any dandy would have taken the man to be one of their own, impressed into the Royal Navy.

"Henry Morton, Bow Street."

"Geoffrey Westcott. It is a pleasure. Do you mind if we slip out of this madhouse? My club is just a few paces off, in St. James's."

Morton had no objections. St. James's Street was home to three of London's most established clubs, White's, Brooks', and Boodle's. It was a street where one seldom saw a woman, and never a woman of quality—at least not an English one. The young bucks who lounged in the club windows, quizzing glasses in hand, had long since given the street its reputation, and no delicately nurtured young lady would dare venture there for fear of her reputation. St. James's and its environs was a masculine preserve, and many a well-to-do bachelor made his home there—often to the detriment of his fortune.

Morton seldom gambled—he worked too hard for his money to chance losing it—but in London he was almost alone in his dislike of this vice. And the city's great clubs were the many beating hearts of this obsession. Not just wealth changed hands within these imposing preserves. Men were driven out of England for the debts that they incurred in White's and Wattier's. Fortunes were lost, and occasionally won as well.

Captain Westcott set a brisk pace as they passed along the border of St. James's Park, onto which the Admiralty building backed. But then, as they gained a little distance from the Admiralty, the seaman turned and stood looking back. Morton's gaze followed. Atop the building the semaphoric telegraph was just then set in motion, the six wooden shutters pivoting upon their central axes so that they appeared either as thin horizontal lines or as dark rectangles.

"Can you read it?" Morton asked.

Westcott nodded, his aquiline nose seeming to lift a little as though he could sniff the message on the air. The shutters held their position for a few seconds, then changed of an instant so that all six showed their dark faces.

"There," Westcott said, pointing. "That is the letter C." He turned his head to Morton and smiled. "It will almost certainly be replaced by an improved system within a year."

Morton could not help but be impressed. "I find it difficult to imagine that there could be a better system. It's said that messages travel along the line of towers at two hundred miles to the hour!"

"Oh, at the very least," Westcott said. "I've known messages to be sent to Plymouth and an answer received in but half an hour. Of course that is only by day, and then only on days without mist or rain." He glanced back at the telegraph, which continued its display. "But even so it is a great advancement." He looked back at Morton and smiled charmingly. "Can you imagine if you had told a man twenty-five years ago that messages would travel across the land at a speed of two hundred miles to the hour what he would have said of you?" He laughed. "It is an age of wonders, Morton. An age of wonders."

They set off again, speaking of small things as they went—the changes to the city, a fire that had destroyed a row of buildings, the new wines that were arriving at Berry's now that the blockade had been lifted. In this way they were soon in St. James's, through the doors so many aspired to pass, and then into White's itself. The joke among Londoners went that when a boy child was born to an aristocratic family, a servant stopped at White's to enter the child's name in the candidacy book before proceeding to the registry office to record the birth.

Westcott was obviously well known here, and he led Morton to a quiet, walnut-panelled room where brandy was served. A few men sat about smoking, their faces thrust into the daily papers, or talking quietly. One exhausted-looking man, fresh from the gambling room, still wore his coat inside out "for luck" and was just now removing the leather wristbands that protected his lace when he threw the dice. He nodded to Westcott.

"Captain," he said hoarsely, then bobbed his head to Morton. The young man collapsed in a chair, ordered brandy, and promptly fell asleep.

Recognition dawned on Morton.

Westcott read something in Morton's face. "You know our Robbie, Mr. Morton?"

"Only by reputation."

This was Miss Caroline Richardson's brother—and Morton's half-brother. They had never formally met, but Morton had seen him numerous times over the years.

Westcott looked over at the sleeping man, who had now begun to snore softly. "He is gaining something of a reputation. Rather sad for his family." He offered Morton a bitter half-smile.

A group of three young gentlemen entered the room then, spotted Robert Richardson, and with muffled laughter proceeded to prod and tickle the insensible young man, gaining great levity from the sport. They were finally shushed and driven away by a stern look from one of the senior members, who had previously been enjoying his paper.

Westcott took a sip from his brandy and then pushed the errant sons of the aristocracy from his mind. "So, Mr. Morton, did I understand correctly that this unfortunate young woman you found had been subjected to the thumbscrew?"

"I'm afraid it is absolutely true."

The captain made a small gesture of amazement. "Have you found out who she was?"

"Her name was Madame Angelique Desmarches,"

Morton reported. "And she was the mistress of the Comte d'Auvraye."

The captain spread his hands along the edge of the table. "Gerrard d'Auvraye?"

Morton nodded.

Westcott lifted his hands to his temples as if stricken by a sudden headache and paused to consider. "Well, that is news."

Morton thought the man looked a bit shaken. "Do you know the count?" Morton asked. He had no intention of allowing this conversation to be a one-way flow of information.

"I have met him, yes. A few times, in fact. He is a member of Wattier's, as am I."

Wattier's, Morton knew, was the club to join if you fancied yourself a gourmet. The cuisine was French, of course. The club had actually been started by the Prince Regent, in league with a great chef named Wattier. In recent years it was gaining a reputation as a gambling hell.

"Is d'Auvraye known for his temper?"

Westcott still looked shaken. "The opposite, in fact. He is quite . . . softly mannered. At the moment he is representing the interests of King Louis here in London, but the French will soon replace him. D'Auvraye is too kindhearted for such a post."

"I have seen the mildest of men, in moments of passion, perform the most odious acts of violence, Captain."

"I'm sure you have, and I would never say that d'Auvraye is not capable of such an act himself—but it does seem unlikely. And thumbscrews!"

"I don't suppose there are rumours of any . . . deviant peculiarities associated with our erstwhile ambassador?"

Westcott shook his head. "None, but this matter takes

on a whole new significance now. *D'Auvraye!*" he said with feeling.

"This distresses you," Morton observed.

"It does indeed. You see, Mr. Morton, it has recently been my function in the Admiralty to 'watch over' certain groups of French nationals in England, though with the royalists I am more of a liaison."

"It seems a difficult task for one man."

"I am not alone in this endeavour, thankfully." He looked at Morton a moment, as though taking his measure. "I suppose now that the war appears to be finally over, I may say this to you, but I should caution you, Mr. Morton: None of this should be repeated."

Morton nodded his assent.

Westcott hesitated a moment, as though wondering what he might safely reveal and what he might not. "I should, at the very least, have my own ship by now, Mr. Morton, but my mother is French, and I had the misfortune to spend a good part of my childhood in that country—not that I didn't enjoy it. I did, entirely. But it had an unexpected influence on my future endeavours.

"I speak the language as a native, know the customs, the odd little things that a foreigner would never pick up, not if he lived there a dozen years. This accident of birth is the reason I've only reached the rank of post captain at the age of thirty-two. Men I shared the midshipman's berth with are *admirals* now." He took a long breath and visibly calmed himself. "I have spent some part of the war across the Channel, travelling under different names, claiming different purposes. I will flatter myself and say that some of the information I have brought back with me has proven passingly useful to the Admiralty—and for this I have been rewarded with a desk in the Admiralty building and charged with watching over the French expatriates here on our shores. Not all of them, of course, but those who are of interest— men and women suspected of being Bonaparte's agents in England. The various royalist factions. Anyone who might be of use or who might do us harm." He applied himself to his brandy a moment. "You see before you the only commissioned officer in His Majesty's navy, who is not a lord of the Admiralty, to sit at a desk in that venerable building. But I do not mean to grumble. I have given service to my country—not the service I yearned to give, but valuable service all the same."

Morton swirled his brandy in his crystal glass. "I'm sure you have, Captain. You at least have served during the wars. It was my lot to chase criminals through the streets of London, and very few of them were even French, let alone agents of Bonaparte."

Westcott raised a glass to Morton. "I think we understand each other, Mr. Morton. And it seems that we might be of assistance to each other as well."

"I will tell you honestly that I would be grateful for any help," Morton admitted. "I'm something out of my depth in this. D'Auvraye's secretary suggested that Madame Desmarches was murdered by Bonapartists. He even provided a list of names of men he thought likely. But what confuses me is that Bonaparte is in chains—figuratively, at least. What could possibly induce his supporters to torture and then murder d'Auvraye's mistress? Could d'Auvraye, in his rather nominal position, be in possession of . . . state secrets that others would kill to know?"

"Well, there are secrets and there are secrets, aren't there? Of the more trivial kind, he might possess many; of the genuine variety, rather fewer, I would guess.

Certainly someone might think the count knows more
than he actually does."

Westcott caught the attention of a servant and asked
for more brandy. He sat back in his comfortable seat; the
clubs vied with one another to provide the most luxurious chairs. "I shall have to look into this. At the moment
there is nothing I know of d'Auvraye's activities that
would justify someone torturing his mistress in hopes of
gaining information. However, there are gentlemen,
even within the confines of these walls, who might tell
me differently. Let me see what can be learned." He
looked over at Morton. "The count's secretary gave you
a list?"

Morton retrieved the list from his waistcoat pocket
and slid it across the polished table. Westcott unfolded
the paper and examined it. A smile crossed his face. He
laughed in spite of himself.

"I'm pleased this entertains you," Morton said.

Westcott could not stop smiling, and Morton, though
not sure of the joke, found himself smiling as well.

"Do excuse me, Mr. Morton. It appears to have taken
quite a number of Frenchmen to torture and murder
this poor woman. How many names are here?"

"Twenty-two."

"She must have been formidable." He laughed softly.
"Some of the men whose names are recorded here have
been dead for not a few years." Westcott looked up at
Morton over the paper. "How did the secretary arrive at
this list?"

The memory of Rolles diligently writing at the small
desk came back to him, and Morton found his anger beginning to simmer. "Are none of them, then, agents of
Bonaparte?"

"Several of them are—or were—suspected of this, yes." Westcott waved a hand at the list. "But look here: Pierre-Etienne Lalidreaux. We put him in front of a firing squad in Halifax in the year eleven. I'm glad to know he's still suspected in a murder that happened this week!"

Morton tried to smile. "I'm told these royalists have long memories."

"Yes, yes, I know—'they've forgotten nothing and have learned nothing.' But this is extraordinary even by that standard."

"I have wondered if Rolles gave me this list to divert my attention from his master."

"Perhaps so, though when you have the mistress of a prominent royalist subjected to thumbscrews, you can't help but look to the Bonapartists. Let me see," said Westcott more seriously, and studied the list again. "There are only so many men who could do such a thing. It takes a colder heart than most would realise. You will want to have words with De la Touche, and this man Niceron. They have both been busy in England as recently as last year, and they would apply thumbscrews to an infant if they thought it would further their cause. Mind, much has changed in a year. If not them, perhaps Guillet de la Gevrillière—he'll probably be going under the name William Roberts over here. He passes for an Englishman almost as easily as I pass for French."

"And where would I find these gentlemen?"

"They move about, never lodging in the same place more than a few days. They are wary and rather ruthless, though they do not like to draw attention to themselves, which keeps their worst inclinations under control. I should add that at this point they are likely desperate and perhaps disillusioned. I wish I could offer you more assistance, Mr. Morton, but at the moment what we have here is merely a somewhat suspicious murder. If you gain information that indicates with some surety that it was politically motivated and not merely an act of personal revenge...well in that case, please contact me immediately and I will speak with my superiors."

"Kind of you to give me the time you have, Captain." Morton placed hands on the arms of his chair as though about to rise. "I realise it is not the function of the Royal Navy to solve murders for the Bow Street Magistrate."

Westcott raised his hands, as though he'd accidentally offered offence. "I should like nothing more than to assist you in every way, Mr. Morton, but I was ordered by my superior to merely enquire into this matter just to see if it might be of interest. Personally, you may ask anything of me, and if it does not compromise my duties to the Admiralty, I shall do everything in my power to assist. I will certainly ask about to see if I can find more of d'Auvraye's activities here. You may count on that."

"Very generous of you, Captain Westcott."

Westcott smiled. "But of course, gentlemen say such things all the time and don't mean them. I rather go against my caste in that regard. I've always been damnably earnest." A self-deprecating laugh escaped him.

The two men rose, Westcott motioning for Morton to precede him. On the way out they passed Morton's dissolute half-brother, still snoring in his chair, sprawled like many a drunk Morton had seen in less lofty surroundings. He could not help but feel a certain sense of satisfaction at the sight—and a sharp jab of the resentment that never quite went away.

As Morton stood on St. James's Street, where he had parted with Geoffrey Westcott, the sight of the Honorable Robert Richardson, fresh from the gaming room and insensible from drink, would not leave his mind. The young buck's demeanour had not been suggestive of a successful night at the tables.

When he was certain Westcott was out of sight, Morton went back into the club, greeting the footman who had just seen them out.

"Sir?" the man asked, for Morton had both the manner and dress of a gentleman, if not the property.

"I believe I left my snuffbox on our table."

"I'll have someone fetch it—"

But Morton slipped by the man with a smile, trusting that Westcott's standing would grant him a brief immunity from exclusion. "No need to trouble yourself. I know right where it is."

Morton had spent many hours talking to servants in his capacity as a Runner—not that men and women in service were more larcenous than those in other occupations, but they always knew more of the functioning of a house than the people who employed them. As such, their knowledge was invaluable. Perhaps Morton's own history made him particularly suited to dealing with the servants, but no matter how it was explained, he had a touch with them, whether it was through flattery, his apparent respect for their work, or by bribery and "persuasion."

The servant he required was quickly found—the keeper of the gambling book.

"Do you wish to make a wager?" the man asked, eyeing Morton, who was certainly not a member, at least not one who frequented the club with regularity. He was, however, too polite to simply ask, for fear of giving offence. A nearby door swung open, and the clatter of Hazard dice echoed hollowly.

"Not today," Morton said jovially. "I don't feel that lucky." Morton was quickly sizing the man up, wondering which approach would prove most profitable. "I'm curious about a wager, though."

The man raised an eyebrow, and Morton quickly went on.

"To be perfectly honest, I'm worried about the degree of indebtedness of my ... cousin. Though, of course, he'd be mortified to know I'd enquired." Morton leaned close and spoke quietly, slipping the man some silver as he did so. "I might arrange to eliminate his debt for him, if I could."

"Excuse me, sir, but I'm uncertain to whom we refer."

"Lord Robert, son of Viscount Richardson."

"Ah." The man offered a relieved smile. "No need, sir, for he has no debt."

Morton noticed the servant who had let him in hurrying past, clearly looking for someone. The Runner shifted a little, putting the servant to whom he spoke between himself and the door. "Why, you surprise me!" Morton said, and then quietly: "His debt was but recently substantial—or so I was informed by Lady Caroline." Morton reached into his pocket for more silver.

"Yes, but it was paid in full two days past."

"That *is* good news!" Morton responded. "I can't tell you what relief you have provided for my worries. I can hardly thank you enough. Odd, though—the viscount is travelling. But of course it was some other, was it not? Some other who paid down Robbie's debt?"

The man was beginning to look uncomfortable, as

the cost of the information quickly rose. The footman passed again.

Encouraging nods, and what Morton hoped was a re-assuring smile. The servant hesitated. The footman spotted Morton and set off across the room toward him.

Morton thrust his remaining coins into the man's hand.

"Mr. Wilfred Stokes, sir."

"Of course it was!" Morton said with relief. "Who loves Robbie more than I, I ask you? Wilfred Stokes." Then, conspiratorially: "But never a word of this. I won't have Robbie know I even enquired."

The man nodded.

Morton managed only a few steps before he was intercepted by the footman.

"Ah, thank goodness," the Runner said as the man caught him. "I'm completely turned around."

"This way, sir. Did you find what you were looking for?"

Morton patted a pocket. "Indeed. I found it and more."

Out on St. James's again, it occurred to Morton that there was another source of information on the French expatriate community that he had not yet consulted. And this gentleman was too close at hand to ignore.

Chapter 12

Lucy Hammond stood in line trying to ignore the itch that tormented her right knee. Miss Cork, her teacher, was looking elsewhere, and Lucy began to inch her hand down her thigh, but she sprang back to attention when her teacher turned back toward the little muster of students.

They were on the Plymouth Hoe again, gazing out over the sound toward a ship of the line anchored there. Of course, Lucy had been up close to this very ship. Too close, by her estimation. She was not really interested in seeing it again, but she'd never looked through a field glass and was anxious to give it a go.

The brass instrument was mounted on some kind of tall stand, so that the girls had to stand on a wooden crate to reach it. The young first lieutenant, who Lucy noticed was sweet on Miss Cork, stood by protectively, clearly a bit apprehensive about the fate of his glass.

Lucy thought he was a fair-looking cove, but then she'd seen such men in the Otter House, and they were anything but fair. She closed her eyes a moment at the thought. The Otter was the place Mr. Morton and Mrs. Malibrant had rescued her from. It was gone now, burned down, but before that it had been a nanny-ken—to put it more bluntly, a brothel. A brothel that specialised in little girls of Lucy's age.

The girl behind gave her a push. The line was moving again as another student took her place upon the box and put her eye to the brass-ringed lens.

Lucy's turn came finally. The lieutenant glanced briefly through the lens to be sure it was still focussed on the ship and not some empty blue expanse of water.

Lucy looked, and she heard herself laugh with delight. Look! There it was! Like a little ship caught in a glass bottle. But upon this one she could see men moving about, and all around in the waters crowded the flock of boats, the people all waiting.

"Give another a turn, there's a girl, Hammond." Miss Cork put a hand gently on Lucy's shoulder. Miss Cork was the youngest teacher at the school and the most well liked by the girls. Lucy stepped down from the box and curtsied to the young lieutenant.

"Did you see the Corsican?"

Lucy shook her head. "But I did when we went out to the ship!" she added.

"You were out to the *Bellerophon*?" the young man asked, bending down a little to be closer to her height.

"Yes. And a woman drowned!"

"My dear—"

"But she did, Miss Cork. Her boat was overturned by the sailors trying to force everyone back from the ship, and she sank down before any could come to her aid. I saw it."

"Well, it is one thing to see such a tragedy and

another to talk about it. That will be enough." Miss
Cork turned back to the students. "Bell. Step up, now."

"Did you really see him?" the young officer asked quietly.

Lucy cast a sly glance at her teacher and then nodded
quickly. "A chubby little cully," she said, causing the
young man to laugh with delight.

He wiped a tear from his eye. "Do you want to know
something funny about him?" he asked.

"Lieutenant," Miss Cork warned, but Lucy could see
that she was charmed by the man.

"He speaks French with a thick Italian accent!" the
lieutenant said.

The girls all laughed.

"But he's French," one of the girls protested. "He was
even their emperor once."

"Indeed he was, but on the island of Corsica, where
he was born and raised, the people speak Italian. And so
did the 'chubby little cully.' " He laughed again. "An officer of my acquaintance serves on the *Bellerophon*, and
he swears that Bonaparte's French is not as good as
his!"

Lucy wondered if this was true, or if it was one of
those stories adults told to see how foolish children
were. You had to be wary of some of them, who were always up to tricking you and telling you lies—which was
somehow not naughty when a grown-up did it but terribly wicked when done by a child. She would ask Lord
Arthur or Mr. Morton how Bonaparte spoke. They
could be trusted.

A sound hissed over the waters then, and it took Lucy
a moment to realise it was a distant huzzah from the
people gathered about the *Bellerophon*.

"Oh, there he is! There he is!" cried Miss Cork,

bouncing up and down a little like an excited girl. She shaded her eyes and gazed off over the sound.

"Where?" said Katherine Bell as she stared into the field glass. "Where is he?"

"He's difficult to see," Lucy informed her. "He's very small."

Chapter 13

B ut you must at least try *mes petites canetons*!"
Marcel Houde entreated him.

Houde was the head chef at Boodle's, which
stood on the same street as Westcott's club, White's. Of
all the famous clubs in the neighbourhood, Boodle's was
the least political and, traditionally, the most resistant
to foreign innovation. Its members were mainly fox-
hunting men, country gentlemen, and landowners who
haunted the place on their visits to London, and their
tastes, left to their own devices, would probably have
run to beefsteak, port wine, and...more beefsteak. But
management had decided that Boodle's was not to
be left behind by such establishments as White's and
Brooks', at least in matters culinary, and had acquired
their own Frenchman. Houde's pedigree was good, if
not quite so stellar as the famous Carème, who had
cooked for Talleyrand and the Russian tsar and now the
Prince Regent and was rumoured to be headed for the
Pulteney Hotel. But Marcel Houde had learned his art
in the employ of Laetitia Bonaparte, the mother of the

emperor, and since coming to England, he had developed a dedicated following. Among whom was Henry Morton.

A Bow Street Runner, of course, was not the sort of man who would ever be proposed for membership at a Mayfair gentleman's club. But Morton had done some services for Monsieur Houde in a matter of some delicacy, involving a female relative of his who had been persecuted by a rejected English lover. An English justice of the peace, at that. And since then Morton's visits to the master-cook's domain, if only through the servants' entrance, were always welcome. Now and again he sat at Houde's plain oaken worktable and, as the clamour and steam of a great club's kitchen swirled around him, sampled some of the most astonishing delights available to the palate of man.

Morton had declined to try the seven or eight courses currently being readied, despite Marcel Houde's vociferous protests.

"Ah, 'Enri, 'Enri, where is your soul? What could be so important, compare to the embrace of a transcendental cuisine? *Allez, mon cher!*"

A plate of roast duckling was being set before Morton even before he could answer.

"Very well, Marcel, very well. But you must sit with me a moment."

"Deux secondes," the chef promised, and went off to inspect the row of burnished copper kettles ranged along the stovetop that ran down the centre of the big room. Morton could hear his voice above the clatter and rattle of plates and implements, exhorting, shouting insults, laughing sarcastically. Other, subordinate voices were once or twice raised in protest, but resignation predominated in their tones. By the time Houde returned a

few minutes later, looking pleased and wiping his reddened face with the sleeve of his open shirt, the Runner had eaten the entire duckling. He pronounced it food for the gods. As his host beamed and turned to call up something else, Morton reached to put a hand on his forearm, restraining him.

"No, no, *mon ami,* we really must have some words. I am pressed, and I am sure you are, too."

"Ah, if you insist. But *un petit verre.*" Houde poured them both a glass from a bottle of red wine that stood open on the cluttered tabletop.

"I thank you. And this is . . . ?"

"*Un*—let me say it as you poor English do, *un* 'Burgundy,' from Beaune, Ropiteau Frères. Good. Not the very best of that *vignoble,* but good."

And of course he was right. Morton savoured it a moment, then set the glass down.

"Perhaps you can assist me, Marcel. There have been some bloody doings amongst your lot."

"*Comment?* The chefs, they are killing each other now?"

"You know that I mean your compatriots. *Les Français.* And not in France, but here in England."

"Ah." Marcel Houde's manner changed. Morton knew little of his past, but they had occasionally talked on serious themes, and he gathered that the chef had once been a man of passionate conviction—and perhaps of passionate deeds as well. Now he professed to be entirely apolitical and to have brushed such matters from his coat like crumbs, as so many other artists and poets and thinking men had done. All the same, it was apparent that he still favoured the French republicans, and possibly even Bonaparte, at least in his heart. And this made his knowledge, and his acquaintance amongst the expatriates, quite different from Geoffrey Westcott's.

"In fact, there has been a murder," Morton told him.

"*Alors,* this is very vile," breathed out the chef, and sat back. "Who, a royalist? This is why you are coming to me?"

"Yes. We do not know who is responsible, but there are some men we want to have words with. I am in hopes that you can help me find them. Antoine De la Touche. Gilles Niceron. And Robert Guillet de la Gevrillière."

Houde blew air through his lips and shook his head.

"*Mais,* 'Enri. Men like these. Maybe I 'ave 'eard of them, but you know, these are not my friends, not my *camarades*."

"I'm sure they're not. But perhaps you can still assist me?"

"Well, well. *Attend.* I think. Guillet de la Gevrillière, now he I 'ave not 'eard to be in England for—what? Two year, at least. In fact, nobody know what become of 'im, except it is spoken that 'e is in prison, in France."

"The others?"

Marcel Houde sighed. "De la Touche. *Bon.* 'E 'as change of 'eart, conversion. This is a great scandal, for some people. 'E become religious, and 'e love King Louis now, and 'e is in France, too, gone to Provence to be acolyte in the Abbaye de Sénanque. Do not smile. This is true, and I 'ave 'eard many people say it. But, now...Niceron. *Oui,* Gilles Niceron, 'e may be in Londres, or near—yes, I think so."

"Do you know where?"

"No, no, not certainly. But I think 'e once was living with some farmer, some old Huguenot, out in the north of *la ville,* near the Stamford 'ill Turnpike. There is *un petit village* over there, let me think—*oui,* who is called Walt'amstow. Niceron, 'e live there, on the farm, and 'e work for the Huguenot, but I don't know that man's name. But you find 'im, I think, if you go there."

"What manner of a man is he? Niceron."

"Oh, I do not know. I 'av 'eard' he is *grand*, and powerful. Some people are afraid of 'im, but I do not remember why. To me, 'Enri, 'e is just a name."

"Is he active in French matters? In politics?"

" 'Enri! I tell you, I do not know about 'im!" Houde was exasperated.

Morton smiled. "No matter. We shall pay a visit to Citizen Niceron. There is another man, too, whose name we don't know. But he is going about saying he is from what I take to be Malmaison, and he is distinguished by a red stain in his skin, a raspberry mark, on the head."

Now Marcel Houde did not look very happy. He leaned on his elbow and closed his eyes, rubbing his broad forehead vaguely with two fingers. "Ah, *oui, oui,*" he murmured.

"I must take it that you do know him, *mon ami*."

Houde opened eyes that suddenly looked weary. "You know what Malmaison is, 'Enri?"

"I was hoping you could help me there, too."

"It is, or it was, a palace of the emperor, west of Paris. Or *plus précisément,* of his stepdaughter 'Ortense. I forgive *you,* of course, but any Frenchman would know this."

"So," said Morton slowly, "this man is a Bonapartist?"

"Let me ask you this, 'Enri. Would you say that a person who loved Bonaparte, in this country, would be wise to go about introducing 'imself this way?"

"Was the name used in irony, then?"

"*Non, non, jamais.* It is ridiculous, yes. *Ironique,* no.

No, 'Enri, I know quite well this man. But listen to me a minute, before I give you 'is name and you go rushing off to *arrêter* 'im. Because I can tell you he is an *imbécile,* a nothing, a crazed man who is drunk always. You know, don't you, that these royalists 'ate each other even more than they 'ate the rest of us?"

"I have heard it said."

"*Bon.* So why don't you think maybe they are killing each *other*?"

"Perhaps they are. But the royalists I talked to seem to hate Napoleon as thoroughly as one could ask."

"Well, but you are right, of course," the chef went on. "They 'ate the emperor. They 'ate the ideals of the *république*, too, and they 'ate nine-tenths of the French people. They want to go back to the days when the peasants were made to beat the marshes all night, so the aristocrats could sleep without the sound of frogs. They really did that, you know. If you ask me, they 'ate France herself, although no doubt they did not tell you that."

"Anything but. And they don't suspect other royalists. They suspect the followers of Bonaparte. Do you really think they are wrong to do that?"

Houde sighed and seemed to consider a moment. "No, *probablement pas*. Probably they are not entirely wrong. But suspicion is one thing. Who knows what the truth is?"

Morton nodded. "It is hard to unravel. I ask myself the same questions. Why would lovers of the republic, or adherents of the fallen emperor, be attacking the émigrés *now*? The battles are over. I am told that most of the agents, spies, and troublemakers have left England."

"They tell you there will be no more trouble here in England? But it is not true! Not true at all. I don't know why they tell you such a thing. Perhaps they are *idiots*. The danger has not pass, 'Enri, and surely you, as a man who listens to *le peuple,* surely you know this in your 'eart. The danger 'as not pass. For Angleterre, the danger is just begin."

Henry Morton smiled grimly. "So our streets will run in blood, as yours did?"

"I am simply telling that the war is *not* over. Not 'ere, and not in France, neither. It is a war that never end. That is why I retire from it, and I make war now just on the quails and the snails and the trout. And these fat 'appy English I cook for, they make war on the foxes. That is why I like this club. These English, they are stupid and proud, and they are 'appy. You see, I am finish with politics, 'Enri. But *it* is not finish."

"I am not fighting a war, Marcel, just trying to keep the king's peace. The name of the man with the raspberry mark?"

"If I tell you, I do not tell you because I care one dried-up bean for the whole *canaille* of imbecile, parasitic royalists. I hope the ocean rise up and drown every one of them. They 'ave France again now because a great man—a *great* man, 'Enri!—has fallen, destroyed by 'is own destiny, because the 'eavens 'ave say, *Not yet.* But these royalists, they are not worthy to untie 'is shoe latchet, as one say."

Morton took another sip of his wine and waited.

"*Non,* and I do not tell you because I believe your country is correctly govern, or just, or generous to its people. It is not true, and any man with eyes in his 'ead can see this. I do not tell you because tyranny 'as been— but I think you 'ave 'eard my speeches before, 'Enri."

Morton shrugged acquiescence. "Perhaps you tell me because I am your friend," he suggested.

"Well, well, or because I know that you will find 'im anyway, with a mark on 'im like that, and you such a clever, *puissant* police. And really, I care nothing at all for this person, *pas de tout. Alors.* The man with that mark on his pate is name Jean Boulot. He live for many years in the City, in Maiden Lane, or somewhere nearby there, where there are some others like him. I 'ave not ever been there to see them, but this is what people say. Boulot, he is a supporter of the emperor, an *ardent* supporter. Or so I 'ave always heard."

"If he is a supporter of Bonaparte, then why has he been in England for so long?"

Marcel shrugged. "I don't know. 'E say so many things when 'e drink—"

"You know him, then?"

Houde looked slightly embarrassed. "You drink French wine during the war, 'Enri?"

"You know I have."

"Then you 'ave come close to know 'im yourselves. Boulot is an *ami* of the smuggler. I buy the wine and brandy from 'im for many year, but 'e became too drunk and—'ow you say?—unreliable."

"I see. What else can you tell me about him?"

"What *can* I tell you? What *will* I, you should say." Marcel Houde laughed, his old, more cheerful self beginning to return. "I will tell you this. 'Is friends would be very surprise to 'ear that he go about calling 'imself the *gentilhomme de Malmaison*. They will not be please with 'im. Unless it is part of some plan."

"What manner of plan? What kind of capers do this Boulot and his friends get up to?"

"Ah, I do not know that. Maybe all they do is smoke their pipe and talk about *les droits de l'homme* and sing '*Ça Ira*' and '*La Marseillaise*.' Sometime people talk, that they have connections to Fouché, and Veyrat, and the rest of the secret police in Paris. Or at least, that they once did. But, 'Enri, you must not listen to this talk. It is *exagéré*. Perhaps some of them were sent over here from Paris—years ago. Now? *Impossible!* They all used to be fighting against *le comte* d'Artois, the brother of King Louis, and against his spies, his royalist underground in France, and those idiots, the Chevaliers de la Foi and their master, Abbé Jean-Baptiste Lafond. But what does that matter now? Now they are all gone back to France. You understand who I am speaking about, 'Enri?"

In fact, Morton was getting a little lost in the names, and it was hard to keep up with his friend's volubility. He was a London police man, not an intelligence officer in the foreign service, like Westcott. So Houde was forced to explain a bit further. Fouché was *chef* of the French security police, and Inspector-General Veyrat was in his service. In the course of the long war they had struggled against the agents of the Bourbon spymaster Artois, who was next in line for the French crown after his gout-ridden brother Louis. Many had died, on both sides. Neither party had been less ruthless than the other, and there were crimes of every kind. But now all had changed. Fouché, who many years before had helped overthrow Robespierre, the bloody tyrant of *la terreur,* had only a few weeks ago performed the same manoeuvre against the defeated Napoleon. It was Fouché who had forced Bonaparte's second abdication, and Fouché who had now, yet again, changed sides and smoothed the path for the return of the Bourbons, who hated and distrusted him but could not do without him.

"What might all this have to do with the current situation in London?"

"*Rien! Rien de tout!* Nothing! All the important royalists 'ave gone back to the continent. I can see no cause for old *Bonapartiste* spies to do anything but slip away into the woodwork, like cock-a-roaches, and 'ope they will be forgotten. If there are republicans and *Bonapartistes* in England now, 'Enri, it is not because they are 'ere to do *espionage* or to kill people. It is because they are running away from France."

Morton frowned in perplexity.

"All the same, can you tell me the names of any of Boulot's friends, these Bonapartist folk?"

"What, 'ow much betrayal do you want in one day? For one plate of *canetons*?" And now Houde's anger seemed genuine. Henry Morton backed away.

"Marcel, *mon cher,* I had not thought of asking you for betrayal at all. Pray, disregard the question. I am very grateful for your assistance, and I promise you, I shall use what you have told me only to catch a murderer, not to influence the course of political events."

"Per'aps to do one is to do the other."

"Well, I cannot judge of that. A person has been killed. My duty is simple."

Houde relented a little. "Well, 'Enri, I hope that it remain so. *Alors,*" he sighed, "if my old friends the republicans have done a murder, then I give them my curse. Remember you the words of Madame Roland, 'Enri? Madame Roland, as she stood at the foot of *la guillotine*?"

Morton smiled ruefully.

" 'O liberty,' " quoted Houde, " 'what crimes are committed in thy name!' "

"Do you recall the words of Shakespeare?" asked Morton.

"Ah, Shakespeare! *Très bien!* But which?"

" 'A plague on both your houses.' "

Marcel Houde gravely raised his glass in approval.

Chapter 14

It was seven in the evening when Henry Morton and Jimmy Presley descended from their hackney-cab at the west end of Maiden Lane, and bells were clanging in the steeples of the nearby churches of Saint Anne and Saint Botolph. The street in this coaching district was loud with the rattle of heavy vehicles and their teams, and a bustling, noisy traffic of barrows and drays and shouting drivers flowed steadily by the two Bow Street men as they conferred.

"Go gently, Jimmy," Morton told him over the racket. "We don't want him bolting on us."

"Your peacher said there were a parcel of Frenchies in the neighbourhood, didn't he?"

"Aye, so try not to beard any of them, lest they fly and give him warning."

Presley nodded and stepped with a born Londoner's confidence into the busy flood and made his way across. They began to move separately down either side of the lane, ducking here and there into the maze of neighbouring byways. As discreetly as possible, sometimes cupping their hands to make themselves heard, they enquired at doorways, or from people on the street—at least people who looked English. A cove with a raspberry patch on his crown? Did they know him? His place of residence? Frencher, named Boulot?

To Henry Morton, Jean Boulot had somehow seemed a better bet than Gilles Niceron. If Morton had had to explain why he was here, he might have had some trouble. Largely it was a hunch—it seemed too great a coincidence that Boulot would visit the count and that same night d'Auvraye would fly into a rage and order his mistress cast out of her house. Morton was also a little sceptical whenever he sensed another was trying to direct the course of his investigation—as Rolles had done with his list of suspects—some of whom were dead! At any rate, he had let John Townsend be the one to ride out to Walthamstow to look up Niceron.

A diminutive child with a massive topper appeared in Morton's path, surrounded by a gang of smaller children, all equally shabbily dressed, though without the impressive headgear.

"Oy, yer lookin' for a Frenchy lives hereabout?"

"Indeed I am. Do you know him?"

"Might do," the child said, spitting lazily onto the cobbles.

Morton reached into his pocket as though he might find a coin. "A man with a raspberry mark on his bald pate. Where might I find him?"

The child nodded to Morton's hand in his pocket. "Tip us the blunt first. D'ye take us for simkins?"

Morton tossed a couple of copper coins, and the boy snatched them nimbly out of the air.

"The bilker dwells round the corner. Number two, Paul's Court."

The din of the street faded as the two Runners turned into Huggin's Lane, and died away almost entirely as they entered the dark little close called Paul's Court. They paused a moment in the centre, looking about themselves. It was quiet here, and still, the city's commotion now like a distant rushing of water beyond the gaunt-eyed walls. Number 2 was a shabby brick building, wedged in tightly amongst a row of others like it, each seeming to lean against its neighbour for support. Indeed, they all looked to be typical poor men's lodgings, almost indistinguishable from thousands of others like them in the metropolis: decrepit, black with soot, windows unglazed. But to Morton's carefully assessing eye, they seemed far from the worst of the "netherskens." They hadn't a patch on that lowest and most dangerous species of doss house, the sort that filled the criminal "holy land" of St. Giles or lined the back of the Ratcliff Highway. No, these were nigh on respectable, by comparison.

About the police men the usual little knot of onlookers, mostly children, had started to materialise, seeping silently out of the doorways and cellar traps and alleys. It was hard to conceal the arrival of the "horneys" long in a place like this. Morton and Presley bore no visible badge of office and wore no distinctive clothing, but the denizens knew them instantly for what they were.

"Who's the proprietor in there?" Morton demanded, without turning. He pointed to number 2.

"No pr'priet'r, yer honour," piped a sickly looking man. "There's but a deputy, Mr. Wi'm'sun."

"Any Frenchies living in there?"

"Uh-uh, aye, yer honour. And in t'other kens, too."

"Let's at it, then," said Morton to Presley, ignoring the shrill pleas to "tip us a farden, oy!"

Mr. Williamson was to be found in the kitchen at the back of the house, a low room whose blackened beams hung down almost to eye level. The landlord's deputy sat smoking beside the unlit hearth, his elbows resting on a scarred tabletop, a bar of dim light from the single small window at the end of the room passing slantwise across his face. Otherwise the kitchen was deserted except for one slatternly woman who shuffled amongst the clutter of empty benches, gathering up scraps and utensils. There would presumably not be another meal served for hours, but a penetrating smell of cooked fish still hung in the air from the last.

" 'E's been bousing," wheezed the old man. "He's not come out of his room in days. Poxy Frenchman. He's mad. Let 'im die of barrel fever if 'e likes, say I."

"He abides up there by himself?"

"Uh, aye. Except from time to time a buttock-woman, or some of his Frenchy friends."

"Does he pay up regular?" Jimmy Presley wanted to know.

The deputy coughed, richly and long, and then hawked and spat on his stone floor. He shrugged. "I'd not 'ave 'im there if he didn't. All me tenants pay up."

"How long has he been on this binge? Was he in his room three nights ago?"

"Do you traps think I spend all me time spying out what folk do? 'E can come and go as 'e pleases. Tenants have their own doors. I don't lock up. I just know 'e 'asn't been down 'ere to sup or break his fast for a time—days. I 'ear 'im raving up there, and then I 'ear 'im singing, and then I hear 'im laughing or squalling like a baby. 'E's daft. Take him away if it pleases ye. I can get another for his room in an hour. People like this 'ouse. They like I gives them privacy."

"We'll speak with the cove. Take us to him."

"Be on the top floor, at the end, on the left. You can find it for yerselves," he added, his tone openly hostile. "Me tenants don't like traps, and I don't make 'em welcome."

Jimmy Presley thrust his baton close to the old man's crooked nose.

"Someday you'll need this," he said, "and that'll be a sorry day for you, as we don't care for old farts neither."

"You lot don't care for none but yerselves," Williamson muttered, but averted his eyes.

Morton and Presley climbed four stories up a narrow, creaking wooden staircase. The air at the top was close and warm and strongly pungent with the sour fumes of urine, as if people had relieved themselves in the hall or in the stairwell, or the place were full of unemptied chamber pots. Outside the room at the end of the cramped corridor, Morton called out Boulot's name and told him in French to open. There was no response. Impatiently, Presley hammered hard on the flimsy door.

The faintest clicking sound alerted Morton, and he thrust Jimmy Presley violently aside. At almost the same instant the foot of the door was shattered and there was a loud report, stunning their ears in the narrow space. Startled, the two Runners gazed at each other for an instant. Morton looked down and saw in the floor a hole the size of a man's eye.

"Cor!" shouted Jimmy Presley, anger quickly replacing alarm. Both men hurriedly pulled out their batons.

Before they could attack, however, another voice could be heard crying out, on the other side of the door. Morton put a restraining hand on his young partner's arm and gestured to him to hold his peace.

"Ce n'est pas comme vous pensez! Fichez-moi la paix!" someone howled, from within the chamber.

The Runners waited, listening intently.

"Ce n'est pas moi! Je sais rien de tout!" The voice subsided now to a mournful wail. *"C'est vrai, c'est vrai."*

Presley looked questioningly at Morton, but Morton held up his finger to be patient.

The voice now let out a long torrent of slurred French, only some of which Morton could follow. *It's true, it's true,* it said, again and again, *they...she...it wasn't me...I told them nothing...* and other incoherent protestations that the Runner lost entirely. Then whoever it was began to weep. *"Je suis en enfer!"*

There was a solid thump, as of an object being tossed down on the wooden floor. And the clink of a bottle against the rim of a metal cup.

When nothing more came for several long moments, Morton shrugged at Presley and raised his voice. "Bow Street! You, within there! Open this door and throw your weapon out!" Presley stepped quickly over to the other side of the doorway.

"*Bow* Street?" asked the unseen man, groggily.

"Your firearm!" repeated Morton. "Heave it out to us."

"I meant no harm," muttered the voice, now in passable but also slurred English. "It fire...*par hasard.* By accident. I meant you Anglais no harm. Why—why are you here?"

"Your *weapon*!" bellowed Jimmy Presley. "Throw it out here before we break down this bloody door and smash your pate!"

A pause, and the door swung open, inward. Morton glanced cautiously around the jamb and saw a booted foot kicking ineffectually at a pistol on the floor. He stepped swiftly into the room and bent and picked up the gun.

The place was dim, its single window shuttered tightly. There was an even more powerful mixture of odours here, the acrid smell of gunsmoke drifting above a deeper layer of food and stale air and urine. The room was larger than Morton expected and piled with small wine and brandy casks and other boxes, most with their tops pried off and apparently empty. A disorderly bed was heaped up with clothes and books and other matter, but the man, dressed in a filthy linen shirt, was slumped on the floor beside it, his back against the wall. Ranged around him was a little thicket of brandy bottles, mostly empty, and several plates, on which lay old breadcrusts and dried-up scraps of cheese. A second pistol lay amongst them. The man watched impassively as Jimmy Presley took that as well and gently let the cock down.

"Loaded and primed," he said to Morton.

"Monsieur Boulot, I think?" asked Morton with sarcastic politeness, as the two Runners peered down at him.

The man bent over as he struggled slowly to get to his feet, and in the glint of light from the corridor Morton could see the irregular red blotch on his half-bald head. Short but powerfully built, perhaps in his early thirties, he had not shaved in days. *"C'est moi,"* he groaned, and tottered as he came upright, so that the Runners reached out to steady him. "I must ... apologise, *messieurs,* but I have no chair to offer you. But you could sit here on my bed."

He sat on it himself, heavily, and something, perhaps made of china, cracked audibly beneath him. The two Bow Street men remained standing.

"What in hell do you mean, shooting at us?" Presley demanded.

"I am . . . sincerely . . . *désolé* . . . sorry, for that," Boulot pronounced with drunken care. "It were . . . purely accidental, *je vous assure*. I think, you know . . . I think I drink too much, and I get ideas, so I have . . . my pistols, by me. I shoot at phantom. But if you must take me . . . to prison, for this. Then, I am ready."

"Maybe we will," said Presley gruffly.

"Whom were you expecting?" Morton wanted to know. Boulot raised bloodshot eyes to him.

"It was a dream, *monsieur la police*. Or . . . I should say, *un cauchemar*. A nightmare. *Comme ma vie*," he added in a bitter undertone.

"It was no nightmare, monsieur. You expected someone. You were crying out something about a woman, about you not saying anything to someone. What did you mean?"

Boulot blinked at him a moment, as if registering the fact that Morton understood French, or perhaps just trying to remember what he *had* said. "I was raving," he replied. "Nothing is real."

"I think you were talking about Angelique Desmarches," Morton said. "You know she's dead, don't you?"

Boulot's eyes went empty. He seemed to be more in control of himself now, however much he had imbibed. He wiped his wet cheeks with the back of one thick hand and slowly shook his head. "It was not 'er."

"But you do know who she is?"

"If you want to . . . arrest me, gennlemen," he replied with a kind of weary, theatrical, drunken self-pity, "do it. I am guilty, *oui, oui,* I am a man of a thousand crimes! Just tell me which ones I must confess to."

"The murder of Angelique Desmarches."

"That I did not do." A grimace ran quickly over his pale face. He looked up at Morton and shook his head emphatically. "It is true what I say: I am not a good man. In my life I have cheated, and lied, and abandoned the people who loved me. But that, *non, jamais,* never."

"So you have not that on your conscience? But you say you are in hell, monsieur. *'Je suis en enfer.'* Why is that?"

"Does this look like heaven to you?"

"You visited the house of the Count d'Auvraye the same day Madame Desmarches died. What were you doing there?"

Instead of answering, Boulot watched Jimmy Presley, who had put the pistol in a pocket and was unfastening the shutters. He flung them open, letting in a flood of evening light and making the Frenchman squint and shy away in pain. The younger Runner began rooting about in the disorder of the room, searching.

"What were you doing there?" demanded Morton again, more sharply.

"I had some . . . things. I thought *le comte* might be interested."

"You sell smuggled French goods, Monsieur Boulot, but I don't think that is why you visited the count."

The man gazed up at Morton, his eyes unfocused. *"Pardon, monsieur?"*

"After your visit, the count cast off Madame Desmarches. What did you say to him? Did she have another lover? Were you her lover?"

"Was *I*?" Jean Boulot laughed, a harsh, barking explosion, his mood suddenly shifting. "Eh, *monsieur la police,* do I look like I could possess a woman like that?" He bent over in sardonic hilarity. "Ah, *oui,* I had so much to offer her! My fortune, my reputation"—he gestured fancifully around the room—"*mon château*."

"So you knew her. You knew her looks, her character, her connections."

"Knew her? From afar," replied Boulot. "Let us say that." His little outburst of merriment subsided.

"What did you tell the count, dem you! Do you want us to haul you into Bow Street and see what you have to say to the Beak?"

"*Oui,*" said Jean Boulot. "I want that."

Morton folded his arms and frowned at the man. Presley concluded his hunt, getting up from looking under the bed, his face a perfect mask of fastidious working-class disgust. His eyes indicated the slovenliness on all sides.

"Pig," he said bluntly to Boulot.

"Call me name" was the listless reply. "Arrest me." Boulot leaned his head in his hands, as if he were trying to keep it from spinning, and stared blankly ahead.

"I think you are a Bonapartist," said Henry Morton. "I think you hate the count and resented him his beautiful mistress."

Boulot gave a very brief grunt of sour laughter. "These things are crimes, now? Ah, *oui*—I am guilty. I am guilty, like million men of my nation, to have love a man, who gave us...such conquest, such dream. But if I am *Bonapartiste,* after he come back from Elba, why I stayed here? I don't love Bonaparte any longer. But I still love France. I want to see France again. My home! *Non, non, monsieur la police,* Jean Boulot lost his faith. He lost it long ago. He lost it with the hundred thousand brave men who died in the snow on the road from Moscow. He lost it when the man who was to end tyranny put a crown on his own head and made himself the greatest of all tyrants."

"You say that now," muttered Jimmy Presley, "now the British army's dished him up."

"We hear something different, monsieur," said Morton.

"From who?"

"Who was it you were expecting, when we arrived? Who were you asking *to leave you in peace*?"

"Who? You. The world."

Presley and Morton's glances met. Presley's angry energy posed the obvious question. Beat it out of him? The young Runner was ready.

But Morton decided against it.

"We'll be back when you're sober. You want our protection, don't you? That's why you'd like us to haul you over to Bow Street. But you'll have to start singing to get it." He raised the discharged pistol he still held. "If you cooperate, we might even give these back to you."

"I'll never be sober," Boulot mumbled, morosely eyeing his confiscated weapon.

Out in Paul's Court again, Morton and Presley consulted.

"We should have brought him in, Morton," said Presley. "He could have killed somebody. He might still do it, too."

"We might bring him in yet, Jimmy. But Boulot is deathly afraid of someone. I think if we keep a good watch on him, we'll soon find out who, and that will be information worth having."

"Maybe the royalists are going to kill him for what he did to their woman. They'll save Jack Ketch some hemp, maybe."

"Do you think that husk of a man could apply a

thumbscrew to a woman and then throw her out a second-floor window? He can't even piss straight into a chamber pot. But he knew Angelique Desmarches, and he visited the count the night she was killed, and I would have the truth out of him."

Their little group of urchins assembled again.

"Oy, constables! Oy!"

Presley was going to drive them off, but Morton gestured for him to wait.

"And what is it now, young sir?" Morton asked.

The boy with the topper half as high as himself glanced about as though not wanting to be heard by some. "That Frenchy, Boo-low? I can tell ye summat about him!"

"Well, what is it?"

"The blunt first, yer honour! The blunt first."

Morton shook his head sceptically but tossed him twopence more. "Mind it be good."

He of the hat snatched the coins with uncanny quickness. "Here 'tis, yer honour. Boo-low used to tip us some pennies to keep quiet about him livin' hereabouts and to give him warning if there were any askin' 'bout him."

"I'll have my coppers back if you can't do better than that."

The child shook his head, almost flinging off his enormous hat with the motion. "But there have been some others 'quiring after him, yer honour. This very morn. Some Frenchies, one bigger 'an you, and another sad-lookin' one."

Morton and Presley looked at each other.

"I wonder what business they had with Boulot?" Presley asked.

"None, yer honour. They couldn't find him, and we wouldn't tell."

"Then why did you tell us?" Presley asked.

"Because that Frenchy's always half seas over now, and he wouldn't give us a copper for what we done." The child's indignation was exquisite.

"So you saw a chance to gain a little by us," Presley said. "Your loyalty is heartwarming."

At this the child merely looked confused.

Morton bent down to bring his face a little nearer the boy's. "Keep an eye out about this man Boulot, and I'll give you more than you've seen today." Morton fished in his waistcoat pocket and dropped two more coins into the child's small filthy hand.

"Aye, yer honour!" The boy beamed.

"I want to know of anyone who comes here looking for Monsieur Boulot, or anyone who visits him. Can you manage that without everyone on the street knowing what you're up to?"

"No one'll hear a word from us," the urchin swore, glancing around at his friends, who all nodded furious agreement.

"Good. Tell me your name, child."

"William, yer honour. Wil to me mates."

"Deal square with me, Wil, and we'll get along like kin."

The boy's face all but lit up. "Aye, yer honour, and when I'm a flash man, you can count on me to tip you t'all the doin's up and down Maiden Lane!"

Morton smiled sadly. "I admire your desire to better your state, William."

He and Presley left the little knot of aspiring criminals and carried on down the street.

Morton stopped after a few paces. "Jimmy, keep an eye here for a few hours, will ye? I've some calls to pay, but I'll send along someone from Bow Street for relief. If some Frenchmen were looking for Boulot and he's frightened out of his wits, it sets me to wondering."

"I'm thinking the same."

"We'll keep the place round the clock. Try to stay out of view, somewhere in the house maybe, so you can get a good look at them if they come."

Presley was about to turn back toward the rookery off Maiden Lane when Morton felt a sudden cold air of apprehension.

"Jimmy?"

The young Runner turned toward him.

Morton put Boulot's loaded pistol in his hand. "You'll likely have no need of this . . ."

"You're likely right." Presley closed his big fist around it with a nod and set off along the crowded and clamourous thoroughfare.

Chapter 15

The Drury Lane Theatre was as busy as a December night, the public having learned that Mrs. Arabella Malibrant had returned and that her understudy was again relegated to a minor role. This was the final month of Dibden's *Revenge*, and the production had been a resounding success. The theatre was abuzz with speculation about the play now in rehearsals.

Morton stood in the lobby awaiting the evening's leading lady. A stage door existed, but Arabella occasionally had need of the attention of her admirers and would descend among them for a few moments, her unmistakable cumulus red curls making her immediately recognisable. A little ripple of excitement entered the lobby with her, washing through the gathering. Impertinent young men on the stairway turned their quizzing glasses upon her, and gentlemen of more senior years (and in the company of wives) tried not to be seen glancing Arabella's way. Even among the women present she had her admirers.

Morton could not help but warm a little with pride as

she took his arm, so that he might escort her out to their waiting hackney-coach. Arabella nodded and said "So kind" and a hundred variations thereof as they made their way through the throng. Here and there she greeted friends and acquaintances, enquiring after children, husbands, lovers.

For a moment they were held up by the crowd pressing around the doors, and Morton found a lovely pair of brown eyes turned their way. It took a moment for him to realise it was he, not the woman on his arm, who was the object of their interest.

"Mademoiselle Honoria," Morton said, bowing.

"Monsieur Morton," answered the young woman with a curtsy. She was in the company of her family—all but the elder count—who were engaged in an animated conversation in French. The words flew so quickly that Morton barely caught the gist—talk of returning home to France.

Morton would have introduced Arabella, but she was speaking to another, and by the time she had finished, the d'Auvraye clan had moved on, young Monsieur Eustache d'Auvraye leading the way; a tiny wave from the daughter's gloved hand as they passed out through the row of columns.

A moment later Morton handed Arabella up into their carriage, and they set off at a snail's pace in the press of conveyances. Arabella laid her head against his shoulder.

"Tired, my love?"

"It has been a full day, what with rehearsals, performances, and fittings—the latter in the service of Bow Street, mind you."

"You saw Madame De le Cœur?"

"Her daughter came to see me so that I might have a

gown made. It shall cost a small fortune, but perhaps it will be worth it. We shall see."

"I shall pay for it myself," Morton said chivalrously.

"Thank you, Henry, but Arthur has already insisted that the bill come to him."

Morton felt a strong sense of irritation at this news.

"Of course it doesn't matter who pays," Arabella added. "The important thing is that we learn more of poor Madame Desmarches."

"And how go your efforts to that end?"

"First I must gain Miss De le Cœur's confidence. To-morrow we meet again. I shall test the waters then, though when I mentioned Madame Desmarches's name today, Amélie became terribly silent for a time. She knows more than she has told us, I am sure of that."

"Something that can be said of most parties involved in this affair," Morton reflected.

They soon arrived at Arabella's home in Theobald's Road. "Come up, Henry. I need comforting after my long day."

"There is nothing I would rather do, but I must be off to Maiden Lane and relieve the man who is watching over a cully who might know something of this same murder."

Arabella gazed at him in the poor light from her door lamp. "And how is one to compete with Mistress Duty?"

"Easily, if one is the celebrated Mrs. Malibrant. But tonight I could find no other to stand the middle watch."

She smiled only a little. "Well, I shall dream of you as I lie in my warm bed, Henry Morton."

Morton stopped off at his own lodgings in Rupert Street to change from his theatre clothes into something more appropriate to Maiden Lane. Wilkes, his manservant, was still stirring and brought Morton a letter.

"Sent over from the Public Office, sir. They wanted you to have it this night." He held it out to Morton in a tremulous hand, a condition that had cost him his employment among the quality and eventually brought him into service with a lowly Bow Street Runner—much to that Runner's benefit. The older man fetched Morton's frock coat from the wardrobe.

Morton turned the letter over. "And what is this?" he wondered.

"I don't know, sir. Unusual coat of arms, though," Wilkes observed.

"Is it?"

Wilkes nodded to the crest stamped at the top of the fine notepaper. His years amongst people of fashion had made him something of an authority on matters heraldic.

"Three chevrons, saltire"—he wrinkled up his nose—"the cross flory—a little unusual. The beast, I think, is a lion *salient*, although I must say, sir, it looks as much like a hedgehog as it does anything else. Certainly such devices are not English, nor even British. If I were to guess, with such a lion, I would say French."

Morton broke the seal and opened the letter. "You impress me, as ever, Wilkes. It belongs to the Count d'Auvraye, although I do wonder how long he's had it."

"I have not heard of the family, sir. But there are ever so many counts over there, even if one doesn't heed the lot that Bony hatched. Is the letter something important?"

"A request by d'Auvraye, or at least from his secretary, to meet with the count in Barnes tomorrow morning. I shall be in late tonight and up early, I'm afraid."

"I'm sorry to hear it, sir."

Morton smiled at the man, as much a friend and confidant as a servant. "Can't be helped. Will you have a breakfast ready for Mr. Presley and me at six?"

"Six it is. Coffee will be steaming."

"You are a warm hearth in a cold world, Wilkes."

The older man performed a slight gracious bow, his trembling hands held carefully out of sight behind his back.

Chapter 16

Morton was back in Paul's Court a few minutes later, as the church bells were giving midnight to the great city, soon to be almost silent. The dingy little close was even emptier and darker than it had been during the day, with only a faint greyish glow showing in a couple of windows around its narrow space. He climbed the stairs of the doss house and found Presley tucked into the shadows down the hall from Boulot's room, concealed behind a massive crumbling chimney. They spoke in whispers.

"Anything stirring, Jimmy?"

"Some time ago I heard our man jabbering in his cursed language—too drunk for even a Frenchman to understand, I'll warrant. Quiet as the grave, upstairs and down. Couldn't you find anyone to stand watch? Farke or some other?"

"Jacobs is coming at four, and we're up the river at seven. Come by my lodgings at six, and Wilkes will find us somewhat to break our fasts."

"Up the river?"

"The count has invited us up to his country home tomorrow morning. Perhaps for a bit of shooting."

"Ah, I wonder what he has to tell. Remembered something he didn't tell when last you met?"

"Maybe, Jimmy. Maybe. We'll just go up there and see. But for now . . ."

Presley crept back down the rickety stairs, each tread crying out as his weight came to bear, as though they'd carried too much over the years and could stand it no more.

Morton settled himself silently into Jimmy's hiding place, sitting on what seemed to be an old wine cask. Below him the house lay quiet, with only the low murmur of an occasional voice or, somewhere in the deeps, a cough, the sound of a door closing. The fumes of urine, which had assailed his nostrils and eyes like a physical force, gradually faded from his attention, and he began to turn over the day's developments.

He had obtained a new piece of intelligence at Bow Street after he had left Jimmy to stand guard over Boulot. John Townsend had returned from his little jaunt into the country.

"Well, Mr. Morton," the elder Runner had told him, as he leaned on the mantelpiece in Sir Nathaniel Conant's anteroom and stuffed his briar, "Walthamstow's a sleepy place, with one very great advantage for an officer of police. Folk having considerably less excitement in their lives than is normal in our metropolis, they are consequently much starved for subjects of conversation and far more prone to watch for and talk about even the smallest doings of their neighbours. And to do it gratis, I might add."

Morton gave a brief grunt of laughter. "In the public interest only, of course."

"Of course. So it was no great matter for them to direct me toward a Frenchman of the Protestant faith—whose name is Dubois, incidentally—known to have amongst his labourers a hefty-sized man named Gil. But when I sought out Farmer Dubois, I learned from him that his man, Gilles Niceron, had just recently gone off, without warning and without explanation."

"Really? How recently?"

John Townsend had lit his pipe and drew deeply before fixing Morton with a meaningful look.

"Four days past."

Letters would be sent to all the magistrates of London and the surrounding counties, asking them to have their officers look out for one Gilles or "Gil" Niceron—tall, seventeen stone or more, dark of hair and, of course, French-speaking.

Morton shifted now on his hard seat in the top-floor darkness, as he mused. There were connections between Boulot, d'Auvraye, and the woman buried beneath the snowdrift on Surgeon Skelton's bloodstained table. Boulot had not fired his pistols at a phantom, and he had not made that visit to the count by chance, not the very day, the very hour the French aristocrat had turned against his mistress. But what were they? What actually linked these men?

His thoughts were interrupted, however, by sounds in back of him, the opposite direction from Boulot's room. From behind the thin wall against which he leaned, the moans, the cadenced gasps...the age-old sounds of a man and a woman. Morton could not help but listen, his blood stirred a little in mere animal sympathy. But pitifully soon a slight speeding up, the single louder grunt. And then silence. One low mutter, and silence again. Was this how it was, then, in a place like Paul's Court?

The joy that ought to be equal for all, in castles and hovels alike—was it not, in fact, smaller and nastier and shabbier for the poor, the miserable, the denizens of narrow tenements and narrow lives? Henry Morton could well believe it. He had been raised on a steady diet of the improving works of Hannah More and Elizabeth Hamilton, forced down his throat by his Evangelical "aunt." But it was a food he had hated and resisted with every particle of his young soul. He would never, ever accept that *anything* was better in poverty, the way the lady authors and their moralizing ilk constantly claimed. Because nothing was. Not love or friendship, not character, virtue, or human-kindness, not wisdom, nor the simple pleasures. Nothing. The only good poverty ever produced—and then only sometimes—was the passionate desire to get out of it.

In the midst of these morose reflections, he heard, below, the staircase begin its wailing. Morton stood quietly and pulled himself back farther into concealment, listening intently. Slowly they came up. He tried to guess how many. Three at least, perhaps four. At the top of the stairs there was no hesitation—they turned directly toward Boulot's chamber. They'd been here before.

Morton risked a careful glimpse around the flue. But in the dimness of the unlit hall, he could barely see a little cluster of people at the far end. The knock on Boulot's door was quick, soft, confidential.

"Ouvrez. C'est nous."

The demand that he open was also quiet, discreet, although Morton heard an urgency in the tone of the speaker. There was only silence in response.

"Boulot, c'est nous. Ouvrez."

Now one of the other men in the hall—for those who spoke, at least, were certainly men—took it up. But his voice was more husky, and Morton could not follow what he said, except to know that it, too, was a remonstrance, accompanied with more rapping at the door.

Now came the sound of a voice from within—Boulot, low, muffled, maybe still drunken, and too far off for Morton to understand either.

"Non, non," replied the first man in the corridor, his voice rising a little in impatience. *"Il n'y a pas de cause. Pas de danger. Ouvrez!"*

Boulot must have been convinced that there was indeed no danger. After a short hesitation, there was a squeak of hinges, and the visitors all went in. Their voices continued inside, as the door closed behind them. Morton immediately left his place of hiding and went as quietly as he could to Boulot's door.

Within the room they were speaking quickly, intensely. He had almost to press his ear to the door to hear anything. At Bow Street Morton was thought fluent in French, but the truth was, he did better when he could see the speaker, hear clearly what that person was saying, when he could slow the sounds down, hearing them again in his mind. Standing in this dark hallway with his ear almost to the door, trying to follow this rapid babble of foreign voices, angry, voluble, interrupting one another—this was a different matter. It was maddening—he could grasp only fragments, parts of sentences, make out some speakers better than others. They were arguing, he could tell that. Boulot was defending himself, but oddly, his visitors did not seem to be accusing him. They seemed to be trying to mollify him, reassure him of their trust.

But the drunken Boulot kept repeating, *"Ce n'est pas ma faute!"* It was not his fault! He claimed to have had nothing to do with it.

Another voice, lower, impossible for Morton to hear. Calming, reassuring.

Finally Boulot seemed to understand and fell silent. Then the sound of a man weeping—Boulot. No one spoke for a long moment, and then a calm deep voice, almost impossible to hear.

They could not do it without him. *Assassiner*, another said. Assassinate. *"They would assassinate him,"* or something like. Morton felt a growing sense of alarm. Perhaps Boulot was not quite so pathetic as he seemed. But then, he remembered, the word in French was not quite the same as in English. It could mean plain "murder," and perhaps, in the manner of all excitable continentals, they were just flinging their words about loosely, carelessly. Perhaps nothing so serious as assassination was at issue, or even killing of any kind.

Boulot spoke again, his words slurred one into the other. *Oui*, Morton heard. *Un bâtiment. Berman sur le quai. Ratton-berri*. Words Morton could not understand. *Nancy*. *"He could do no more. Leave him in peace."*

The door Morton held his ear to swept suddenly open, so that Morton all but fell into the room. The pale blur of five surprised faces, and then the largest of them charged him, catching him before he'd regained his balance and throwing him across the hallway and almost over the banister into the stairwell.

The others shot out the door in a panic. Morton made a grab for one, his fingers grasping futilely at the coarse buckram of a jacket. Cursing, he lashed out with his foot, half-tripping one of them, who careened into the stairwell after his fellows. Making a sprawling dive, Morton stabbed his hand though the banister posts, briefly catching the man's shoe, upsetting him completely and sending him spilling head over heels down the groaning stairs. A voice cried in panic, then grunted with an impact, thumping sounds, and other voices shouting out in fear, as he must have fallen onto them. In an instant Morton had regained his feet, scooped up his baton, and pulled himself round the newel post to give chase down the staircase. But his quarry seemed all to have managed to regain their balance and resume their own descent. He charged after them, bellowing out to the inhabitants of the house to stop the thieves in the name of the king.

Down they all went, thumping and clattering in the lightless shaft, taking three and four steps at a bound, causing the flimsy staircase to shake and scream. By the time they reached the bottom hall, Morton had almost caught them up. They were just ahead of him, struggling through the front vestibule. Reaching out as he surged forward, he was just about to seize the hindmost—when he fell over something solid and went sprawling face-first. He had been tripped by a booted foot, thrust deftly out from one of the rooms. It withdrew in a trice, and the door of the room clapped closed again. The "traps" had no friends here.

Henry Morton had fallen hard. For a moment he lay stunned, wheezing and gasping to regain his breath. Then slowly, painfully, he pulled himself to his feet again. His knee throbbing, he pushed through the front door and stumbled out into the cooler air of Paul's Court. But from the darkness there came only the echo of receding footfalls.

Morton went a few paces down the almost black street, then gave it up and hobbled back. Boulot would not proclaim his innocence now. *Assassiner,* they had said, whatever the specific meaning of the word. Morton would drag the drunkard down to Bow Street and keep him from his bottle until he'd told everything he knew.

Morton made his slow way up the stair, at each step his knee screaming in concert with the tread itself. When he reached the door to Boulot's room, he found it wide open, a lone candle guttering, and Boulot gone.

Chapter 17

The slick surface of the Thames, that July morning, was scattered with boats of all shapes and purposes, from the river wherry that carried Morton and Presley, to swimmies and stumpies, dobles and peter boats. Morton could see the lightermen on their barges, lying alongside or to anchors, waiting for the tide to turn, searching the sky for signs of a breath of wind below the bridges. The river was a high road of commerce and transportation through the heart of London and out to the sea and the great world beyond.

"Tide'll turn in two hour," their waterman said. "Carry you back downriver afterward, sir, if you've a mind to return. I could tarry if ye not be too long."

"We shan't be more than an hour or so, I wouldn't think," Morton said.

"I'll abide then, if it pleases ye."

Morton nodded his assent.

"Well," Presley said, "we shan't find that poxy Frenchman in a temperance meeting. Beyond that the city is large, and we are few."

"It is unfortunate. I thought Boulot too drunk to make any kind of escape, but when I returned to his rooms, I could find him nowhere." Morton had waited for Jacobs, and the two of them had given the area around Maiden Lane a good combing. The estimable Boulot was not to be seen. Leaving Jacobs in Boulot's room, Morton had stumbled home in time to break his fast with Presley, and now the two were off to Barnes Terrace to keep the appointment with the Count d'Auvraye. Morton's poor brain hummed a high faint note from fatigue.

They'd found their waterman on the stairs at Beaufort Wharfs, where they'd also realised the reason for the early hour of their appointment—the count knew the tides on the river and when a boat might travel up to Barnes and when it might not.

Once they passed Vauxhall vinegar works, the London stench subsided rapidly, and it turned into a very fine morning to be on the water, with the summer sun shining, the green fields sliding by on either hand, and the casual traffic of barges and wherries causing no great congestion.

Morton had sent Wilkes with a note to Sir Nathaniel informing him of the talk he'd heard inside Boulot's room—threats of "assassinations"—but he'd felt a little foolish. After all, he had no notion of whom the victim might be. Or if, indeed, it really was to be an assassination, a murder, or was just wild talk.

"What are those Frenchies up to, then?" Presley wondered aloud.

Morton shrugged. "If Boulot is indeed a Bonapartist, then it would seem their intended victim must be a royalist of some stripe."

"If they needed a ship, as you say, it could even be across the Channel."

"I've thought the same thing. There are any number of prominent royalists who might be targets, including Louis himself."

"Would you know them again were you to see them?" Presley asked.

"Nay, it were too dark, Jimmy. It's a demnable shame I couldn't keep hold of at least one of them."

The younger man's beefy face frowned in thought as he squinted into the sun. He had his top hat on his knee, and the breeze was ruffling his thick brown hair. Morton watched as the steeple of St. Mary's, Chelsea, slipped slowly past on their right.

"Won't these folk have taken alarm now, what with them seeing you?" asked Presley.

"Perhaps. But I'm not sure they recognised I overheard any of what they said. They were skittish, though, that I'll say. I flushed them like a covey of quail. I wonder who they thought I was, for they ran me over before I said a word. They were fearful men. Fearful and suspicious."

"Do you think they're the ones what murdered the count's mistress?"

"I don't know, Jimmy. They weren't visiting our drunken friend to buy wine, that's certain." With that Morton lay down in the bottom of their wherry and let the ancient river rock him into a dreamless sleep.

Two hours later, as they came slowly around the final bend and Barnes village swung into view, Presley shook Morton awake. The two police men straightened themselves and put their hats back on, preparing to leave the untroubled world of the river behind. The elegant row of facades that made up Barnes Terrace was nestled prettily in the curve, rising over the stone wall against which the waters lapped. But now they caught a flurry of motion there.

"What's the to-do?" muttered Henry Morton. Through the screen of trees a crowd of people could be seen, milling about on the terrace. As they drew closer, a babble of voices drifted across to them.

As the boat nudged into the wall, they leapt ashore and climbed a set of slippery steps. The commotion when they got up to the top was intense. Somewhere a woman was weeping, crying out hysterically, then again weeping and sobbing. The front door of one house was open, and a group of apparent neighbours gathered there, whispering amongst themselves.

"What's happened?" Presley asked a woman.

"Happened?" she said. "Murder, sir! Coldhearted murder."

"We're from Bow Street," Morton said, and pointed toward the open door. "There?"

"Yes." Then she called out to the people before the open door, "Call the constable, the Runners are here."

The gathering on the steps gave way to let the Bow Street men pass inside, and a heavy red-faced man met them at the door.

"Good lord, sirs! How did you come so quickly?"

"We've come to Barnes on another errand," Morton said. "But what has happened?"

This was clearly the village constable, who looked as though he might swoon. Nothing of the sort had happened to him before, and he was clearly unequal to the situation.

"Two of 'em, sir. Two! Master and man."

Now Morton's eye caught the trail, the spotted spoor of red that led up the steps, and without even looking at the number, he knew whose house this was. He looked at Presley, who had made the same assumption, and then the younger man pressed himself past the constable and into the door.

"I didn't see them, sir," the constable rambled on. "I've just come. Fetched by Mrs. Barkling."

"This is d'Auvraye's house?" Morton asked. "Gerrard d'Auvraye?"

"So it is, sir."

The Runner cursed.

"Morton!" Presley called from inside. His voice was hard. "Best come up."

"None of you leave," Morton ordered the crowd. "But keep yourselves back from this door."

Inside, a man in servant's livery was sprawled face-down in the vestibule at the bottom of the stairs, his bald head toward them. A round pool of red spread visibly from his right side. Above him a bright rivulet of blood spilled, like a miniature waterfall, over the polished edges of the bottom three stairs, following him. Everything was motionless except that strange, slow falling of blood, as if the house were entranced. The crying of the woman was louder here, coming from the upper floor of the house.

The two Runners glanced at each other, and vaulting awkwardly over the body, Morton led the way upward.

"Who's there? Bow Street!"

At the top of the stairs they found that the voice of the woman, gasping and shrieking incessantly, came from the nearest of three open doors. Morton strode in. A bed-chamber. A woman sitting on a chair, rocking, crying, her mouth contorted. Lying on his back on the silken-canopied bed, his hands spread out on each side, his head bent as if he were gazing down in fascination at his own bare chest, the white-haired corpse of the Count d'Auvraye. In his chest a round red hole.

"Surgeon! Send for a surgeon!" bellowed Presley back down the stairwell.

But Morton knew, as surely as if he'd seen a guillotine fall, that d'Auvraye was dead. He felt for a pulse in the neck, and though the body was still warm with life, no heart beat.

"The other chambers," Morton said. The two Runners went down the hall, tense with readiness. But the rooms were empty—ordinary, sunlit, empty.

"This mustn't have happened more than ten minutes ago," Presley said. "How far can they have gone?"

"Not far. Go out and see if you can find anyone who saw them and where they went."

Presley nodded.

As his younger colleague ran back down the steps, Morton returned to the Count d'Auvraye's bedchamber. The young woman, gasping convulsively, looked up at him, desperate, her face swimming in tears. She was wearing housemaid's garb, Morton noticed.

"You are safe," he tried to reassure her. "You are safe. We are the king's men."

At this, the maid suddenly found her legs and with a wild cry leapt to her feet and rushed after Presley. Morton did not try to prevent her. He could hear her feet pounding rapidly downward.

"But you must not leave the house!" he called after her. For a moment more he looked at the dead man. The count was clad in a green silk-damask dressing gown, which had sagged open to reveal his motionless chest. On the floor beside the bed were the spilled and shattered contents of a breakfast tray, and the tray itself. Nothing else seemed out of order.

He went out of the room. From the bottom of the stairs the Barnes constable called up.

"Sir? This one's still alive!"

Morton clattered down the stairs. He and the constable and one of the bystanders lifted the man as gently as they could and laid him on his back on a long ottoman in the adjoining room. But there were two wounds in his chest, and the blood was coming fast. They applied hastily fashioned cloth compresses, but these were deep fountains, and nothing seemed to help. The man's eyes were squinted closed, in pain, and he was trembling. But he made no sound at all.

"What is his name?" Morton turned and demanded of the press of people who had edged into the room, despite his commands, and were watching.

"Armand, sir. French fellow—the count's butler."

Morton bent urgently over him.

"Armand, there's a doctor coming, *un médecin*. We shall save you, bear up now, bear up, *tu vas vivre*." The man made no response. It was not clear he had even heard. "Now Armand, if you can speak. If you can tell us, who was it did this? *Qui a fait ça?* Did you know them?" But now suddenly the butler's eyes did spring open, staring wide. He began to cough violently, spraying droplets of blood up onto Morton's face and neckcloth, and then to choke, in slow, retching, horrible convulsions. He was still choking a few moments later when the surgeon hurried in. Five minutes after that he was dead.

As the surgeon straightened, Morton slapped his hands together once in angry frustration and spun away.

⚜

Presley returned about an hour later. "It appears they went down the river," he said, bleakly.

"Then they must have passed us!"

Presley nodded his head, chagrined. "Not a few boats went by while you slept." He shrugged helplessly. "We pulled downstream a fair piece, but the tide's changed and swept them on toward the city. They might have gone ashore anywhere."

"Un bâtiment," Morton said to himself.

"A *what*?" There was always a touch of disapproval in the young man's voice when his friend spoke French. Certain kinds of knowledge did not reflect well on their possessors.

"A ship, Jimmy. That's what Boulot said, and I thought that's what he meant, but he was drunk. He must have meant a *bachot*—a wherry. His friends were saying they could not do it without his help." Morton put his hands over his burning eyes for a moment. "And the other word I understood was *assassiner*—assassinate—but I did not understand it well enough."

"Then you think it was our drunken Frenchman?"

"He had something to do with it, I'll wager, he and his Bonapartist friends."

"And just minutes before we got here!" exclaimed the younger man. "A trice sooner, and we'd have had them! The nerve! In broad daylight!"

"Not just in broad daylight, but as the tide turned. They couldn't have done it before—not and escaped by the river. Look here." Morton led him through the still-open door and pointed at the red trail down the outside steps of the house. It was smudged from being trod on but visible yet. "One of them was wounded, and not just a scratch, by the look of it."

As Presley bent to examine the trail, Morton went on:

"I have assembled everyone who might have aught to tell us. We'd do better to talk to them now, while it's fresh in their minds."

The younger Runner rose. "Shall I start with them outside?"

"Aye. I will see what can be got from the servants."

The village constable hovered, uncertain. Morton turned to him.

"Mr. . . . ?"

"Wainwright, sir, Silas Wainwright."

"Mr. Wainwright, if you would be so good, perhaps you can attend me as I interview the women. I'm sure they will be reassured by the presence of a familiar face."

"Thank you, sir," stammered back the constable gratefully. "Anything I can do, sir, to be of assistance."

Morton led him through into the small parlour at the back of the building. Here the domestics of the house sat waiting; this was a larger establishment than that of Angelique Desmarches, and there were half a dozen people in the room. Most of them had small crystal glasses in hand, held with an odd, unfamiliar primness. In the centre of the carpet, on a small pedestal table, lay a wooden-stocked flintlock pistol. Morton recognised the thin-faced, bow-mouthed young maidservant from upstairs, calmer now, eyes red but no longer weeping. Beside her sat an older woman, with an arm protectively round her shoulder. As Morton came in, this latter woman released the younger and rose.

"I am Mrs. Barkling, sir. I have taken the liberty of dispensing some sherry-wine for the female domestics, as a prop to them, given the circumstances."

"I am sure it is justified, ma'am. I will vouch for you, if asked."

Mrs. Barkling's eye was steady and her voice strong and deep. She wore a coarse grey-blue smock and an apron over her stocky figure, and Morton's observant glance caught a piece of white sticking-plaster on the bottom of one of her ears.

"I am normally a downstairs maid, sir. But I do some cooking and other work when the count's proper chef is up in London with the family, and I generally have charge of things. We are ready to tell you what we saw. Miss Boynton and I saw the most, so perhaps you will wish to begin with us."

"Let us do that," Morton said. He remained standing, using his great height to advantage. He could be an intimidating presence when necessary.

"Gladys?" As the cook turned to the younger woman, her voice softened. "Are you up to it, my girl?" The maid swallowed and nodded dimly.

"Begin with your name," Morton said.

"Gladys Boynton," the young woman said hoarsely.

"And where were you when this all began, Miss Boynton?" Morton asked softly. "What did you see and hear?"

"I was serving the count his breakfast, sir," she began, punctuating her discourse with deep gasps, as though still unable to catch her breath after what had happened, "and suddenly I heard two very loud reports downstairs. I—I dropped my tray." She took two long deep breaths. "At almost the same moment the door was flung open, and a man strode into the chamber." She covered her eyes, gasped several times. "He raised a pistol and...and he just...sh-sh—" Sobbing interrupted her, and Mrs. Barkling gravely comforted her, slipping her arm again around the younger woman's frail shoulders, while the others watched with blank sombre faces.

"He just sh-*shot* him, without so much as a word, and th-then..." Her tears were even stronger now, as some greater crisis in her story seemed to have been reached. Morton leaned forward, his bowels tightening. Another young woman, another violent intruder. "And th-then, he...produced another pistol, and *pointed it at me,* and—" Again she had to pause, as Morton waited, his face set. "I th-think he was going to...to do something...but then Andrea, Mrs. Barkling, that is...was calling up from below the stairs...and he stopped... and he went down...and there was another shot...and I thought he had killed her...and I can't remember any more!"

"Nay, good lass, good, 'tis well done. There was no more." Mrs. Barkling gave another reassuring squeeze with her arm before removing it, while others in the room sniffed and dabbed at their eyes in sympathy.

"Now, Miss Boynton," said Morton, "did you know this man who came into the room?"

She shook her head.

"Are you certain that the Count d'Auvraye and he had no words, no words at all?"

"Yes—I mean no, they had none. The master and me just stared at him, so surprised we were."

"And what did he look like?"

The attempt to recall the scene was obviously upsetting, and tears rose again. "I don't know! He were big!"

"I believe I may have seen him better, sir," said Mrs. Barkling, and even smiled grimly. "I'll warrant I did."

"Yes. Thank you, Miss Boynton." Morton looked thoughtfully at her, as she dried her tears on Mrs. Barkling's proffered apron. He turned to the older woman.

"Mrs. Barkling, then, if you please. Perhaps from the start."

"Very good, sir." The contrast of the cook's voice and manner with that of young Gladys could hardly have been greater. Mrs. Barkling's self-possession was complete. There was even an edge of resentment in her tone as she told her story, a resentment whose source Morton could not quite discern. Was it the usual dislike of the Runners? Yes, probably, but something a bit more, as well. Something habitual, and just slightly contemptuous—part of the attitude with which this formidable woman faced the world.

"I had come up from the kitchen, sir, from the cellar, after finishing the count's omelette, and I was standing at the back garden door for a breath of air. Just here." She pointed out the place, behind and around the corner from where Morton sat. "I heard Armand speaking to someone in the front hallway. He spoke in French, sir, which I don't understand. But he sounded surprised, which made me heed. His voice rose at the end, as if he were asking a question. The last word of what he was saying was *monsieur*, and 'twas a short sentence."

"Was he angry? Frightened?"

"No, sir. Surprised."

"Did the other answer?"

"Not so as I heard. Not in like manner."

"Can you recall any of the other words Armand said, or what they sounded like?"

"I should not like to venture, were it a matter of evidence before the bar, sir."

"But merely as a guess, to assist us in our enquiries?"

"Very well, as such, then. I believe the other sounds may have included something like *poor-kwah* and *zee-see*."

"Pourquoi êtes-vous ici, monsieur?" ventured Henry Morton, after a moment's thought. "Did it sound like that?"

Mrs. Barkling's estimation of Morton's abilities seemed to rise. "Indeed, sir, it was very like that. And what does that mean, sir, if I may ask?"

" 'Why are you here, sir?' Please go on, ma'am."

"Then there were two loud noises, shots, and I heard someone fall down the steps. Directly I went back downstairs and fetched my small cleaver, which lay on the cutting-board below, as I had been using it for the onions. 'Twas the first thing to come to hand, although there were better implements in the rack, I expect. While I did so, I heard a third report, from higher up in the house. As I came back up, I could hear Armand groaning in the front hall."

"You did not stay in safety, in the kitchen?"

Mrs. Barkling's indignation rose. "Miss Boynton was upstairs, sir! I called to her as I came, telling her to hold fast and I would soon be there. As I came into the drawing room, I could hear the man coming down the stairs. I feared the worst, sir. I mean, that he'd done some harm to Gladys." It was not fear that Morton saw in her blunt-featured face now, but anger, the hunger for battle rising in her again as she remembered.

"Pray, continue."

"The man and I reached the doorway from the drawing room together. We faced each other. There were no words between us, sir, as it was perfectly clear what both of us were about. He had pistols in both his hands, and he raised the one in his right hand and pointed it at my face, while at the same instant I struck at him with my cleaver. I hit his arm, here"—she patted her forearm—"and at the same second his pistol discharged and

took off part of my ear." Morton could see now the proof
of this, dark stains on the back of her collar that were
out of view before. He could see burns on that side of her
cheek, too, from the closeness of the muzzle-blast. Mrs.
Barkling had obviously tidied herself, washed off the
black powder, and put on a fresh apron to cover most
of the blood, but the angry red marks on her face remained.

"So," she said, "then we stood a moment taking
breath and looking at each other. The pistol had fallen
from his grip—here it is." Morton reached for the
weapon on the little table and examined it as Mrs.
Barkling continued. "For my own part, I still had my
cleaver in hand, so I think he decided to try no more
throws with me. He ran out the door. Then upstairs I
heard the blessed sound of Miss Boynton's voice, weeping and wailing. I thought of going up to her at once, but
as she was giving such hearty voice, I felt sure she was
not hurt, and it seemed better to fetch the constable
from around the corner first. Then, after Mr. Wainwright went running on ahead, my legs went all to jelly,
and I had to rest against a railing. 'Twas pure weakness,
sir, and with my Gladys wanting me, but I admit it to
you. After that I came on and arrived back here just as
she ran back downstairs, and you gentlemen were help-
ing Armand."

"How much time had elapsed, ma'am, do you think?"

"It seemed long, but mayhap 'twas not. A matter of a
few minutes. But you wished to know the appearance of
this man, with whom I had the set-to. Firstly, he was a
stranger to me—I never laid eyes upon him before. Sec-
ondly, he was a very large man, as Miss Boynton has
said, above six feet, and eighteen or nineteen stone. He
wore tradesman's garb, sir, or that of a mechanic—

rough breeches and an old woolen shirt, open at the neck. He had no proper beard, but he had not shaved of several days, neither. His hair was...no, sir, I cannot recollect anything of his hair. His eyes—they were black, or brown. Yes, I can aver so. Not blue. Oh, yes. His teeth were crooked, and gappy, and stained. Yes, his mouth was a fright."

Morton waited as Mrs. Barkling considered. But she could call back nothing more, so he asked: "The other man, ma'am. Did you see him?"

"No, sir, I did not."

"Are you quite sure there were two?"

"There were four shots fired in all, sir. Does that not suggest two men, each with two pistols? I think the second man had already gone out the house door when I encountered the other. The door was open."

"Did the count say or do anything that seemed unusual or out of place to you, Mrs. Barkling?"

"Well, sir." She considered. "He were...moody, Mr. Morton. Not his usual self, and he and Monsieur Rolles were closeted up, talking—even more than usual."

The count had cast off his mistress for betrayal, and then she was murdered. Morton would have been more surprised to find that the old man was not moody.

"Did anyone visit?"

"No, sir. No one since the Count d'Auvraye arrived yesterday afternoon. He comes here to get away from all that, I think, Mr. Morton. I've never been there, but it's said his house in London is a regular hive of comings and goings." She raised a finger. "Though there was one man, sir, last week when the count was in residence."

Morton leaned forward. "Who?"

"I am sorry to tell you I don't know his name. None of us liked the looks of him, though. The master seemed to feel the same way, and so did Monsieur Rolles. They were both very agitated after he'd left."

"You mention Monsieur Rolles, ma'am. I do not see him here today. Did he not come down from London, then? I mean, this time."

"He came with the count yesterday afternoon. But then the count sent him back to London, in the early evening. I believe he had a message of some sort for him to deliver. After that the count was alone. Neither Madame Countess, nor the two misses, nor anyone else were with him last night. But 'twas not unusual."

"What did last week's visitor look like?"

"A man of normal height, aged some thirty years, dressed as you might expect a foreign music-master or wine-agent to dress. Nothing much to distinguish him, sir, except that he had a red stain on his head—a raspberry-mark."

Morton sat back and gazed at the estimable Mrs. Barkling. Boulot, again.

"How did these two men get into the house?" he wondered aloud. "I suppose Armand must have answered the door and let them in. Did anyone hear the knocker?"

None of the women in the room could recall hearing it. Morton spent some time questioning these other women, while Mrs. Barkling listened impassively, side by side with Gladys Boynton. No one else had seen either of the two men or heard Armand's words. Most of them had been either in the kitchen or on the second floor. One had been out to market. At the sound of shots, they had all hidden themselves. One or two had seen the visitor the previous week but could say nothing more about him. There had been an air of secrecy about his visit.

Finally Henry Morton drew back, and his attention returned to Mrs. Barkling. One strong hand lay in her

aproned lap, and her severe features were set in a frown.
Morton's imagination called back to his mind's eye the
moment of confrontation. The peaceful house suddenly,
unexpectedly, erupting with noise and terror. And below,
that unhesitating response, reaching for a weapon and
heading straight for the danger itself. Then, face-to-face
with murder—and not backing down.

"I salute you, ma'am," he said, moved. "You are a
woman of spirit. The wound you inflicted will not be
easy to conceal. With luck, you have delivered these vi-
cious persons into our hands."

But Mrs. Barkling was impervious to flattery. Her response was sharp.

"See that they are caught and hung, sir, and you'll re-
pay our trust in you. Innocent working folk are not to be
threatened in their places of employment, whilst going
about their proper tasks. Now, if you have nothing
more, we must be about laying out these two bodies."

He asked them not to do this yet, as the coroner
would very certainly need to see them in their current
condition. He would surely be up from London before
the day was out and would also doubtless be planning
an inquest. They should rest now, and after he had
taken a last look at things as they lay, they could perhaps
put the house to rights. He warned them, too, that there
would be an onslaught of people—officers of the crown
but also writers from the newspapers, and the merely
curious. A double murder, and one of them of a notable
foreign personage, was not so usual a thing in England.

He found Jimmy Presley in the White Hart, the tavern
at the west end of the terrace, where he had set up shop
in the taproom, questioning the townsmen.

"There are a half dozen of them as say they saw the murderers, Morton. Four of them say there was but two, and the other two, *they* say there were *three*."

Morton tossed his hat down on the oaken table and laid the murderer's pistol beside it with a sigh. He gestured to the tapster for refreshment.

This was about average. Folks' stories never matched up exactly. The third man might have been one of the party, or an unrelated man, glanced in the distance. Or he might have been a product of the imagination altogether.

"How did they describe them?"

This too was not very consistent. The large man, whom Mrs. Barkling had wounded, seemed to come through in some of the descriptions, as did the not-very-helpful observation that the other man was smaller. No one mentioned anything that sounded particularly like Boulot. But plainly enough no one had seen any of the men close up or for more than an instant.

Morton picked up the pistol that lay on the table and turned it slowly in his hands. The caustic odor of black powder still clung to the steel. A fine inlay of silver wire decorated the grip and stock, and upon the lock a stand of arms stood proud. It was a greatcoat pistol, smaller than a duelling pistol—about ten inches long. It was not a new gun, dated 1783, though by the looks of the steel it had been lightly used. The maker's name, engraved upon the barrel, was Twigg, London.

"That's a fine gun," Presley said.

"Yes." Morton tested the grip. "Made for someone with a small hand." He held it up, aiming toward a post not a few feet away, cocked it, and pulled the trigger. A small shower of sparks scattered off the steel as the flint struck. He slid the gun across the table to Presley. "See if you can find its mate," the older Runner said.

Presley picked up the pistol, gave it a cursory examination, then slid it into a pocket. "I shall go speak with Mr. Twigg, gun maker."

"Unfortunately, John Twigg left the gun maker's trade before you were born." Morton glanced round the room. "We shall have to linger here until the other Bow Street men arrive," he said, as he received his ale and bread. "Then we're for London again, to speak with the count's family and consult with Mr. Townsend. We need to find Boulot more than ever now."

Presley wanted to know what the maidservant had seen, and Morton relayed to him the tales he had heard in the house. At the description of Mrs. Barkling's battle with the tall intruder, the young Runner whistled.

"All to protect her master. There's loyalty."

"I'm not so sure it was her master she was protecting," Morton said quietly. But he went no further. There were certain kinds of truth he suspected Jimmy Presley was not quite ready for, and Morton had no desire just now to listen to shocked denunciations or crude jests. His knowledge of Mrs. Barkling, and everything she was, he kept for himself, in a place he could do it honour.

Chapter 18

Arabella stood upon a small footstool while the costumer, Madame Beliveau, draped silk about her. They were in the costumer's chambers in the upper reaches of the theatre, the noise of the city only a dim rumble, punctuated sporadically by the voices of the rehearsing players.

"The skirt will fall like so," she said. "Do you see?"

Arabella admired her reflection in a mirror.

The elfin dressmaker glanced up at the mirror herself, assessing the effect. "Good, yes?"

"Très belle, oui," Arabella agreed.

"Then the lace. Can you hold...?"

Arabella pinched the fabric between her fingers and held it tight to her waist. Madame Beliveau found a swath of lace.

"That is exquisitely made," Arabella said.

"Yes, it is from France," the other woman said in her clear, almost unaccented English. She seemed to offer only the occasional French word, for emphasis, not out of necessity. "There is none finer. We use nothing else."

"It must have been difficult to come by, these last years."

"It has been difficult at times, but Madeleine De le Cœur has kept me supplied."

Arabella smiled at her reflection in the mirror. It was interesting, the way the smuggling had worked over the years of the blockade. The government had gone to great efforts to stop the illegal trade, while its members drank smuggled wine, ate smuggled cheese, and dressed their wives in smuggled fabrics often sewn into dresses in the French style!

"Have you known the De le Cœurs a long time?"

"Oh, yes. For much of our lives."

"Madame De le Cœur told me she dressed the ladies of the court of Versailles."

Madame Beliveau laughed charmingly. "Well, we can both make such a claim, I suppose."

"Which means you did, or you did not?"

The costumer pinned the lace in place, regarded Arabella in the mirror a moment, and then shook her head. The lace came off. "We were both seamstresses, a long time past now. Too long. We learned our trade under the great Catharine Brehl. That is how we came here, to London. We fled... what is now called *le terreur*. But it is true Madame Brehl made many dresses for the great ladies of the court, and we seamstresses sewed them, stitch by stitch."

She readjusted the lace and stopped to peer at Arabella in the looking-glass. *"Non, non, impossible!"* she pronounced, and tossed the lace onto a chair. A swath of creamy silk was plucked from among the rainbow of fabrics spread over tables, benches, and chairs.

"Ah!" she said. *"Peut-être celui-ci*—this one." She arranged it over Arabella's shoulders, folding it expertly.

"Perhaps too much décolletage?" Arabella wondered.

"Your character is a saint?"

"No, not really."

"Well, then. You have a fine bosom." She rearranged the fabric—for the sake of Arabella's modesty presumably, though Arabella thought the difference slight.

"So you came to London, and then ... ?"

"Well, we continued as we had in France, though the gowns were not so—*très ornée*—ornate—if that is the word. Then Madame Brehl retired. Madeleine went back to France, and I eventually found my way into the theatre, as you see."

"But Madame De le Cœur did not stay in France."

"No, of course. She was there a few years and prospered somewhat. She made gowns for Josephine—Napoleon's Josephine. But then she came back to England. France had changed too much, I think, and her hero had crowned himself *l'empereur*. That was the end for her."

"I see." Arabella gazed at the small woman as she busied herself about Arabella's person, tucking the material here, pinning it there. "Then she was once a supporter of Bonaparte?"

"Many were, madame. Many were."

Arabella wanted to ask if Madame Beliveau had counted herself among them but thought the question might be too personal. She was, after all, seeking information about the De le Cœurs, not Jacqueline Beliveau.

"Do you know this man who supplied the De le Cœurs with their French lace and fine wine? Oh, what was his name—Boulot?"

"Jean Boulot? I have only met him once or twice. He tried for some time to make his way on the London stage. Perhaps you met him yourself? He was a singer in Paris. Not of the opera, but the comic opera. Many thought he would one day be a singer *renommé*—famous. But here in England his talents fell on dark ears."

"Deaf," Arabella said before she'd thought.

"Pardon?"

"Deaf ears."

"*Oui,* deaf ears." The small woman continued to busy herself about Arabella, tucking fabric here, letting it out there.

"So he became a smuggler?"

"He became *un ivrogne.* A victim of his own wares, a drunkard. But he has a friend among the smugglers. Someone who admires his talent—that is what people say at least, though it might be a joke."

"It sounds a little like," Arabella ventured. "How did Boulot come to be in London, I wonder. He was not a nobleman, was he?"

"Jean Boulot?!" The Frenchwoman laughed. "No, he is not a nobleman. What was it people said? I can't remember. *Ah, oui.* He had friends among the intellectuals—as *artistes* sometimes do—and they ran afoul of Fouché. These men were dragged off to prison, but when the secret police came for Boulot, he was not home, and he was warned. His escape to England was managed through some relative or friend who dealt with the smugglers. And now he is here, nothing but a vestige of the Jean Boulot who once sang for the Parisian audience and had ladies throwing him flowers. You see, madame, we French do not grow well in soil that is not French. It is *une vérité*—well, a sad truth. Beyond our borders we do not prosper. And now they have taken Napoleon away from France, and he will be like Jean Boulot, but more *tragique*—sorrowful—and *humilié*—humiliated."

And it will all be well deserved, thought Arabella, but she kept this to herself.

Chapter 19

While waiting to speak with Sir Nathaniel, Henry Morton wrote a quick note to Geoffrey Westcott and had it delivered to the Admiralty. Westcott no doubt had his own sources, but few of them would have been as close to the location of the murder as Morton—and he was quite sure that Captain Westcott would want to know about the death of such a prominent royalist.

Just as the message boy went out, John Townsend came in, a newspaper in his hand, a pipe clasped tightly between stained teeth. The sweet smell of tobacco preceded him, emanating from his clothes.

"Mr. Townsend?"

The old man stopped, not having noticed the Runner who had once been his protégé.

"Ah, Morton. There you are. Did you catch them? These men who did for the count?"

"I didn't. They slipped down the river on the tide, and we could not find them."

The old man made an angry noise and cursed under

his breath. He took the pipe stem from between his teeth. "Mistress and man," he pronounced. "The woman tortured to learn what schemes her lover set in motion, the man murdered to stop him from doing—what, I do not know."

"It does seem a pretty snug fit," Morton said.

"You'll not find another boot better suited to that particular foot, I think. But what was this man d'Auvraye up to? Do you know?"

"I don't, John, that's the hell of it."

The two men took seats in the little panelled antechamber to Sir Nathaniel's office. Townsend waved his creased newspaper at Morton, then slapped it against his palm. "What are the French royalists most concerned with at this moment in time?"

"Securing their nation, I should say."

"As right as morning. And what will they do to accomplish this?" the old man asked. "Raise an army to protect them from their own people, whom they now greatly fear. *And* rid themselves once and for all time of this scoundrel Bonaparte! For the first they need gold; for the latter they need we English to find some way of securing Bonaparte that will last. But how would a people, even a people as clever as the English, accomplish that?"

"There is only one sure way," Morton said, happy to play the foil. "A noose around his neck."

"There are, no doubt, a hundred sure ways, but they all amount to the same thing—Bonaparte dead. I fear we English will not oblige them in this, for we have our laws, and those laws cannot be twisted quite enough to allow it. No, we will not execute Bonaparte, but there are many within France who wish we would and are applying pressure to our government to do them this favour. Do it here on English soil, out of sight of the French people. Do it and let the rabble find out after. I would think that the French king would be chief among those demanding that our government do away with Bonaparte. And who is the voice of the French king on these shores but the late Comte d'Auvraye?" The old man sat back in his chair and looked directly at Morton as if to say, *Find a hole in that!*

"So you think d'Auvraye was lobbying our government to have Bonaparte executed, and somehow the ex-emperor's supporters caught wind of it and killed him?"

Townsend made a gesture with mouth and shoulders that appeared somewhat noncommittal.

"But why would they torture Angelique if they already had wind of this? It doesn't make sense."

"Particulars," Townsend said.

Morton felt an eyebrow rise. "Particulars?"

"Aye. Whatever the count was up to, there must have been some particulars that the emperor's supporters needed to know. Or at least they believed they needed to know."

"Or maybe they needed particulars to plan their murder of d'Auvraye," Morton said. "I've been wondering all day if the count's murderers had a key. No one heard them knock."

"Did this poor, misused woman have a key to the house in Barnes?"

"I don't know. Her servants said that she had sometimes gone away for short periods of time—a day or two—never telling them where. Visiting the count at Barnes Terrace seems a likely possibility. The servants there might know. I never thought to ask them. Boulot visited the count there, though. About a week ago. He would have had the lay of the place." Morton realised that Townsend was gazing at him thoughtfully, while he was staring off into the void.

"The odd thing is that Boulot did not seem terribly keen to co-operate with the men I overheard. He finally gave them a man's name and then bade them leave him in peace."

"Still, he knows who the men are, assisted them knowingly. Did they not say they would assassinate a man?"

"I heard the French word *assassiner* but little more."

"Well, that is clear enough. They needed a boat, Boulot gave them a name, and the next morning the count is murdered by men who then escape by boat. Find Boulot. That will give you your answers."

"Yes, it will, but at the moment all I have is a question: Where is Boulot?"

Two hours of sleep on the floorboards of a wherry was not nearly enough, and Morton felt the effects. His mind was sluggish, words slipping away just as he went to utter them. His brief discussion with Sir Nathaniel left him feeling chagrined—he had not come at all close to solving the murder of Angelique Desmarches, and now the Count d'Auvraye was dead as well. What made it worse was that he had heard the men planning the murder and had not realised it or managed to apprehend a single one of them.

Mistress and man both dead, and Morton did not know why.

Geoffrey Westcott arrived as Morton left the Magistrate's presence. He looked red-faced, as though he had run all the way.

"Is this true?" the navy man blurted out before even uttering a greeting. "D'Auvraye is dead?"

"Yes, murdered, and if I'd been but a few minutes earlier, I might have prevented it."

Westcott strode away a few paces, too agitated to be still. "Well, this will cause an uproar," he said to no one in particular. He turned back to Morton. "And who do you think has done it?" he demanded, his tone a little accusatory.

"I was going to ask the same question of you."

"Bonapartists," Westcott said.

"That is the obvious answer," Morton said.

"Meaning what, Mr. Morton?"

"I don't know." Morton's exhausted brain could not find words for what was barely more than a vague uneasiness. "I suppose I distrust the obvious sometimes."

Westcott stood looking at him for a moment, his face unreadable. "How will you proceed now?"

"I will interview the count's son and continue searching for Jean Boulot. There is also this man Berman on the quay, whom I overheard them speaking of at Paul's Court, when his friends visited Boulot. I have men out beating the riverbank looking for any man who goes by that name, and the River Police are offering their assistance."

Westcott took a long breath and appeared to turn pale. "The King of France will be writing to the Prince Regent, Mr. Morton, and to the First Minister, lamenting the murder of his erstwhile ambassador. Louis will be demanding justice."

"And we will deliver nothing less, Captain Westcott," Morton said.

Westcott nodded, his face softening. "I'm sure you will. I have no doubt of it. I'm just..." He shifted his hat from beneath one arm to the other. "My superiors at the Admiralty will want to know how a man of d'Auvraye's importance could be assassinated here without my having wind of it."

"And what will you tell them?" Morton wondered.

"I will tell them that it is a mystery we will quickly solve. And that the men who pursue these murderers are the finest in England. We can do no better."

Morton offered a small bow to this compliment and went off to write a note to the coroner.

Turning from the comparatively quiet thoroughfare that was Bow Street, Henry Morton made his way into the redolent hubbub of Covent Garden, where London's busiest food market was in full cry. He himself was hungry to the point of distraction and decided to seek out some quick sustenance in one of the chop houses beyond. As he worked his way through the clamour of barking market folk and their teeming customers, a seemingly unsupported top hat emerged from the throng and appeared to hover about the Runner's waist.

"Oy! Oy!" The piping voice rose shrilly over the racket. "Remember Wil?"

"I never forget a hat," Morton said, stopping to gaze down at the freckled, gap-toothed urchin. "And what brings young Wil to my eye today?"

"I've summat for ye!"

But it was clearly too loud, and too public, to talk here. Forsaking ceremony, the tall Runner bent and hoisted the child onto his shoulders. Skirting the barrows and bulling through the crowd, he found them some sanctuary in the stinky shadows of the portico on the north side of the Garden.

"That French cully was back sniffing around Maiden Lane!" Wil burst out, as soon as he had been set on his pins again. A couple of his confederates had somehow followed and now stood silently at his back, apparently in awe of his audacity.

"Boulot?"

"That's him. Came sniffing around his old doss house, but some 'un warned him off."

Morton still had a man in Boulot's room. He cursed under his breath.

"No need for oaths, yer honour. We followed him, didn't we, lads?" His silent followers nodded enthusiastically.

"Followed him where?"

"To a snoozing ken!"

Morton was a little surprised to hear Boulot would go to a brothel. Not that such an establishment wouldn't make a good place to hide, but he wondered how Boulot could afford the fare.

"And where might this snoozing ken be?"

"It's by that slap-bang shop on Oxendon Street."

"Mrs. Mott's?" Morton said, incredulous.

"Aye, that's she."

Morton fished some coins from his pocket. "If this turns out to be true, my friend William, you shall have greater reward than this." He dropped the coins into the boy's small hand.

Morton looked once longingly in the direction of the chop houses, ignored the growling of his stomach, and set off toward Long Acre to find a hackney-coach.

Chapter 20

A little to his shame, Henry Morton had once been to Mrs. Mott's in Oxendon Street himself. It was some years past, and he had been under the influence of a certain curiosity, a dark impulse, and rather too much brandy, in about that order. And even then the thing was perhaps aided a bit by proximity, as Mrs. Mott's establishment was but a block away from Morton's own lodgings in Rupert Street. A longer journey, and he might have turned back before he'd got there, if only on consideration of expense.

Mrs. Mott's was not quite an ordinary house of entertainment. It was not aimed at any well-defined taste. In fact, it was a place whose reputation was all in its ability to surprise, in its sometimes exotic and always shifting bill of fare. It was discreet, of course, and folk could merely rent a chamber for whatever purpose they contemplated. But for the initially unattached, it was a place where one might hope to encounter . . . well, not the usual sorts of choices. An equally curious, darkly influenced female adventurer, of one's own or a better class, likewise experimenting? Or, if not quite so singular a thing, perhaps a stranded traveller from some foreign shore, genteel, but far from the judging eyes of her native land and needing a smallish sum to tide herself over or buy her passage home? Or at the very least, an actress and dancer languishing a little between engagements, perhaps just arrived in town and of as-yet-underappreciated talents. At any rate, whoever it was, she would be new. It was one of Mrs. Mott's principles (if such a word applied) never to allow her house to become a habitual recourse for any female visitor. A week was the utmost limit of her stay, so a man could be sure never to see the same face twice, unless it were Mrs. Mott's own. That man, though, was of course himself very welcome to come back as oft as he pleased. And pay high for the privilege.

Morton descended from his hired coach, paid the driver, and stood staring a moment at Mrs. Mott's. It appeared to be but another house on this obscure street. The home of a minor barrister, perhaps. Morton walked a few paces down and found the second address he was seeking—or at least the door to it, which was hidden down a few stone steps. A slap-bang shop was commonly an establishment where no credit was given. Cash had to be paid down, slap-bang on the counter. But in the cant of thieves, the name applied to a thieves' cellar—a place where stolen goods were bought, sold, or traded. No credit was offered there, either.

Certain thieves' cellars had their usual patrons, as did Mrs. Mott's no doubt, and a few were by so frequently that Morton was confident he could find one to help. The local flash men all knew Mrs. Mott, and though they might not have the finances to afford her wares, they "procured" things for her as needed, so a

warm little friendship grew up between the local thieves
and the brothel matron.

Morton waited about for half of the hour, his stomach
grumbling of its need for food, his head bemoaning its
lack of sleep. And then an angler he recognised appeared on the street, a sack over his shoulder. Morton
stepped behind a slow-moving cart and, when he
judged his position right, set off across the thoroughfare
to nab this unwary angler from behind.

"Well, well. Aberdeen Sumner Fox. And what have
you caught today?"

The youth cringed away in surprise, collapsing
against the wall of a house as he staggered back from the
Runner. The look of utter shock and consternation was
immediately replaced by one of defeat and anguish. The
young man, barely more than a boy, cursed under his
breath and looked as though he might weep.

Morton stared at him a moment, his hand keeping a
strong grip on the boy's jacket. Anglers used a hooked
stick to steal goods from shop windows and from between gratings. As London's criminal classes went, they
were of a lower order—small fish, so to speak—but they
had a quality that Morton had to admire: They were almost invisible, even in the smallest gathering. The angler was the man whose face you would never recall.
But Henry Morton was possessed of almost perfect
memory, and criminals of all stripes were his business in
more ways than people realised. And he was about to
transact a piece of business with this dismayed young
man.

"Have you mackerel in there? I ask myself. Or oys-
ters, maybe?" Morton sniffed the air. "No, doesn't smell
like either of those. Doesn't smell like fish at all. You
know what I think you have in there? A stay in Newgate

Prison—if you're lucky. If the magistrate thinks what
you have is worth more than forty pounds—well then,
it's a hemp necktie."

"It's nothing, Mr. Morton, sir," the young man said,
overcoming his initial distress. "Hardly worth a pound.
And I found it on the street. Fell off a wagon, I judge."

Morton gave the man a shake, banging him roughly
against the wall. "Do the flash men tell you that Henry
Morton's a fool?"

"No, Mr. Morton, they don't say that."

Morton eased his hold on Fox, though not enough
that he might twist away. For a moment the Runner regarded the sandy-haired youth, perhaps eighteen years
old. He was slight and quick, his features almost unnaturally regular—neither handsome nor plain. His cap
had fallen off, and Morton noted his hair was already
thinning.

"I'll tell you what, young Mr. Fox. If you can offer me
a little of what I need to know, I might be induced not to
look into your sack at all."

The youth glanced up at him, measuring, wondering
if he was being lied to. But Morton had a reputation for
keeping his word. He only hoped news of it had reached
this young man's ears.

"I don't know much, Mr. Morton, and that's the
truth."

"I don't want to know anything about your thieving
friends, if that's your worry." Morton motioned with his
head. "The snoozing ken down the street."

"Mrs. Mott's?"

"Yes, Mott's. Is it not said that you spend a bit of time
there?"

"It's a bit rich for the likes of me," the boy said.

Morton tightened his grip.

"But I know one of the maids."

"Good. We need have a little talk with her."

Morton escorted the young man along the street, the afternoon sun glancing off high windowpanes and throwing rectangles of light down onto the uneven cobbles. Morton, who'd been poisoned with religion when a child and would not partake of this unguent now, wondered if some higher power cast these little patches of divine light down on the city of London. Perhaps he and this petty thief with the ridiculous name could walk through one and achieve a state of grace. But it did not seem to be so. It was nothing but the reflected glory of some greater power, and when Morton and Fox had passed through, the Runner felt unchanged, no more charitable or at peace with the world.

They took the steps down to the cellar door and rang. A moment later a man's face appeared. Morton kept back, out of the man's line of sight.

"Mr. Fox!" the man said. "And what have you for us today?"

"Nothing, nothing. I only wonder if Katie's in, is all."

"Well, she's a busy girl, you know."

"I know. It is most important that I see her."

"I'll tell her, but you mustn't expect her to come running down."

Fox nodded.

Morton must have underestimated the attractions of Aberdeen Sumner Fox, for the maid Katie appeared a few moments later, and to the Runner's surprise, she was a maid—that is to say, a servant.

"Aberdeen Fox," she said. "I thought you'd forgotten my name."

"Not at all, Katie lass. Not at all." He looked nervously back at Morton, whom the girl could not see.

"I'm in a bit of trouble," the thief blurted out.

The girl noticed his gaze flicking back up the steps and chanced a look out from the door. She dodged back in and would have slammed the door, but Morton was quick enough to get his baton in the opening.

Morton had hold of the girl now and pulled her outside onto the narrow landing at the stair's foot before she could scream.

"You've nothing to fear from me," Morton said soothingly. "I'm a Runner, it's true, but I've no cause to disturb our good Mrs. Mott or her fine establishment. I'm just looking for a man who's staying here. Frenchman named Boulot, though he might be calling himself something else. He's a bald cully with a raspberry stain on his pate. Do you know him?"

The frightened girl nodded. Morton released his hold of her.

"Just tell him what he wants," Fox implored her. "I'm for Newgate otherwise."

"He was here," the young woman whispered. "But he's gone."

"Where?"

She shook her head. "The priest might know."

"What priest?"

"French priest, named Lafond, though we're not supposed to know his real name. Your man visited him."

"And where is the priest?"

Her eyes went upward, and she cocked her head a little.

"Inside?"

"Yes."

"Can you take me to him?"

"No, I'd be seen. Mrs. Mott'll have for me as it is, talking to a horney about her patrons."

"All right, Katie girl. You've done well. Well enough that I'm thinking of letting your friend here go free."

"Thank you, sir," she breathed.

But Morton had a last thought. "What name was Boulot using here, do you know?"

"No name. Mrs. Mott just called him the Frenchman. No, wait. I heard her call him the man from Malmaison. Does that sound right?"

"Indeed it does, I'm afraid." He let the girl go, and she slipped back in the door, frightened and angry.

"She won't be speaking to Aberdeen Sumner Fox again," the boy lamented.

"Let me have a look in your sack, Fox," Morton said. He assured himself that the stolen property was of little value and not likely something that he would find an owner for, and sent the angler on his way.

For a few moments he paced up and down the street, considering what to do next. He was also trying to remember where he had heard the name Lafond before. He sifted through the conversations he'd had with Westcott to no avail, then tried to recall the details of his conversation with Marcel Houde. The chef had dropped so many names. But, yes! Jean-Baptiste Lafond. Abbé Lafond. A royalist connected to some secretive faction.

Morton decided that it was time to try the front door.

Morton was shown into Mrs. M.'s intimate first-floor salon, where the Lady Abbess herself sat at piquet, her tea things at her side, and her fellow players—all women— ranged a bit uneasily about her. Mrs. Mott, however, was very much at her ease, like any other woman of fashion at home to a select circle of her friends. Or almost like. A large woman, dressed in a low-cut gown in which her massive bosom was just a trifle more than modestly gleaming, she gave Morton a slightly harder look than many ladies might have bestowed upon a guest. He suspected that, like himself, Mrs. Mott never forgot a face.

Nonetheless she smiled toothily and bade the Runner welcome. What manner of . . . introduction might he be seeking?

"I will speak with a Frenchman named Jean-Baptiste Lafond."

Mrs. Mott did not seem pleased.

"Here is not the place for such capers," she remarked bluntly. The anomalous women round the piquet table all frowned a little.

"You mistake me. I merely wish to speak to him, upon a private matter. But madame, permit me to say this much. I am from Bow Street, and while I expect you operate more or less within the bounds of the law here, I'm sure you recognise that there are ways I could make your life exceedingly difficult. Lafond is here. Do not trifle with me, as I can come back with a force. You know how your . . . reputation might suffer."

Mrs. Mott's expression was now very sour.

"There are those as might be interested to know their fine Bow Street man 'as been an intimate of this house on past occasions," she muttered darkly.

"One occasion. And you're welcome to tell anyone you can find to listen. But if you slander me, I'll have you before the Magistrate double quick. Now, is Monsieur Lafond here or not?"

A moment of hesitation. "I can enquire. He may or may not wish to be disturbed."

"Do not enquire. I shall disturb either him or your entire clientele for some time—the choice is yours."

Mrs. Mott glared at him for a moment but finally chose the lesser of evils and called for a servant. A little stick of a serving-girl was summoned and led Morton up the stairs.

Morton ascended silently, on steps heavily muffled with a rich Oriental carpet. At the top was a dim, sumptuous hallway, with sinumbra lamps in golden brackets. The first door on the left was ajar. Morton tapped on it. From within a muffled voice. "Who is it?"

"C'est moi," Morton said in his best accent.

"Entrez" came the reply, and Morton went in.

It was a bedchamber, and in its centre stood a richly draped four-poster, with a green top valance and rich swags of silk curtaining. At a desk against the far wall, with his back to Morton, sat a man in black breeches and a loose linen shirt, bent over and apparently writing. The bed was in disorder, its pillows fallen to the floor and its coverlets swept aside down to the blue-grey sheets. Along their surface stretched the very white form of an unclothed woman.

She was reclining on her side with her face toward Morton, leaning on one elbow and watching him with blank eyes. As he quietly closed the door behind him, he took her in. She seemed almost without hair—on her head, it was drawn back so tightly as hardly to be visible, between her thighs the merest wisp—which made her that much more starkly, somehow embarrassingly naked. Her face was sharp and almost masculine, and her long shape was boyish too, chest just dimpled with small pointed breasts, jutting hip angular and gaunt. To Morton she seemed like a parody of an erotic painting, a bleached and bony odalisque, a meagre Venus striking the incongruous pose of the goddess of love. Her age was unguessable but not young, and the empty gaze with

which she met his regard was quite without shame, or
self-consciousness, or human response of any kind.
Above one breast an ugly blue half-circle showed in
stark relief.

Without turning, the man in the chair said, *"Alors, tu
as décidé. C'est assez tard. Mais"*—and here he sighed
with impatience—*"mais il faut prendre un navire, ou un
autre. Il faut choisir."*

Morton did not reply but stood just inside the door
with folded arms. Except for the bed and its nude, the
chamber was very orderly, almost prim. The man's
buckled shoes were arranged neatly together beside the
unlit fireplace, and Morton noticed his black frock coat
hung very precisely over the other chair in the corner.

The priest made a final stroke and set his pen down,
blotted his work briefly, and turned, still speaking.
"Bon. Maintenant—"

And then he stopped, seeing Morton.

"Now?" softly asked Morton.

The other stared at him, his face set but showing no
particular alarm. Jean-Baptiste Lafond's face was trian-
gular, his broad white brow narrowing through high
cheekbones to a small, almost lipless mouth and a
sharp, closely shaven chin. His head was tonsured, and
he wore small round golden-framed spectacles. They
stared at each other a long moment, before Morton
spoke.

"Henry Morton, of Bow Street. Monsieur Lafond?"

"Abbé Lafond, yes."

"Ah, Father Lafond," murmured Morton, and his eye
could not help another brief, sardonic glance to the
naked woman.

A flicker of irritation crossed the Frenchman's face—
not embarrassment—and without turning he made a

curt gesture to her with his hand, motioning toward the
door. The woman obediently swung her bare feet over
and sat up. She rose stiffly, as if weary, and bent slowly
to gather up the articles of feminine dress that were scattered on the floor amongst the bedclothes. As the two
men waited in silence, she began to transform herself. A
filmy undershift she arranged slowly, then pulled it over
her head and drew it down over her nakedness, rather
awkwardly. Then a silk pelisse and belt, sandal shoes,
and a neck scarf, and the whore began slowly but certainly to disappear, to be replaced by the woman of fashion, a hard-featured but well-bred Englishwoman, a
little past her prime, Morton could now see, perhaps five
and forty even, a bit brittle but refined, erect. Now from
the side cabinet she took up her discarded ornaments,
slipped rings onto her fingers, and over her flat breast
draped a thin silver chain, from which depended a small
silver cross. Fully clad, transformed, she turned toward
Lafond, head bent. He extended his ring-hand. She curtsied and bowed to kiss it, without ever raising her eyes
to him. As she limped toward Morton, he stepped aside.
The sourness of her sweated body, and the odour of ven-
ery, faint but unmistakable, touched his nostrils as she
passed him.

When she was gone, he pulled the door closed again
and turned back to Lafond, repugnance and suspicion
stirring within him.

"What is it you want, Mr. Morton?"

Morton frowned. "Your countryman, the Count
d'Auvraye, is dead, as is his mistress, and Jean Boulot is
suspected of aiding the murderers. Boulot recently visited you, and I wish to know why."

The priest tilted his sharp chin very slightly downward, causing the lens of his spectacles to glint for a

moment and deny Morton the sight of his eyes. But it was only a moment, and then Lafond was once again meeting his gaze steadily.

"Is everyone who has had speech with Jean Boulot a suspect, then?"

"No, but you are affiliated with the Chevaliers de la Foi, who have resorted to violence and murder in the past."

"Who told you this?"

"It is my job to know these things."

"The Comte d'Auvraye was a royalist. I am a royalist. We had common cause."

To Morton as well, the royalists would seem to have common cause, but both Westcott and Houde had said they fought amongst themselves, sometimes violently. "But you are an ally of the Count d'Artois, whose brother, Louis, ascended the throne. Louis's faction won."

"God will set the right man upon the throne of France. You need not fear."

"So you are not such an ally of the Count d'Auvraye after all."

"Nor am I enough of an enemy to have him killed."

Morton tapped his baton in the palm of his hand. "Why did Boulot visit you?"

"Jean Boulot has been a traitor to his God and to his king," Lafond replied tonelessly. "But it came to my attention that he was wishing to repent his sinful folly and make amends. Had he done so—made proper penance and bent his will to divine instruction—I might have been prepared to take steps toward his reinstatement as a French subject and as a Christian."

Morton wondered how he could not have seen this before. "He came to you after the Count d'Auvraye had refused him. Why?"

"D'Auvraye was utterly without influence in court."

"Or in heaven, no doubt, unlike yourself."

"Why are you here, sir? Is someone attempting to attribute these murders to me?"

"Or to your faction, les Chevaliers."

Lafond swore, shaking his head in disgust. "Let me be very plain with you, Mr. Morton. The brotherhood you have just named is a friend to your government. We have done much to assist your government during the recent wars. Our activities have always been confined to France—"

"Then what are you doing in England, Father?" Morton's eyes glanced toward the now-deserted bed. "Sight-seeing?"

The man stared at him defiantly. "Yes, that is what I do."

"I think you are in England because Bonaparte is here. What else could draw you away from France at this critical time?"

The priest removed his spectacles and cleaned the lenses on his shirttail. "It is our hope that your government will not fail us in the matter of the Corsican."

Yet another Frenchman hoping to influence British policy. But would he kill d'Auvraye over this? Only if the count had been recommending leniency in Bonaparte's case, and Morton could hardly imagine that was true.

"Why did you ask 'upon which ship will you sail'? Is Jean Boulot about to embark for France?"

"What Monsieur Boulot does is of no concern to me."

"Did you know the late Madame Desmarches and the count?"

"A whore and a fool, Mr. Morton. Why would I associate with such people?"

"You are in a brothel, Father, in case you did not know."

"Beware whom you judge, monsieur," said the priest evenly. "My master and my purposes are greater than you comprehend."

"You serve them in curious ways," observed Morton. "Do you know a man named Gilles Niceron?"

Father Lafond, still sitting in his chair, bent his head in thought again for a moment. "This name . . . is familiar. But it is . . . from some time past. He was amongst the enemies of God and our king."

"If the Chevaliers de la Foi did not murder the Count d'Auvraye or Madame Desmarches, who might have done such things?"

"I don't know. Finding them is your duty, not mine. I suggest you do it."

Morton eyed Lafond for a moment. And then on an angry impulse, he asked, "Do you hurt women in the service of your king, Father Lafond, or only for your own private purposes?"

Lafond for a moment said nothing and seemed almost to drop into a reverie. "I do not feel a need to answer any further questions."

"Perhaps you don't. But Angelique Desmarches was tortured before she was murdered, Father Lafond, and that makes you, a man with your vices, a suspect in her murder. In a court of law you will answer all my questions, and no English judge will care that you are a priest. They will grant you no earthly immunity. Good day, monsieur."

Chapter 21

"You could almost feel it at a distance," Arabella said. "The power of the man was—well, it made my head swim a little, though I hope you won't repeat that," she said to Amélie De le Cœur. The two women were drinking tea in the boudoir of Arabella's town house on Theobald's Road. Swatches of fabric lay all about them, as though they took their leisure upon a rainbow.

"That is what others have said," Amélie agreed. "That he has a magnetism, a greatness that cannot be denied."

"Everyone felt it, in all the boats. We even raised a cheer, spontaneously."

Amélie clasped her hands together in rapture. "Ah, madame!"

"Oh, I'm glad to find another who feels as I do," Arabella said confidentially. "What the English government is doing to him..." She shook her head. "I don't mind telling you that whenever I find myself in the company of anyone of influence, and of course they all come to the theatre, I tell them that justice is paramount. We must not cast our own laws aside. If the emperor cannot be brought before an English court, then he is innocent and must be released. I suppose I've had no influence at all, but I cannot help but speak out."

Amélie nodded, eyes aglitter. She glanced reverently over at the picture of Napoleon that Arabella had purchased and hung on her wall that very morning. The sunlight streamed in the tall windows and washed over the room, illuminating the image of the now-fallen hero. It was a copy of the celebrated portrait of Bonaparte on the battlefield of Eylau by Baron Gros, and showed the emperor on horseback, gesturing as a follower kissed his boot and dying soldiers lay all about, some of them raising faltering hands toward him, like Lazarus reaching out to Jesus. Actually, it was a wretched daub, even from the point of view of technique, but Arabella was trusting that young Amélie wouldn't know the difference. Or care.

"I wish I had been with you!" said the dressmaker's daughter. "My mama made gowns for Josephine. Did you know?"

"I did not. Did she ever meet...?"

Amélie leaned a little closer. "Once, yes. The emperor came into Josephine's salon at Malmaison—well, he was not yet the emperor—and they spoke for a time with my mama present. He nodded to her as he left. She was..." There did not seem to be a word in either French or English that could describe what she was, but the near rapture upon the young woman's face was enough. Finally Amélie gave up the search and shrugged. "She has never forgotten."

"I would imagine not!" Arabella said. "Would you not do anything to free him now?"

"Anything," the younger woman agreed.

Arabella reached out and squeezed her hand.

"Does it not offend you to see these royalist women, these arrogant, empty-headed cows, traipsing back to France as though they have conquered? As though the natural order has been restored!"

"It is very difficult, yes, but..."

Arabella said nothing, only raising her eyebrows and nodding a little in encouragement.

Amélie's gaze fell away. "But look at the hour! I must be off." The young woman rose to her feet.

"When you find a fellow spirit..." Arabella offered as she stood, but Amélie only smiled. In a few moments she and her servant had bustled out the door.

"Well," Arabella said to the empty room. The dressmaker's daughter had slipped out before Arabella could ask her question—not that she really felt she needed to now. It was all perfectly obvious to her. She crossed to the small desk and began writing a note to Henry Morton.

Christabel came in to clear away the tea service.

"Christabel?"

"Ma'am?"

"Tell me, why would a woman who made gowns for Josephine, and is an admirer of Napoleon, come to London and claim to be a staunch royalist, making gowns for the wives of all the prominent royalists—the people who have opposed Bonaparte from the beginning?"

"I don't know, ma'am. Why?"

"Because she is a spy, Christabel. She has been spying on Bonaparte's enemies here in England and is no doubt hoping that no one will ever learn the truth. I wonder what these foolish royalist women have been telling her? And all through the war she has had her

French fabrics and lace—carried to England by the smugglers. Mr. Morton's friend Boulot is known to her, and he was a smuggler or a dealer in their wares. Who better to carry the things she learns back to France than a smuggler? And she was acquainted with Madame Desmarches, who was the mistress of the Count d'Auvraye. Too many coincidences. She is a spy, and perhaps her daughter is, too."

Cristobal looked pensive, her pretty brow wrinkled in thought. "Who is Boulot, ma'am?"

"Never mind."

Christabel turned to take her tea tray out.

"Christabel?"

"Yes, ma'am?"

"Would you take that bloody painting off the wall?"

"With pleasure, ma'am."

Chapter 22

News of the death of the Count d'Auvraye must have reached Spanish Place by midmorning, but when Morton arrived in the late afternoon, the house seemed strangely untroubled, with no obvious signs of disorder or upset. A footman in mourning ribbons showed him silently into the same white and gold retiring room in which he had waited two days before. This time it also held John Townsend, who was quietly smoking and reading a copy of the *Times*.

"Ah, Morton, here you are. Good, good." He tapped his paper before folding it. "Still no decision about Bonaparte. The cabinet in constant session, and the city in a turmoil. And now this Scotsman trying to get him ashore with legal stratagems! It is like a farce. Should he succeed, it appears His Majesty's government would be on very shaky legal ground indeed, as far as holding or charging him goes. Strange days, are they not?"

Morton nodded, then gestured upward, toward the private part of the house. "Have you spoken to them yet?"

"No, but we are promised an interview with the son, Monsieur Eustache."

"I presume he has taken the title and is the Count d'Auvraye now."

" 'Tis so," muttered the old man. Townsend's mood had grown more subdued since one murder had become three. "At any rate, he wanted to wait until you came, that he might hear directly about matters in Barnes."

"It's Rolles I really want to talk to. Is he here?"

"I believe he is. But before we go up, tell me in private what you have found."

As his elder colleague listened in sober silence, Morton did so, and then added, "I've sent Jimmy across to Maiden Lane to take our watcher from Boulot's rooms. Someone tipped Boulot to that, so he won't show his face there for a while, I don't imagine."

"Unless he has money hidden away there," Townsend said.

"Any money that cully had went into the bottle."

Townsend nodded, distracted by something, it seemed. "What interests me," he mused, "is your Mrs. Barkling's description of the tall Frenchman she wounded. I expect it's to be concluded this is Niceron."

"Too soon to form conclusions, I daresay," Morton answered, but smiled. "Perhaps you have turned this Niceron up, whilst we were in Barnes?"

"No, no, that I have not," admitted the old man. "But you have noticed a certain discrepancy in the descriptions, perhaps?"

"I have," agreed Morton.

"Still," went on Townsend, "a large Frenchman, a supporter of Bonaparte, drops out of sight. Some days later a large Frenchman is reported killing a royalist count. It must be the same man. Yes, really it must," he added as he rose to summon the footman.

A few moments later they were ushered into another room on the next floor. This was more genuinely a study than the old count's cabinet below, with fewer ornaments and more books. A long oaken table was covered with opened volumes and papers. Beside it, resting one hand lightly on its surface, stood the thin young man whom Morton had met on his first visit. Behind him, hovering deferentially, was Rolles. Both were clad in deep mourning, after the French style.

Eustache d'Auvraye bowed formally, and they returned the salutation. The face of the young count was pale against his black silks, but he showed no other sign of emotional disarray. His expression was grave, thoughtful, inward-looking. To Morton's covert eye, his movements as he bowed were precisely the same as they had been before. If this was a parody of courtly manners, it was one he practised habitually.

Having been previously introduced, Morton took the lead and presented John Townsend. The veteran Runner was greeted by another silent bow.

"I hope *monsieur le comte* will accept our most genuine and heartfelt condolences," began Townsend, who was entirely in his element with elaborate displays of courtesy. "The death of your father, *le comte* d'Auvraye, is a great loss to the civilised nations. I think that I may safely speak, as his loyal officer, for His Royal Highness the Prince Regent, in adding his own profoundest personal regrets."

Another bow, and the Runners caught this time a faint waft of perfume from the young man's garments. Eustache d'Auvraye's voice, when he spoke, was soft, melodious and, unlike the elder count's, slightly accented. Given the extravagant pretences of the odd old police man, it was also surprisingly polite.

"I must thank Monsieur. You are acquainted, then, with the Prince Regent?"

"Monsieur, I have that honour," replied Townsend with some complacency. And in fact, it was even true, Morton reflected. After a fashion.

"He is an illustrious sovereign," quietly pronounced the young Frenchman.

The son's manners were not, as one might have expected from a younger man, less formal than those of his father—if anything, they were more so. His bearing was stately, his gestures restrained, his self-possession complete. But somehow this was not off-putting. Though not so handsome as the elder count, he nevertheless had something indefinably superior, a charm, a delicacy even, that compensated.

"I have just come from Barnes Terrace," Morton told him. "I understand that you wish to hear the particulars of the crime."

"If you would be so good, monsieur."

There was something else that distinguished son from father, Morton at this moment also remarked: the brightness of his black eyes, the complete, focussed attention, the stillness. Unless Morton was greatly mistaken, the new Count d'Auvraye was rather more intelligent than the old.

He told the count about his father's death, watching carefully the young man's reaction.

"No one, then, can identify my father's murderers?"

Townsend chose to answer. "As of yet, *monsieur le comte*, we don't know who they were."

"There is something, though," Morton said. "A French expatriate named Jean Boulot had visited the count at Barnes last week. He called upon him again here the day before Madame Desmarches was found dead. He had come both times to ask the count to intercede for him with Monsieur Fouché in Paris, so that he might be allowed to return to France. I believe the count refused him."

The new count did look surprised, and his pale brow furrowed. He turned and glanced enquiringly at Monsieur Rolles.

"Do you know this man, *monsieur le comte*?" Morton asked.

Young d'Auvraye turned back and seemed to consider for a moment before answering, meeting Morton's eye steadily as he did. "Monsieur, I do not. But I was informed that a stranger had an interview in this house, at which I was not present. I did not know, however, that he had also called upon *le comte* d'Auvraye at Barnes Terrace. Were you aware of this, Monsieur Rolles?" he asked, without looking round again.

Rolles murmured that he was not.

"Did Jean Boulot leave this place in anger, *monsieur le comte*?" Morton asked.

Eustache d'Auvraye was silent a moment, but his eyes were dark with thought and feeling. "I think it is best," he said eventually, "that you direct this question to Monsieur Rolles, who was present at the interview."

"His ostensible purpose," Rolles began, "was to try to sell *le comte* d'Auvraye some goods from France—wine and other commodities. You are right, that was the name he gave: Jean Boulot."

"He was a person of no reputation, no family, nothing at all," murmured Eustache d'Auvraye. "*Monsieur le comte* should never have received him."

"I was not present for the entire interview, Monsieur

Morton," Rolles went on, "but he did ask that *le comte* d'Auvraye intercede for him. He wished to return to France, where he was once a minor *artiste*. He had fallen afoul of the police there and had fled to England. The count did not so much refuse as demur. He wished to know more of this Boulot, for he would not return the seditious to our country."

"But did Boulot leave this house in anger, Monsieur Rolles?"

"Anger? No, I don't think so."

"But the count was angry. What else passed between them? Did Boulot offer some proof of Madame Desmarches's betrayal?"

At the mention of this name, the young gentleman balled a fist, which hovered for a second over the table. "I would ask that you not mention that woman's name in this house where my mother is mourning," he said in a controlled voice.

"I'm sorry, *monsieur le comte,* but I am investigating three murders. Three murders that are likely connected. To solve one will almost certainly mean the solution of all."

The count nodded once stiffly, but he was not happy with this response.

You are not back in France yet, Morton thought. *Your word is not law here.*

"Monsieur Rolles, what passed between the count and this man Boulot that caused the count so much agitation?"

"Monsieur Morton, I was not present for the entire interview. I was called out for a moment on another matter, and when I returned, the count had ordered Boulot removed."

"And he was in a rage."

Rolles's gaze drifted over to his new employer for an instant. "He was distressed, yes."

"And why was that?"

"I don't know, monsieur. He ordered me to go and eject...this woman you have named from her dwelling. You know what I then did."

Morton nodded. "He gave you no indication of his reason for doing this?"

"No, and I did not question him."

"What did you presume at the time? Why did you think the count did this?"

Again the hesitation, the eyes flicking toward his new employer. "I thought that this man Boulot must have said something to turn *le comte* against...this woman, but I knew not what."

"But you were in the count's confidence. You told me as much."

"As much as any man was, yes, but *le comte* d'Auvraye was a private man, monsieur."

Eustache d'Auvraye broke in. "Does it not appear to you, monsieur, that this Boulot was merely trying to gain access to *le comte* with murderous purpose? The unexpected presence of Monsieur Rolles may have restrained him on the occasion of which we speak. This morning, in Barnes Terrace, with the help of some republican *scélérat*—some thug, as you English might term him—he must have succeeded."

Morton nodded. It was plausible enough. There remained a difficulty, however. And it was a difficulty that secretary Rolles would have to meet.

"How is it, Monsieur Rolles, that you made no reference to this visit of Boulot, when I wished to know the circumstances of the death of Madame Angelique Desmarches? How is it that Boulot's name was not amongst the considerable list of Bonapartists that you provided me on that occasion?"

"I did not know him to be a Bonapartist," replied Rolles. "His troubles with the French police occurred while the French court was in exile. This would indicate the man was not a supporter of the Corsican."

This had not really occurred to Morton, and he did not even begin to know how to address it. Houde had called Boulot a supporter of Bonaparte, yet the man was exiled to England through most of the Corsican's reign. Perhaps Houde was not wrong, and Boulot was merely a common criminal who had fled the French police. "Why did the count later send word to see me?"

"I do not know, monsieur."

"But you wrote the note to Bow Street, did you not? And you even carried it to town?"

Rolles bowed slightly. "The count was considerably troubled, I believe, and meditated long, in private, before giving me this note. I did not ask, for he was clearly in some distress."

John Townsend now stepped in, full of sympathy and conciliation. He apologised for Morton's plain-spoken manner and assured the count that it was only in the conduct of their duties that they were required to say disagreeable things, and that of course not the slightest hint of disrespect was intended toward the ladies of the house, and that all these enquiries would, of course, remain in the strictest confidence.

At these words the young count seemed to relax a little and waved his hand negligently. "This is not needed, monsieur. I am sure that an ability to ask unpleasant questions, without undue delicacy, is an advantage in your profession. In which case I ought to be grateful for present rudeness, in anticipation of future success."

But Morton broke in.

"As *messieurs* have acknowledged the necessity for disagreeable questions, permit me to ask one more. Where were you, Monsieur Rolles, this morning? And who can avouch for it?"

The face of the little secretary reddened, and he began to draw himself up to retort. But it was the young count who turned to Morton with a calm smile.

"Monsieur Rolles passed last night under this roof, after delivering *le comte* d'Auvraye's message to Bow Street. He spent much of this morning with me, in discussions of a private nature. I vouch for him."

Now Townsend again, mild and accommodating.

"Thank you. That is, of course, as much as is needed. *Monsieur le comte,* may I only ask, did you speak to your father before he went to Barnes yesterday? Did he say anything, related to matters of state or to any other subject, that might throw light upon subsequent events?"

There was now a slight hesitation before the son replied. "*Le comte d'Auvraye* and I had some few words of a personal nature and not, I think, germane to your enquiries. I was not privy to his affairs of state or of other kinds. He did not...much honour me with his confidence. He was much more likely to speak to Monsieur Rolles on any such matters."

"Were your...views different?"

Again, a short silence. Now the young count's smile was reflective. Morton wondered whether he was thinking of how to phrase his response or administering a quiet reproof for their probing so intimate a matter.

"The late gentleman and I were in unity on the fundamental need to restore the glory of France and of her royal family and nobility. We had some differences of opinion as to the most expeditious and honourable means of achieving this goal. But these differences were of little consequence, as I had no practical role in *monsieur le comte*'s undertakings."

Was there bitterness in these phrases? Henry Morton was becoming more interested in Eustache d'Auvraye than he had quite expected to be.

"Would it be possible, *monsieur le comte*," John Townsend went on, "to speak to your mother or your sisters? They may perhaps have overheard something that will aid us."

"It would greatly surprise me, monsieur, if the ladies of this house were any better informed upon these matters than I. In *le comte* d'Auvraye's conception of his role as head of this family, it was his privilege, and no doubt also his duty, to keep strictly to himself all such concerns, as well as the decisions related to them. In any case, I am sure you will appreciate that for the moment the ladies are deeply distressed and indisposed to converse with strangers. At the present time the effort would be insupportable for them."

"Ah yes, monsieur, this is quite to be understood. Of course." But now, as he and Morton seemed poised to go, Townsend asked in a considerate tone, "Will *monsieur le comte* be returning soon to France?" The young count blinked at him a moment. For some reason, of all the questions they had posed, this seemed the one he was least prepared for.

"I—I—do not know, monsieur. I have not thought so far. Perhaps I shall. Yes, perhaps. But I believe I would prefer to remain in your country, at least until vengeance is exacted for *le comte* d'Auvraye's murder."

"In England, *monsieur le comte*," muttered Morton, "we would rather speak of justice."

Instead of taking umbrage, Eustache d'Auvraye looked straight at Henry Morton, and the polite smile he had been maintaining faded. There was a kind of appeal in the slightly melancholy expression that remained, and as their eyes met, Morton felt an odd moment of connection, of unexpected sympathy.

"I humbly beg Monsieur's pardon," d'Auvraye corrected himself. "He is entirely in the right. Even on such a day as this, it is of *la justice* we should speak. This was, in fact, one of *le comte* d'Auvraye's most cherished notions. *Let justice be done, though heaven should fall.*"

Outside the house on Spanish Place, Morton looked over at the worn and lined face of his fellow Runner. "What is it they are not telling us, I wonder."

"A great deal, I think," Townsend answered, and reached for his pipe. As they walked, he filled the bowl, tamping the tobacco down expertly. "But why they are keeping things from us might be more interesting than the information they will not divulge."

"If it is relevant to the count's murder, you would think they would be more forthcoming."

Townsend lit his pipe and drew deeply of the scented smoke. Three carefully formed rings appeared before him. "In my experience families hide certain kinds of truths. A family such as the d'Auvrayes might have even more reasons to keep things back. They have great pride, Mr. Morton, a terrible failing. What if the old count had flirted with the republican cause or had tried to return to France during Bonaparte's reign? Some did, you know. But given present circumstances such knowledge would best be kept to themselves. Perhaps Jean Boulot had wind of this and was blackmailing them."

"Well, I had not considered that. Though it has occurred to me just now that Boulot was very likely one of Bonaparte's spies. The cook Marcel Houde told me Boulot was a well-known supporter of Bonaparte, yet Boulot claimed to be exiled here even though his hero was in power. Does that not seem odd?"

"Indeed, though if I were a spy for Bonaparte, I should not come to England and go about calling myself an admirer of the Corsican. It seems a sure way to draw attention to oneself."

"I suppose."

Morton and Townsend walked down the comparatively quiet street.

"What will you do now?" the old man asked.

"Why, I will go back to my friend the *chef de cuisine*."

Townsend turned his charming smile on Morton and, from the centre of a cloud of smoke, said, "Well, ask him who murdered the count and his mistress so that we can stop chasing our tails through the streets of London."

Boodle's in St. James's Street was thus Morton's next destination, hurrying, as the evening wore quickly on. He felt at a loss for motives in this sea of French names and faces. Their politics and sense of honour and pride were all foreign to him. So he returned, looking for Marcel Houde.

As he entered the door, he narrowly escaped a collision with a bowl of soup, carried by a rushing servitor who shouted an insult at him over his shoulder as he careened onward.

"You ask me where Houde is?" shouted a harried young manager over the busy confusion of the kitchen at late supper hour. "No! I ask *you*! Where in God's name is he? We've not seen him all day! Do you think we can keep this up?" he demanded, indicating the crowded room with a sweep of his arm. "Do you think we can produce *that* menu by ourselves?"

"He's gone?" Morton said, utterly surprised. "Have you tried his lodgings?"

"Do you think I'm a stark, staring idiot? Of course I've tried his bloody lodgings. But look now, what a bit 'o luck. Here's bloody Bow Street. Why don't *you* find him, before every man jack in this room loses his place and is thrown out onto the street!"

And it was certainly true that, even to Morton's unpractised eye, the kitchen looked dangerously ill-regulated, almost chaotic. People were running, whereas in Marcel's presence they seemed only ever to walk. In one corner an underchef was berating one of his assistants in a voice that seemed dangerously near hysteria, shouting over and over, *"Non! Non! Non!"* Indeed, there was something wrong in the aromas in the air, too—the odour of burning, not just cooking food.

The Runner retreated out onto the street and wondered a moment. Houde was responsible in the extreme—to desert his post would be so out of character that Morton would have bet considerable sums against it.

"Marcel, my friend," he whispered, "what is it you do?"

Chapter 23

Morton made his way back to the Magistrate's Court at number 4 Bow Street, where he found two notes. First, from Arabella:

Dear Henry:

Here is some news that I think will cheer you. Madame De le Cœur and her daughter are unquestionably great admirers of that short man I saw in Plymouth Harbour but a few days ago. Do you think they could have been using their access to the wives of both the royalists and London's powerful to gather information for the Corsican? And did you not say that this Frenchman (Bol-something) was smuggling French goods, such as French lace and fabrics, things the De le Cœurs possess in quantity?

You are invited to Portman House after the

*theatre, where I expect to be suitably rewarded for
my efforts.*

*Love,
Arabella*

Morton sat down heavily upon a bench. His head
swam from lack of food and rest. *Were* the dressmakers
spying for the French—or more specifically, for
Bonaparte? Had they learned something from Madame
Desmarches that had led to her torture and death?

The second note was brief: Westcott asking if Morton
could meet him at White's that evening. His belly empty
and mood sour, Morton scribbled a note and had it delivered to White's saying that he would be at the Golden
Apple in the Strand. There he hoped to fill the void in
his stomach and find some fellow Bow Street men with
whom to commiserate.

As it turned out, Presley was happily ensconced at a
corner table, nursing a mug and watching a gang of bitter midshipmen—all without futures in the navy now—
get foully drunk.

"Morton!" the young Runner said, his great ham of a
face lighting with a smile, a smile that quickly disappeared. "What's happened?"

"I have not eaten since we broke our fast this morning, and I am as confused as I have ever been in my days
at Bow Street."

Presley looked sympathetic. "Well, I was hoping you
might explain all these doings to me."

Morton waved down a servant and called for bread
and a rasher of bacon. They had some pork pie, too, so
he took that, a cherry tart, and a mug of cider to wash it
all down.

When the servant left, Presley leaned forward and said, "The young count had Henshawe dismissed earlier this day—the stableman I talked to."

Morton tried to fight off weariness. This day? Could this really still be the same day that had begun with himself and Presley on the river? He considered closing his eyes and having a brief sleep while he awaited his meal.

But instead he asked Presley, "Henshawe knew about the old count's death?"

"Oh, aye. Seems just after the news came, the young count had Rolles make him walk the carpet, then sent him on his way."

"Curious. It would not be many men's first reaction to hearing of the death of their father."

"Aye, well, Henshawe says if he hadn't talked to me, he might have been all right."

"I thought the two of you met somewhere out of sight."

"So we did, but not out of sight enough, seems. That Henshawe's a bit of a clever cove. He's not a man I much take to, but I will say for him, he's sharper than a saw. Serving in the d'Auvraye house, he's managed to gather up enough threads and scraps of their parlee-vous to patch it a bit. But they never knew it. So when Rolles gives him his wages, just as he's turning away, he mutters to himself, in their lingo, 'Tell *that* to the English.'" Presley drained his mug of beer. "That's what Henshawe took from it, anyway."

Morton frowned. "Did he tell you anything else?"

"The day the old count went up to Barnes, he and his son had a row. 'Twas heard all over the house."

Morton's tired brain tried to keep it straight. This

must have happened the day he and Presley paid their first visit to Spanish Place. "What was their dispute?"

Presley gave a grunt of laughter. "Appears Henshawe's French is not so fine as all that. He couldn't say. Apparently 'tweren't so strange for them to quarrel, although never so badly as this, from the sound of it. He thinks maybe they were arguing about his mistress."

Morton's food began to arrive, and he ate and drank as he listened.

"What I don't understand," Presley went on, "is why the son would care. Henshawe told me all these Frenchy swells is like that, having their madge on the side, it being their privilege, as they think. Well, English lords, too, for that matter."

Morton grimaced slightly. This last was hardly a proposition he was in a position to dispute. Of course, his young colleague knew nothing of Morton's own parentage or of his current domestic arrangements.

The bacon dealt with, Morton tucked hungrily into his pork pie. A tall naval officer entered the smoky room, and Morton realised it was Westcott. The man walked past the table of midshipmen, who all stood to acknowledge a superior officer. After that, their drunken banter fell quiet.

"Ah, Morton, there you are," Westcott said.

"Do you know Mr. Presley?"

The navy man shook hands with Presley and sat down, calling for a glass of wine. He regarded Morton for a moment, his manner rather grim.

"I must tell you, d'Auvraye's murder has caused something of a row in the halls of government. Have you learned anything more of it?"

Morton took a pull of his cider and shook his head. "The count's son and his secretary were not terribly helpful, other than to say it was the Bonapartists, of whom they have already given me a list. The finer points of law seem to elude them. Even if we could find these men, we would still have to have some proof that they committed the crimes. Being on a list is not a crime in this country."

Westcott rubbed an eye delicately, as though he were as tired as Morton.

"What do you know of Jean-Baptiste Lafond?" Morton asked the seaman.

Westcott stopped rubbing his eye and made an empty gesture with his hands. "Lafond is a tool of the Count d'Artois, the brother of King Louis. They worked secretly against Bonaparte all these long years and had a formidable league in France. Lafond himself is a bit of a mystery. Not many have met him. He was in England briefly years ago but has not been seen in some time."

"I spoke with him this afternoon."

Westcott sat back in his chair, a smile of admiration appearing as he regarded Morton. "Well, I don't know why I'm telling you anything. Lafond is here, in London?"

Morton continued to eat, too hungry to worry about manners. "Yes, and I'm wondering why. The only possible answer I can find is that Bonaparte is in England. Do you think that Bonaparte could be shot from a small boat as he takes his daily turn on the deck of His Majesty's ship *Bellerophon*?"

This brought Westcott up short. He took a sip of his wine, considering.

"Well, I suppose it is possible—these rifled barrels are much more accurate. But even if someone did manage it, he would never get away. The press about the ship is great, and small boats are locked in. There would be no escape. And the assassin would have to be quick, or someone nearby would stop him before he took aim."

"But if someone did not care what happened to him? If he did not care that he was caught or killed or hung, then it could be done?"

"Possibly, yes. Do you know of such a plot?"

"No, but Lafond is not in England to take the waters. D'Auvraye, a prominent royalist, is murdered, as is his mistress. Jean Boulot, a French national once known to have been an admirer of Bonaparte, seems to have had something to do with at least one of these murders if not both. I can think of no other explanation than the royalists are plotting to kill Bonaparte, and the Corsican's supporters are trying to stop them. You should alert the Admiralty to this."

"You know, Morton, the royalists are something of a speciality of mine. I've worked with them in many capacities for much of my time in the service. They have been our allies throughout the war. Are you now suggesting that they've become our enemies?"

"Mr. Morton, sir?"

Morton looked up to find one of the boys who cleared the tables and swept the floors standing respectfully at his elbow.

"A wee squib of a boy in a ruined topper is asking for you at the door. He won't tell me his name."

Morton lifted his mug and indelicately gulped down some cider, then rose. "Excuse me a moment."

Outside the door he looked around in the dim street.

"Mr. Morton?" came a small voice.

"Wil?"

The child emerged from a shadow, somehow not his brazen self. And where were his gaggle of followers?

Morton crouched down. "What brings you here at such an hour?"

"A man at Bow Street said you might be here."

The boy came a little closer, and in the light from the Golden Apple, Morton saw the shadowy pool of bruise around his eye, and his lip was swollen and split.

"What's happened to you, lad?"

"Some of the flash men found out I'd been taking dust from a horney," he said quietly, his manner subdued, "and this bandy dubber and a lumper give me a drubbing. I told them it was just the Frenchies I was peaching on, but they was half-seas-over and didn't listen. You mightn't come around Maiden Lane looking for me, Mr. Morton. I'll come to you, if you don't mind, sir."

"Step into the light, Wil. Let me look at you. Can you see out of that eye?"

"Well enough, sir. Well enough to know those two bastards who did me over. I shan't be a minikin all me life. They should have thought of that."

Poor child, Morton thought. He would always be small, like so many children of poverty in this city.

Unsure of what to do, Morton reached into a pocket and took out some silver, feeling low and mean as he did so. The boy closed his fingers around the coins, which shone dully in the poor light.

"Thank ye, Mr. Morton," the boy said softly.

"Don't thank me, Wil. It was your association with me that gained you the drubbing."

"I've had worse for less," the boy said. "But I'm forgetting, Mr. Morton. I'm forgetting why I've come for you. I've found your Frenchy again! The cully with the raspberry pate!"

"Boulot? Where?"

"Cheapside, sir! Not so far off, not so far. At the White Bear, sir, there in Basing'all Street. He come prowling back round his old doss house—he's a friend there seems he was trying to touch for money. And I followed him again."

"Well done!" Morton reached out and put a hand on the boy's shoulder. "You keep away from these flash men, Wil. Can't have anyone as valuable as you getting beaten. Now you be off, and keep that silver out of sight!"

Morton retreated inside to find Presley and Westcott and tell them his news. Westcott had his coach, it turned out, and he hurried off to bring it round while Morton tried to swallow a few more mouthfuls of his now-cold pie. A few moments later the officer drew up before the Golden Apple, himself up in the driver's bench, four in hand.

"What's become of your driver?"

"I've just sent him off with regrets to friends. I shan't be meeting them for supper as I'd hoped this evening."

Morton climbed up on the bench beside him, leaving Presley to ride in state.

"Should we be rushing into this unarmed, do you think?" asked Westcott, as he snapped his whip and put the vehicle in motion. "I could swing us round to the Admiralty and fetch a cutlass or my carriage pistols."

Morton considered. "Yes, I agree," he said, raising his voice to be heard over the clatter of hooves and the rumble of the wheels on the cobbles. "We should not go unprepared, this time. Who knows who else might be there? And if Boulot was involved in the murder of d'Auvraye, he will not likely come peaceably. But the Admiralty is too far. Take a turn by Bow Street, if you will."

Chapter 24

Arabella gazed at her face in the looking-glass. Makeup would be the ruin of her complexion. It dried her skin terribly, the putting it on, then washing it off.

"I shall look seventy at thirty-five," she lamented to her reflection.

A soft knock on her dressing-cabinet door interrupted her lamentation. She was annoyed, but then it occurred to her it might be Morton.

"Yes?" she sang out.

"Mrs. Malibrant, a young woman to see you."

Arabella looked at her reflection in the mirror and sighed. Some nights she was simply too exhausted at the end of a performance.

A whispering outside her door.

"Mrs. Malibrant? The young woman's name is Miss Honoria d'Auvraye, and she assures me she is here on a matter of utmost importance."

Arabella rose immediately and swept open the door.

A young woman stood there accompanied by a man who worked for the theatre. She was dressed entirely in black.

"My apologies, Mrs. Malibrant," the woman said without trace of accent. "I am Honoria d'Auvraye. May I have a moment of your time?"

"Yes, by all means. Please come in."

The space was small, hardly room for Arabella to apply her makeup and dress. Costumes hung on the wall or were spread over a miniature divan provided for the star to rest upon when not needed on the stage. Arabella swept up the costumes.

"Please—"

"I cannot," the young woman said. "I am on my way to church for midnight mass. It was with great difficulty that I arranged this meeting."

Beneath her hat and veil Arabella could see a handsome young woman, dark-eyed, full-mouthed. She was glad Henry was not here.

"Among your acquaintances you count Mr. Morton, the Bow Street Runner?"

"Yes, I do."

"I have something for him," she said, reaching into a small reticule, from which she withdrew a folded sheet of paper.

"I removed this letter from my father's study. It has caused a great deal of trouble. A man brought it to my father, the Count d'Auvraye, a few nights before he was killed." She crossed herself, her eyes pressing closed for just an instant. "Please give it to Mr. Morton."

Honoria turned to go, her black-gloved hand coming to rest on the door handle.

"But have you nothing more to say?" Arabella said. "Do you know who killed your father?"

The young woman leaned her cheek against the door for a second as she pulled it open. "I—I hope I do not know, madame," she said.

"Mrs. M.?" came a familiar voice from beyond.

Honoria nodded to Arabella and swept out past a surprised Arthur Darley.

"Do you need a few more minutes?" Darley began, but then regarded her strangely. "Has something distressed you, my dear?"

"I don't quite know. Come in, please." She reached out and drew the nobleman into her small chamber. "That was a daughter of the Count d'Auvraye. She left me this letter, saying Henry must have it." Arabella unfolded the letter, holding it up to the light. She lowered herself to the chair before the mirror, and Darley sat upon the divan, where he read over her shoulder.

"It is signed by Fouché!" Darley said.

"That I can see. But who is he again?"

"The man who forced Bonaparte to abdicate and smoothed the way for the Bourbons to return. The great survivor. It was Fouché who brought down Robespierre. He has served as head of the secret police to every French government since: Republican, Bonaparte, Bourbon. It does not matter. They are all too afraid of him to do him harm. It is said of Fouché, if he were stranded alone on a desert island, he would form a conspiracy against the sand."

Arabella puzzled over the French a moment. "I don't understand. What does it say, exactly?"

Darley took a corner of the paper, angling it a little his way. "It's a bit ambiguous, but essentially:

My dear Comte d'Auvraye:

Events move very quickly now, and we must not hesitate or they will sweep beyond our control. The government of England must not be allowed to falter or to permit their own petty notions of justice to stop them from doing what is right. Bonaparte must be sent off to some remote station and as quickly as possible. The longer he remains on a ship in an English harbour, the more likely it is that legal arguments will allow him to escape true justice. Final arrangements have been made for the little general. But he must be sent away to some remote place with his suite of followers.

Do not fail in this. History will judge us harshly.

Fouché

"It hardly seems momentous," Arabella said, wondering why it was so important that this reach Morton.

"No," Darley said, taking it from her and examining it closely, "but there is a great deal written between the lines; most importantly this last: 'Final arrangements have been made for the little general. But he must be sent away to some remote place with his suite of followers.'"

"They've arranged his murder," Arabella said.

Darley looked very grave and troubled. "It is certainly the interpretation that I would choose."

Arabella leaned closer to Darley so that their shoulders touched and their heads came gently together. She stabbed a finger at the paper. "But this was not written by Fouché," she pronounced. "It is the hand of a woman—look."

Darley turned the paper so that it caught the light. "It is

rather elegant and feminine, I must agree." Darley turned
the letter over. "And it has no sealing wax. It is a copy."

"A copy made by a woman..." Arabella said, the re-
alisation dawning. "And not young Honoria, for she says
she snatched it from her father's desk. The woman must
be Angelique Desmarches. That is why Honoria wants
Henry to see it. She doesn't care about what happens to
Bonaparte. She wants her father's murderer found.
That man Boulot brought this to d'Auvraye, I will wager you anything. Boulot came by it somehow and carried it to d'Auvraye to prove that the mistress was
spying on him. And the mistress was a friend of the De le
Coeurs, who are almost certainly spies for Bonaparte."

"I do not like the sound of that," Darley said, leaning
back against the wall. "It would almost certainly mean
that d'Auvraye had his mistress tortured to find out
what she knew or what her Bonapartist friends were up
to." Darley shook his head. "I would have said the count
could never do such a thing. But there it is."

But to Arabella nothing was obvious. "Why would
the count's daughter give us a letter that incriminates
her own father?"

Laughter in the hallway beyond distracted them a
moment.

"No doubt she was not as astute as you, my dear,"
Darley went on when the noise subsided. "She likely did
not realise this letter was a copy but thought it from
Fouché himself."

Arabella considered the woman who had entered her
cabinet—how she had reacted when asked if she knew
who had murdered her father: "*I hope I do not know,
madame.*"

"Should this letter not go to the proper people in our
government?" Arabella wondered.

"I suppose, though if it was sent through the mail, the government will be aware of its contents already."

This caused Arabella to lift an eyebrow in question.

"Well, it isn't well known, even within the government itself, but there is a little suite of rooms in Whitehall, near the Foreign Office, where the mail of certain people is opened and read, and diplomatic codes are deciphered."

Arabella's other eyebrow rose, and Darley smiled.

"It is perfectly legal, my dear—or at least it has been sanctioned. The Secret Department, so called, reports to the foreign secretary. The post office intercepts the mail and sends it along to Whitehall, where it is copied and closed again so that no one can tell it has been opened. The seals of the embassies and of many individuals have been copied."

Arabella laughed—she could not help it. "Are you telling me that this goes on within the confines of Whitehall and no one knows of it?"

"Well, certainly Fouché knows, which might explain the veiled language—though he might have sent this by courier so that it did not pass through the Secret Department, in which case I should alert certain people to its existence. But unfortunately it is only a copy of a letter that we *believe* was written by Fouché. Without the original letter, or the d'Auvraye family vouching for its authenticity, I rather doubt it will be taken too seriously. So someone might be plotting to murder Napoleon—but even that is open to interpretation. I rather doubt the government will care."

"Well, let's take it to Henry, at the very least. He should know that the count likely murdered his own mistress. And Bonaparte's followers murdered him in revenge."

"I agree. Morton should see this immediately." Darley looked at her warmly. "But where will we find him?"

Chapter 25

They were a moment at Bow Street finding someone with the key to the gun cabinet.

"You've one for me, I hope," Westcott said as
Morton and Presley each primed and loaded a brace of
pistols. Morton wished he had his own Wogdon's or his
old turn-off pistols.

"I wish I had, Captain," he said as he tipped a powder
flask, opening it to deposit a measure of black powder
into the neck. He shook a little powder into the pan and
closed it. The rest went down the muzzle. "But you're
not one of Sir Nathaniel's constables, and I can't provide you with a weapon, at risk of my own position."

Westcott looked a bit vexed but then nodded. "I'm
sure you don't want firearms in just anyone's hands,
though I am an excellent shot at twenty paces."

"I'm sure you are," Morton said. "Let us hope that
none of us has need to fire a weapon."

A moment later they were off through the warm,
dark streets of London, the coach lamps casting the dim
shadows of their straining horses on the cobbles before

them. Linkmen passed, their charges huddled beneath their lanterns, for London's night streets were dark and never wholly without threat.

By mistake, they turned into a blind alley and had to climb down and take hold of the horses' bridles to back them slowly out. By the time they reached Basinghall Street, the night was far advanced. A hunchback moon swam in the blur over the jumbled rooftops, and below, the windows of the buildings were dark or only dimly lit. The slow *clop clop* of a horse as it drew a tradesman's cart along the distant street was the only interruption to the quiet.

"There is the inn," Morton said, pointing. "Draw up here. We'll go forward quietly on foot. Boulot might be ready to bolt at the slightest sign of a threat." Morton felt a liquid rumbling in his stomach, a foreboding. Perhaps it was the dark deserted street or the ominous-looking White Bear, its dark mass like a ship on a silent sea. Boulot had fired a pistol at them before—accidentally, he claimed, but he was likely more desperate now. And how many friends had he here?

Westcott drew the carriage up in the shadow of a building and applied the brake. They climbed down onto the street, and Presley wedged himself out through the small door of the carriage. In the poor light Morton could just make out the young Runner's grim face. Westcott's dark blue coat would have hidden him well had his breeches not been white. The navy man looked alert, ready, perhaps even excited. Morton wondered how much the man had missed the action of a fighting ship these last years.

"You and I will go in alone, Jimmy, and see what we can learn about Boulot. If the owner of the inn is

English, he might tell us all we need to know, but if he should be French, it could be another story."

"Should we have brought reinforcements?" Westcott asked.

"We can still send for help if it seems necessary," Morton answered, pitching his voice low. "But let's get the lay of the land first."

One of the inn's side doors opened at that moment, a fan of light spreading over the uneven cobbles. Men emerged, shadowy at this distance, and then one of them broke and ran. He hadn't gone five paces before he was run down by a larger man who punched him hard and then dragged him to his feet. Two others came up, one pointing a pistol, and words in French reached Morton's ears.

He drew a pistol and shouted, "Hold! Bow Street!"

A muffled shout in French.

Westcott cursed.

The three shadow men all stopped at once, then one levelled a pistol and fired. Morton and Presley threw themselves back against the building, but Westcott stood in the open, as officers did on the decks of their ships.

The shadow men dragged their captive round the corner and out of sight. Morton and Presley went pounding across the paving stones, shouting as they went, but they hadn't gone far when someone leaned out from behind the building, and the muzzle flash of a pistol stopped them. The report echoed down the street, the ball passing so close that Westcott's horses reared back, lumbering into each other.

"Dem!" Morton swore, and they ran on, staying to the shadows.

The clatter of horses reached them as they rounded

the corner, and the sound of wheels rattling over paving stones. A large, old-fashioned carriage bounced off down the narrow avenue. Morton raised a pistol, cocked it, and fired once, but to no visible effect.

They turned back, shouting for Westcott, who immediately brought the carriage up. Morton leapt up beside the navy man.

"Was that Boulot?" Westcott asked as he cracked a whip over his team's heads.

"Yes, I'm sure it was. I heard him call out," Morton shouted over the clatter of horses and carriage.

They rounded the corner, narrowly avoiding a few people who had spilled out of the White Bear to see what all the fuss was about. The carriage whisking the captive Boulot away was barely visible now, its lamps disappearing round a curve in the street.

Westcott was a skilled driver, but he was noticeably unwilling to destroy his fine carriage in the chase, and the other vehicle was soon lost to sight.

"Difficult to imagine worse luck than that," the captain said as he slowed his team to a walk.

"Yes," Morton said. "We seem always to be arriving a moment too late." He was still breathing hard from their run and the sudden unexpected fire. He wondered if those were the same men who'd escaped him outside Boulot's door, but in the dark and with the distance, he could not say. Certainly it was likely to be no one else—unless Abbé Lafond was somehow involved. "Can you find us a hackney-coach, do you think?"

"I'll take you wherever you want to go," Westcott offered.

"If you'll carry us out to the toll gate by Apsley House, I'll be much in your debt."

"The Hyde Park toll gate it is," Westcott said, then snapped his whip, and set them off at a good speed.

The man at the toll gate stood with a lantern in his hand. He looked as though he had been asleep, though there was traffic through this gate both day and night. "Aye. Not an hour ago," he said. "Big berlin, but ornate and foreign looking."

"Did the man who paid you have an accent?"

"He didn't say a word, yer honour. Just paid his toll and set off. They'd been in some rush to get here—horses were all in a lather."

"Sounds like our men," Presley offered, stepping out onto the roadside.

Morton considered for only a second. "Let's find some saddle horses, Jimmy, and see if we can't run these men down."

"I'll take you on," Westcott said. "But who do you think they are?"

Morton was wondering the same thing. "Supporters of Bonaparte. They used Boulot to find the waterman who assisted them in their murder of the Count d'Auvraye. Boulot may not have co-operated freely, but he did give them Berman's name—Berman on the quay. I think they've taken Boulot now because he is known among the smugglers."

"But taken him for what purpose?"

"I do not know," Morton said. "To kill more royalists, I fear."

"Then we must go on with all haste." Westcott turned to the man, still standing with his lantern. "Lift the bar," the navy man ordered. "We are on the king's business."

Chapter 26

The moonlight brightened as they passed out of the city of London, the sky overhead clearing until it was bright with stars. The Great West Road curved away before them beneath rows of swaying trees. Morton sat up beside Westcott, who had donned a greatcoat and gloves in imitation of the mail-coach drivers.

For a seaman he was a skilled driver, Morton thought, though among a certain set this was a mark of some distinction. You could see them in Regent's Park on Sunday afternoons, gentry who aped not only the dress of the mail-coach drivers but their manner of speech and other habits as well—not all of these habits worthy of gentlemen. A few young men of good families had gone so far as to take positions driving mail coaches, and one titled gentlemen was said to be planning the purchase of the London/Brighton route so that he might drive whenever the desire struck. It appeared that Westcott was a follower of this fashion, though Morton would not complain of it this night.

The moonlit country sped by, the carriage rocking and jouncing along the wide white road. Occasionally the coach lamps of a London-bound vehicle swam up out of the obscurity on their right. The clatter of the team, the rattle of wheels, and the other coach went by, its driver cocking his whip in brief salutation. Then solitude and the dark again, into which Westcott sent them plunging steadily. Morton was all but falling from his perch with fatigue but was not ready to sleep yet. He still hoped to catch the carriage and the men who had taken Boulot.

"You think these men are going to Plymouth?" Westcott asked over the pounding of the horses' hooves, the squeaking of the carriage springs.

"Yes. I wonder if we should try to alert the port admiral there. Can we use the telegraph?" The Admiralty's semaphoric telegraph had been stretched to Plymouth a decade before, the tall, boxy towers set on high points of land, each about ten miles from the next.

Westcott shook his head. "No. We should have done that from London. The men in the towers will not let even an officer send a message." Westcott shifted in his seat. "You asked if I thought Bonaparte could be shot on the deck of the *Bellerophon*. Do you have some basis to believe that this is planned?"

"None. But these Bonapartists are killing royalists for a reason. You wouldn't be sorry to see the Corsican shot, I collect?"

A dark smile crossed the seaman's face. "I confess I would not, but it is my duty to stop such a plot. And I shall do my duty. It is not for Geoffrey Westcott to decide the fate of Napoleon Bonaparte."

"Quite so." Morton rubbed his burning eyes. "Friends went out into the sound to see the little general. Their description of the press of boats and people about the *Bellerophon* was nothing less than astonishing."

"It is peculiar, isn't it? They say he's not shown the least animosity. As though he were really an emperor on an imperial visit, rather than the scoundrel who has spilt English blood on countless battlefields and in all the seas. He is a wonder, I will admit that. Have you ever raised horses, Morton?"

"I confess I have not."

"My father bred horses for racing for many years. It was instructive, I will tell you. Every once in a great while a horse of no particular bloodline would appear and beat all the best horses of its day. The odd thing was, the greatness of this beast was almost never passed down. The blood did not run true. Bonaparte is like that, I think. There will be no one left to follow him. This son of his will come to nothing, mark my words."

"The republicans don't much like to hear such arguments."

Westcott cracked his whip over the head of one horse—"the laggard," as he called her. "No, I suppose they don't, but I can make the argument work from the opposite direction just as well. I have been closely associated with the French royalists for much of the war. There are exceptions, of course, but for the most part it is as though they have been breeding the worst stock to the worst, creating a race of idiots who have no concerns beyond honour and privilege." He was silent for a moment. "But I was in France in the early days of the Revolution, during some of the Terror, even. I saw what men, ungoverned, were capable of. I fear for France, Morton. I fear for the land of my mother. The Bourbons are doomed. They will not hold the nation. France is a ship without a captain. The officers will squabble amongst themselves, and the men before the mast will cease taking orders. Such a ship is bound for the rocks, Morton, bound for the rocks."

"You think Bonaparte will come back?"

"I do not count him out. The man is a phoenix. But he has made war on England and her allies for far too long. It's time we put an end to that threat."

"Hang him, then?"

An odd, shrugging grimace was all the answer Morton received.

They arrived at the first posting station then and swept into its dim yard beneath a veil of dust.

Jimmy Presley tumbled out of the carriage, an unlikely-looking passenger of such a conveyance. The dark mass of the inn leaned over them, blocking out the moon. The smell of horses and dung was strong here, mixed with the sweeter smell of hay and grain dust. Three barking dogs appeared, wagging their tails. Presley immediately made friends with them, and they fell silent. An ostler and two boys roused themselves in a few moments; one of them carried a lantern that sent the shadows fleeing and then rushing back across the yard as it swung in his hand.

"No rest for the deevil or the ostler," muttered the ostler, a heavy, slow shadow of a man.

"Did a big berlin come this way, traveling west?" Morton asked.

"Aye. A passel of Frenchies, wanting everything done double quick, as though they were the bloody Prince of Wales."

All of them? Morton wanted to ask. "When did they set out from here?"

The man rubbed his head.

"Pardon me, sir," one of the boys interjected. "Just after three. I heard the inn's clock chime."

The ostler gave the boy a sour look.

Morton could not read his watch in the poor light but guessed sunrise was not far off. "They're just shy of two hours ahead," he told Westcott, "which means we are not closing the gap at all. In truth, they have gained a little." Morton considered their situation. The mail coaches did not leave London until night. He looked over at Presley. "We'll have to hire horses and try to run Boulot and his captors down. Can you manage that?"

"I'll do what needs to be done," Presley said. He was not much of a horseman, being born to London's working class.

"We can take my carriage," Westcott said without hesitation.

Morton turned to the navy man. "The cost of hiring post horses would be too great, Captain. My magistrate would never countenance it."

"Then the Admiralty shall pay," Westcott said firmly. "And if they refuse, I will bear the cost myself. And I will brook no argument on this." Westcott turned to the ostler. "At the risk of being mistaken for the bloody Prince of Wales," he said, "we shall need everything done triple quick. But I shall make it worth your while."

Morton reclined as best he could in the small carriage, falling into dream only to be shaken to wakefulness by the carriage lurching or shaking. He rolled down the curtain against the morning sun, but it still found its way through the cracks, throwing stark lines of light about the carriage in a mad race.

He had sent a note back to Sir Nathaniel telling him

what went on and asking that he alert the government to the possible threat to Bonaparte, but he was still not completely convinced himself. Oh, something went on, that was certain, and the man at the centre of it was the drunkard Boulot, who had once supported Bonaparte and had then become a friend of smugglers. A young woman was dead, and an old nobleman and his manservant. Lafond, a general of the Chevaliers de la Foi, was in London for the first time in years—perhaps. And Bonaparte was on a ship in Plymouth harbour. These were all threads of the same cloth, Morton was sure of that, but he could not weave them all together.

What made the most sense was that the royalists planned to murder Bonaparte. The Bonapartists had got wind of the plan from Madame De le Cœur, who almost certainly had learned of it from Angelique Desmarches, the count's mistress. The supporters of Bonaparte had then tortured Madame Desmarches to find out what the royalists were planning. They had then murdered the Count d'Auvraye in an attempt to stop the royalists.

And what of Boulot? He was the betrayer. He'd gone to the count and told him his mistress had passed information to the supporters of the Corsican. No doubt he'd offered some proof. Boulot would have known about Angelique Desmarches because he still had friends among the Bonapartists. But this betrayal hadn't swayed d'Auvraye, who refused to intercede with Fouché on Boulot's behalf, perhaps even out of anger at what Boulot had told him. The count had then cast off his mistress, thinking her in league with his enemies. It had then been easy for the Bonapartists to convince Boulot to help them assassinate d'Auvraye. The sot had provided the name of a waterman who could be involved in such a scheme or who would give them a boat but not talk to the police. But what use did the supporters of Bonaparte have for the little drunkard now?

Before he could puzzle this out any further, Morton fell into a dream. Faceless men ran from darkened doorway to alley to doorway. On a balcony overlooking the street stood the Corsican, silhouetted by a dim light from behind. The shadow men became still, and when they advanced were as stealthy as spiders. Morton could see them, but he could neither move nor cry out. A loud report, and Morton was thrown hard against the side of the carriage.

He heard Westcott talking soothingly to his team, slowing it. The carriage jounced to a halt, and Morton stepped down to the ground. It was bright morning, the summer birds in full song, swallows swooping over a field of green hay. From the driver's seat, Westcott and Presley climbed stiffly down. The navy man crouched to look under his carriage, examining each wheel, handling the spokes to be sure they were not cracked.

"Sorry to give you such a shake, Morton," the seaman said. "Found an abyss in the road. We seem to be in one piece."

Morton offered to drive for a time, and after Westcott had assured himself that Morton could handle four in hand, he climbed into the carriage so that he might try to sleep. The two Runners sat out in the English sun, the breeze cooling them only a little. Morton pressed the horses on, but they were tiring, and the team would have to be changed if they hoped to catch up to Boulot and his abductors.

As they crested a hill, Morton saw a large carriage disappearing beneath the elms below and set the horses to race. Presley took out a pistol and sat grimly holding on, staring at the road ahead. The carriage was soon overtaken and proved to be a very English family, their smiling faces filling the carriage windows.

Morton called to the driver: "Have you seen a large berlin, traveling west, and in a hurry?"

The man nodded. "Two hours ago. Perhaps a little more."

Morton pressed the horses on.

Chapter 27

The setting sun lit all the clouds in the western sky aflame, some burning down to charcoal grey, others still molten bright—oranges and reds and liquid golds. The green rolling hills extended to every point of the compass, the shadows of trees and hedges stretched long and thin across fields and pastures. Dusk seemed to seep out of the shadows, spreading over the Somersetshire countryside, as though the darkness bled out of the earth itself.

Morton and Westcott sat up on the box, Westcott with reins and whip in hand. They had not spoken much for the past hour, watching a sky overwhelmed with transient beauty. They had stopped at a posting inn two hours earlier, where some navy men had paused en route to London. Westcott had avoided them, Morton noticed, almost to the point of hiding himself away. Morton, curious by profession, wondered why.

"You knew those officers at the inn?" the Runner said at last, having first considered several variations on the wording of his question.

"Not all of them, no," Westcott answered softly. "Thamesly was midshipman with me briefly on the *Ajax*. He's a rear admiral now."

Morton felt this was more explanation than he needed. Westcott's bitterness at having spent the war ashore was a wound Morton did not want to open. They drove on in silence, the sky burning itself out, dusk spreading over the lands. Once or twice Morton thought Westcott would speak, but then he did not.

Finally the navy man said, "You are, if I'm not mistaken, Morton, a man who takes his duty seriously. Do you ever wonder if you have not been too much of a slave to duty? If you have served her, but she has not served you in return? After all, Morton, you are also a man of considerable ability. You could have made your fortune in commerce or trade. Lesser men than you have done it. Look at Soanes—an architect now, but was his father not a bricklayer?"

Morton was about to answer that duty had no obligation to serve in return, but the question was seriously and honestly asked, and he felt it deserved an answer in kind. "I have at times felt resentment at others who have taken a path less difficult than mine, and not so narrow, and yet achieved great acclaim for their efforts. I'm sure the navy is full of men who have performed difficult service that will never be recognised. In wars, many serve but few are noticed. Some give their lives."

Westcott nodded. "Yes. I should not grumble. Men I've known did lose their lives in the wars against Bonaparte. They served with distinction and in the end were rewarded with a white shroud, a shot of chain, and a forty-fathom grave. I've fared better than they. I should not grumble. You're quite right, Morton. I should not."

He shifted in his seat, glancing round. "It is time to light the lamps, I think."

The dusky little coaching town of Ilchester appeared as a close scattering of dim lights, and soon the dark houses and buildings pressed in around them. Westcott negotiated the turn beneath the arch and on into the yard of the inn. Beneath the dim light of a few lamps the paving stones glittered, apparently wet from a light rain, though Morton and his companions had been spared this as they travelled.

Despite the hour the innyard was full of the usual noise and confusion: a crowd of milling dark figures, vehicles, hills of baggage, stamping horses. As the coach came to rest, Morton stood, casting a weary eye over the scene. The mail coach, which had recently overtaken them on the road, exchanged its team, the passengers alighting, looking as though they'd just wakened, and then, one by one, wandering into the coffee room for refreshment.

On all sides the yard was surrounded by buildings: the inn to the fore and down one side, a stable to the left, and in the back the dark bulk of an outbuilding that Morton could not name. Another arch led out there, so that the coaches should not have to be turned in such a confined space. Several more carriages stood in a shadowy corner, but there was no lamp lit near them, and Morton guessed they would remain where they were for the night.

"Do they have horses for us, I wonder?" Westcott asked.

Morton climbed down from the high seat, joints cracking at the effort. "So I hope," he said. He was having

trouble forcing his mind to wake and seemed to be drifting in some near-dream state. How long had it been since
he'd enjoyed the luxury of a full night's sleep in his own
bed? He waved a hand toward the back of the yard.
"There are carriages down the way. I'll see they're not our
berlin, then we'll find the inn manager." He rapped on the
carriage door. "Jimmy? Time for an ale, lad."

The rocking of the carriage signalled the young Runner's attempt to rouse himself.

As Morton left the oblong of dim illumination and
approached the dark carriages, a small man detached
himself from their shadow and hurried across the yard
into one of the stable's open doors.

Morton took another pace and realised that he was
looking at the berlin they had chased through the streets
of London! He snapped awake. Before he could call out
to Westcott and Presley, a muffled cry caused him to step
into the shadow of a carriage. A pistol flashed, from just
inside one of the stable doors, the report echoing down
the length of the yard, bringing everything to a stop for a
long moment. And then everyone began to run.

Morton sprinted for an open door of the stable, ducking in and keeping low.

He cursed silently. Someone had tried to call out to
him—Boulot. It could only have been Boulot.

He pulled out his pistols and cocked them, the grips
cool and solid in his hands. A single lamp pushed a few
shadows away from its immediate vicinity, but the rest
of the barn was very dark. Shapes suggested beams and
stalls, grain bins and haystacks. Morton stood with his
back to a massive post and gazed into the darkness
around him, watching for the smallest movement. He
strained to hear, but the shot had frightened everyone,

and outside there was pandemonium and little could be heard over it.

Inside, the horses in their rows of standing-stalls were casting their heads from side to side, pulling at their tethers and trying to back out into the alley. Morton ducked down and poked his head out to look down the alleyway. All he could make out was a long row of horses' hindquarters, shadows, bits of straw bedding, dung awaiting a shovel. The sweet smell of hay was mixed here with the noisome odours of the carriage trade.

A man dodged out into the alley, then disappeared into shadow. Morton was sure he'd held a pistol in his hand. How many were there? Then he heard voices whispering—in French, he was almost certain.

"We are from Bow Street!" Morton called out. "You cannot get away now. Give yourselves up!"

A pistol fired again, and a horse, not a yard away, whinnied, dancing to one side.

Morton stood and fired toward the muzzle-flash, but he saw no one. The smell of smoke touched his nostrils, and he heard some desperate stamping. A flame licked up from behind the standing-stalls very near to where the man had fired. The shadows of men were suddenly thrown against a wall.

"Morton?" Presley's voice came from outside, but Morton dared not answer.

The hay in the mangers was going up now, a high, quick crackling sound that made the hair on Morton's neck stand on end. Flames spread out and upward, until they lapped at the ceiling, illuminating the scene in eerie orange light. The horses were in terror now, struggling wildly to free themselves, hooves scraping harshly on stone as they pulled at their tethers. Their backs were like a moving sea—a storm of fear and panic.

Smoke began to burn Morton's eyes, and he ducked low, moving forward, one hand on the cool stone floor. A man shouted in French—words Morton did not recognise. And then dark shapes dodged out of the smoke. Morton raised his second pistol and pulled the trigger, but it hung fire, only a spray of sparks erupting from the pan. A wild-eyed horse rushed toward him, its nostrils flaring.

He spun and raced out the door, dodging the horse that had broken free. Outside Morton found Westcott and Presley pressed against the wall, each with one of Jimmy's pistols in hand.

Dim shadows leapt onto the berlin.

"There they are!" Morton shouted.

Both Presley and Westcott raised their pistols and fired, but it was impossible to see if they'd hit anything. The berlin lumbered into motion, picked up speed, and disappeared under the archway at the back of the inn.

More horses were breaking their tethers and charging out of the barn, where they ran in circles, endangering anyone who came near. Some tried to force their way back in again, so panicked were they.

Presley stood by an open door, and when he judged no horses were coming out, he dashed into the stable.

"Jimmy!" Morton called. "You'll be trampled."

Morton and Westcott were retreating along the wall, fearful of the horses and driven back by the smoke.

"You!" someone called from behind, and Morton turned to find a frightened man with a blunderbuss pointed at them. "You will put down your pistols!"

"I'm a Bow Street Runner," Morton called over the

noise. "We're pursuing murderers, Frenchmen in a big berlin."

The big muzzle of the gun wavered.

"Put that weapon down!" Westcott ordered the man. "We are the king's men on the king's business. You'll lose your stable and buildings if you don't jump to it."

Slowly the sweating man lowered the muzzle. Presley came barrelling out of the building and was knocked down by a horse that shot out behind him. He picked himself up, coughing into a handkerchief he held over his mouth.

"I freed as many horses as I could, but they're running in circles, knocking each other down." He looked about at the scene of madness in the yard, frightened horses running every which way, the flickering light of the growing fire glittering off their flanks. Wide-eyed men and boys came pounding across the yard with buckets.

Westcott reached out to take a bucket from a man, but Morton stayed his hand.

"No!" he shouted over the cacophony. "We can't let them escape." He pointed back toward Westcott's carriage.

"But this inn will go up," Westcott protested.

"We are pursuing murderers, Captain. We cannot waver."

Morton herded his reluctant companions back to the carriage. They were some time turning it round in the madness of the innyard, but then they were out into the roadway, where men on foot and horse came hurrying to the fire.

With one backward look at the rising glow, Westcott turned the carriage onto the western road and cracked his whip over the heads of their tired team.

Chapter 28

A t first they seemed almost unearthly, a strange dancing circle of yellowish-orange lights, bobbing in the dark emptiness of the night above him. Morton was by himself on the box, and he blinked his weary eyes a moment in confusion, the reins slack in his hands. Plymouth was still some twenty-five miles off, it was well past midnight, and all around, unseen below an overcast sky, lay the barren upland wastes of Dartmoor. It was the most deserted stretch of country he and his companions had traversed since leaving London—he had not seen lights of any kind for hours, since they had passed the lonely signal tower at the edge of the moor, its shutters motionless, a single dim lamp burning in an upper window. Now, from nowhere, a faerie circle of illumination seemed to hover and vibrate over the invisible earth.

But as he urged his team cautiously on and felt the coach begin once more to ascend, he recognised that they weren't in midair at all, but only on the brow of the next height of the Great Western Road. Drawing slowly up the slope, he could make out a little knot of men with lanterns, standing oddly across the way and blocking it. As he stopped a few yards short of them, a deep silence fell, and the crickets could be heard pulsing on all sides.

Only then did he notice the weapons—the musket barrels, the glint of blades. Too late. Several of them were setting down their lanterns, taking up their arms. Presley and Westcott remained asleep in the compartment. Morton moved his hand unobtrusively to his pistol. The sound of the men's boots on the gravel road seemed very loud as they walked deliberately up. Their stern faces loomed into the glow cast by his own coach-lamps.

But when Morton saw them more clearly, he relaxed. Whatever their expression, these were country faces. Yeomen, farmers, clad in dark corduroys and fustian. He knew such weathered features and such clothes well enough; he drew his hand unobtrusively away from his weapon.

"Even to ye, zir. Ye'll be vrom London-way, expect."

The West Country accent was unmistakable.

"Good evening to you. Aye, from London. What's the matter, then?"

Four of them had drawn up around the dusty vehicle and were gazing up at him with an earnestly appraising look. They were not quick to reply. When they did, it was the first man again, a tall, dark fellow with a fowling piece cradled, muzzle down, in the crook of his arm.

"H'a ye zeen aught amiss on the road tonight, zir?"

"Nay. Is aught amiss here?"

"Aye. There be. H'a ye zeen a great dark painted carriage? Vrenchmen, it might be. Travelling hard."

"Why do you ask?" Morton peered at him in surprise and got a long guarded look in response. He could feel the coach sway a little on its springs as the passengers in the cabin below him shifted. Presently he heard the door open. The Devonshire men watched with steady eyes, but Morton noticed the grip on their weapons get a little tighter. They were on edge, for all their phlegmatic country manners.

Jimmy Presley clambered out into the night air, yawning, bending at the waist to stretch himself.

"Aye," slowly resumed the tall man, watching Morton's young colleague. "Vrench zoldier-men, appears, as have broken their parole and gone off from the gaol on t'moors there by Princeton. They were zeen hereabout."

"Aye," said another. "The colonel at Princeton zays they've t'an horse vrom his stable, but they must've thieved a carriage from zomeone."

"They've been zeen," repeated one of the other men flatly.

"Like enough they'll be bound for the coast," said another voice, at Morton's back. Geoffrey Westcott also yawned and gave a perfunctory nod of greeting to the country men. "They're a-weary of our company, I daresay. The Home Office tells us they've been wandering off all over England," he told Morton with a wry smile. "They're trying to find passage for France, one way or another. There's smuggler folk along the coast south of here who'll be glad enough to ferry them over for a fee. I think you'll find them lost and harmless."

The four men regarded Westcott steadily for a moment, and Morton saw, even if Westcott couldn't, that they knew more than they had said.

"Nay so harmless" was the cryptic response of the tall man.

"We're from the Bow Street Magistrate's office, in

London," Jimmy Presley announced brusquely. "We're after some other Frenchies in a dark painted coach and four—a berlin, heading westward."

The Devon men took sober note of this and looked at one another questioningly.

"Ess, Humphrey," one of them eventually addressed the tall man. "Here be zummut. Zir Godfrey'll want 'em, sure."

Jimmy was impatient. "Speak up, lads! Don't mumble. Have ye seen these folk in the coach, yea or nay? They'd like have been passing along this road."

They all regarded him another moment, unsmiling, blank. The tall man, Humphrey, cleared his throat.

"If ye be the king's men, our justice of the peace'll want ye. He's zent for. There be zummut that ye best look on."

They would be no more specific. Humphrey went ahead on horseback, leading the carriage with the Bow Street men and their companion away from the high road and along a narrow, deeply shadowed lane overgrown on both sides by furze bushes and straggling hedgerows of thorn and briar. The way was pitted and eroded by the floods of other seasons, and their wheels rocked perilously as they jounced over it; but then the way became smoother, gravel crunching beneath the iron-shod feet of their team and beneath the wheels. Someone had repaired the lane out of sight of the main road.

Below a low stone bridge, invisible water muttered and rattled endlessly in a rocky bed. Once there came the shrill cry of a plover out of the surrounding obscurity. Then silence again, and the rank perfume of midsummer heather hanging oppressively in the muggy air.

At length the path seemed just to peter out. Their yellow lamps cast a sulphurous glow over an unkempt yard, filled with dim forms: a broken rick and other decayed and half-seen things—rusting spade, scythe handle, a heap of shattered crockery—all overrun with knapweed.

They found a decrepit barn, newly thatched, set back in a grove of scraggy trees that clung to the hillside. As the London men and their guide approached, a dark form detached itself and moved toward them.

"Lemuel?"

"Here, Maister Albright."

A gaunt young man came into the light, a musket at port. From the familiar way he held it, Morton guessed him to be a discharged soldier.

"Zir Godfrey's not come?"

"Been, and 's gone to Ashburton for the crowner and some other volk. Come again anon, 'a zays."

"Nought's stirred here?"

Lemuel's beardless lips formed a slight sardonic smile. "Nay," he replied, "nor like to, 'll guess."

Albright grimaced and gestured for the visitors to come in. As he followed, Morton's chest tightened, and he tried to prepare himself. But something about the wretchedness of this place, perched on the margins of the barren moor, something in the grim air of the men, and an indescribable charge of anxiety that seemed to hang unreleased in the very boughs of the stunted trees and in the eerily still ghost-forms of shrubbery on either side of the path, all combined to fill his fatigued mind with a deeper dread, a feeling shapeless and uncanny.

A little wave of almost panicky resistance coursed through him, and he badly wanted not to have to go into this barn, not to confront what was there. For a moment it seemed almost to take hold of his body, to be physically impeding him, and it was an enormous struggle to place one foot ahead of the other. But leadenly, doggedly, he continued to walk.

Humphrey Albright was the first through the low, wide door that already stood open. Morton went next, breathing deep. The barn was open, large, the light not strong enough to banish all the shadows. But there was no hay here, and any stalls or pens had been torn out. The floor was stacked with small four-gallon barrels, and boxes of all sizes, many marked with writing in French.

"A smugglers' den," Presley said. "Out here!"

"Not zo var vrom Tor Bay, Teignmouth, and Dalish," the other man said, then reached up to hang his lantern on a beam hook, illuminating a hellish tableau.

Morton registered the blood first. Darkened blood everywhere, splashed, smeared, drabbled across the rough stone floor. But there were other things. Grey stuff spilled across the stones, viscous, amidst which were scraps of white, glistening in the lamplight. A man's brains, and bits of his broken skull. And then the man himself, on the floor. Beyond an overturned plank table a second man, partly hidden from Morton's view.

Somehow, now that he actually had the thing before him, Henry Morton was better able to control his emotions. The worst, the horrible foreboding, seemed to pass, after one light-headed moment. For Jimmy Presley it was otherwise, and with a choking gasp, he abruptly turned and blundered back out. A moment later, through the narrow, broken window, they heard him bellow—a strange, half-throttled cry of protest and horror and shock. Then he fell silent. Albright nodded his head slowly, looking down. Beside him Westcott was impassive. It occurred rather disconnectedly to Morton

that he must have seen worse on the decks of His
Majesty's warships.

No. As bad perhaps. Not worse.

But it also flickered through his mind that these
sailors were hard men. Harder than one might otherwise have supposed.

In fact, it was Westcott who spoke. "Who was he?"

"Him? Don't know. The other's a foreign cove," murmured Albright. "Lived here some zeven year now, by
himself. Gervais, by name."

Morton stepped over the corpse to gain a better view
of the second body. A man of good size and strong
build—nearly sixty, Morton guessed. He had what appeared to be two wounds—one in his chest, the other in
the brow just above his eye.

"Master Gervais was shot," Morton told the others.

Stepping away, he bent again to have a closer look at
the other man. He had been large, bigger than Morton.
As he grew more steady, the Runner noticed more.
There seemed to be a single wound to the man's skull,
though it had caused enormous damage—a testament to
the force behind it.

"Is that Boulot, Morton?" Westcott asked.

"No." Morton noticed something beneath the man's
torn sleeve. "This man has a dressing on his forearm. I
would venture he is the same man d'Auvraye's Mrs.
Barkling wounded with a cleaver." He bent forward and
pulled open the man's mouth a little more, repelled by
the feel of cold lifeless flesh. "He fits the description—
even the bad teeth."

"Well, that's one saved from the hangman," Westcott
said softly. "Here's the weapon."

Morton rose to find Westcott holding a greatcoat
pistol.

"It hasn't been fired!" the navy man said. "And look at this." He handed it butt first to Morton, who found a scar across the top of the octagonal barrel, as though it had been struck by a sharp object or considerable weight. The scar cut through the maker's name: *Twigg*.

"I've seen this pistol before—or rather another just like it. D'Auvraye's murderer dropped one in the entry of the count's house in Barnes."

"Here's what did for the murderer, then." Westcott bent over a pile of packing straw and retrieved a hand axe, bloodied, its handle broken off just below the head.

"Leave it as it lies," Morton told them. "The coroner will want to see it."

Westcott eyed him from across the field of carnage. "Who killed these men? Boulot?"

"If these are the men who killed the Count d'Auvraye, as I suspect they are, then it makes little sense that Bonapartists killed them. But who, then, is Boulot traveling with? Let's out."

In the open again, gratefully breathing the fresh night air, they wandered from the yard, through an overgrown paddock, and stood together a moment, mute, looking sightlessly out into the darkness. Morton wordlessly offered Westcott a cheroot, and they lit them from the lantern, while Humphrey Albright pulled a briar pipe from his pocket.

In the lantern light Morton opened his pocket watch: almost five. There was a hint of pewter in the eastern sky, he thought.

A few moments later Presley came up, white-faced.

"Morton . . ." he began, hollowly.

"Nay, Jimmy." Morton waved his apology away, the red tip of his cigar tracing a short arc in the night.

Presley bent his head for a moment, then looked up again. His voice was still unsteady.

"I've never seen a man with his brains spilled out like that. Every thought he ever had, every memory, spread out on the stone..."

The farmer made a low, sympathetic noise in his throat, and Westcott blew smoke reflectively into the dark air.

Morton asked, "Who found them?"

Albright nodded. " 'Twas a boy named Parsons, as brought Gervais potatoes and cabbages vrom the varm over the way. That were early this even. As he comes over the vield, the boy zees a carriage going down the lane to the road. These Vrenchmen must have ztolen it zomewhere."

"How did the boy know they were French?"

"This man here be Vrench, and a smuggler, sure. Mayhap he won't carry them over t' Channel." The Devon man shrugged. " 'Tis Vrenchmen be missing from Princetown."

"This crime wasn't committed by some escaped French soldiers. When you find them, remember that. This was done by men who believe that entire nations are at stake and that individual lives count for nothing. We've no time to await Sir Godfrey but will send word back if we learn anything that bears upon this." Morton motioned toward the barn; then the three London men climbed aboard the carriage and set off down the shadowy lane.

Presley and Morton went back up onto the driver's bench, manoeuvring them back onto the highway to Plymouth. Morton set the horses to a good pace, realising that the carriage carrying Boulot had gained much time on them. Exhaustion and anxiety both preyed on him now. Angelique Desmarches, the Count d'Auvraye, his manservant, and now these two out on the lonely moor. Five deaths. The first involving torture; the count and his servant cold, quick, calculated. Almost certainly revenge. The brutal murders he had just seen—and these too were likely revenge for the murder of the count. But then who had abducted Boulot? Why would Bonapartists kill the man who had murdered the count? Perhaps the supporters of Bonaparte were making war amongst themselves, though for what reason he could not imagine.

Whoever was aboard the berlin, one thing was certain—they did not hesitate. The murders in the barn were not crimes of passion, to be regretted later. These men would not go to their confessors and repent. Murder was nothing to them—the man who had wielded the axe would have split wood with the same dispassion.

"Jimmy?"

"Aye, Morton."

"When we catch these murderers up, remember, they'll kill you if they can. Don't forget what you saw in that barn. These are not men who will give themselves over to justice when they are finally caught. They have never known pity or remorse. And we cannot indulge them either."

Presley nodded. "Aye, Morton. I've my pistols ready."

"Pistols are ever unreliable. But our nerve—when it falters, we are lost."

Chapter 29

Ilchester appeared where and when Darley had predicted, and the driver made his way toward the coaching inn. As they passed into the yard, however, the stench of charred wood assailed their nostrils, and a terrible sight greeted their eyes.

"What a fire they have had!" Darley said.

The driver brought the coach up before the inn's doors, a crowd of gawkers moving slowly aside.

Darley handed Arabella down from the carriage, and they stood gazing at the blackened mass, the burnt remains of beams and posts jutting out at odd angles, the slate roof collapsed, its back twisted and broken. Smoke still spiralled up in thin plumes here and there, and a few young men with buckets picked their way through the half-fallen building, dousing any places where the fire threatened to rise up again.

"It is a miracle the whole inn was not lost," Darley said.

A woman standing nearby turned to them and said,

"It is a miracle, sir, but God sent rain and the fire was quelched."

"Quenched," Arabella corrected her. "But thank the Lord, all the same."

"How did it start?" Darley enquired.

The woman, who was exceptionally pious-looking, turned to them. "'Twas the Bow Street men chasing some poor men for the reward money as did it. Set the hay afire with the flash from their pistols. Poor Mr. Berry will have them to court, he will. Lost half his stable of horses, and men were burned and laid low with smoke fighting the fire."

"Bow Street?" Arabella said, turning on the woman, whom she towered over. "When was this?"

"Last night, ma'am."

"Were they hurt? The Bow Street men?"

"I'm sorry to say they weren't, ma'am. They went off after the men they were chasing lest their rewards get away. Didn't stay to help quelch the fire they started."

Arabella and Darley looked at each other. "Can we get horses here?" Darley wondered.

The woman shook her head. "Mr. Berry's doing his best, sir. You'd best talk to him."

More careful enquiries assured them that indeed men claiming to be from Bow Street had been there, and everyone thought they'd started the fire in the stables, where shots had been fired.

Arabella was sure that only Darley could have found fresh horses in such a situation, for they were back on the road and pressing on in little more than an hour.

After Arabella's unexpected visit from Honoria d'Auvraye, she and Darley had gone looking for Morton. Mr. Townsend told them that Morton and Presley had stopped at Bow Street for firearms earlier in the evening, but no one had seen them since.

After that they had retreated to Morton's rooms to wait. A concerned Wilkes hovered over them, bringing café au lait and dainty cakes. Mr. Townsend had finally arrived saying that a note had come from Morton for Sir Nathaniel. Morton and Presley had gone with Captain Westcott in pursuit of supporters of Bonaparte who were suspected of murder. They had set out down the Great West Road that very night.

Darley had hesitated only a moment, then proposed they set out in pursuit.

"But where are they going?" Arabella had asked.

"Where is Bonaparte?" Darley had answered.

"Plymouth, as you know very well."

"Then that is where we will go, too, for there we shall find Mr. Morton."

Chapter 30

It was early afternoon when they finally reached
Plymouth, and as he climbed stiffly from the coach,
Henry Morton could smell the sea, heavy with the
dull reek of fish. But he could see nothing. A thick wall
of white fog hung before them, immense and motionless
and uncanny in the cool, still air.

In the last miles of their journey they had had a horse
go lame and had limped into the town, tradesmen's
carts fairly flying past. But then they were rewarded. In
the courtyard of the inn where they brought their post
horses, casually parked amongst the other vehicles,
stood their quarry. The phantom berlin they had been
chasing across the English countryside was empty, however, its team gone, its dark shape hunched spiderlike in
the blur. Morton crossed the yard to be sure of what he
saw.

After looking into the deserted compartment, his eye
was caught by something on the door. Scooping up a
handful of hay, he wiped away some of the caked grey
dirt, revealing a painted line. Scrubbing harder—one

would almost think the grime had been plastered on deliberately—he gradually revealed the whole design. A coat of arms. Westcott and Presley appeared to either side of him.

"Where did this lot get hold of a carriage like this?" Jimmy wondered. "Some toff's, obviously."

Morton peered hard at the crest, the dim gold and blue chevrons, the odd, sketchily rendered little animal. Yes, odd. Like a hedgehog—wasn't that what Wilkes had said? But when you looked closer, maybe a lion, its hind paws together on the ground, forepaws together in the air. A lion *salient*.

"Do you recognise these devices, Captain?" Morton asked.

Westcott stared a moment. "No, I think not. Might they be French?"

"I think they are, and I have seen them before. It has just taken me a moment to recall where. This same crest was on a letter I received but the other day. It belongs to the Count d'Auvraye."

The surprise of his companions hung a moment wordless in the air, then Westcott swore.

"I am constantly dumbfounded by this matter," the seaman muttered.

Presley wiped at his eyes and gave his head a shake. "I thought we were chasing bloody Boulot and some of his Bonapartist friends!"

"So did I," Morton said, "but it seems we've got that wrong—like too many things."

Morton turned to Westcott, who still stared at the coat of arms, his look grim and distant.

"You'd best alert your admiral to what goes on here, Captain. Until we have these folk in hand, they should not allow Bonaparte out on the deck or anywhere else he might be a target for a sharpshooter."

Westcott nodded. "Yes. I'll go down and try to see Keith immediately. He's likely to think me an alarmist, but I shall suffer that if need be." He turned his measuring gaze to Morton. "And what of you?"

"We'll begin the search for—"

"Well, who?" Jimmy interrupted.

Morton looked back at the berlin. "For Eustache d'Auvraye, or his secretary, Rolles—or both. I cannot say."

"Royalists!" said Jimmy, still trying to grasp it.

"And what charges will you lay at their feet?" Westcott quietly wondered.

"The abduction of Jean Boulot, to begin. The murder of Napoleon Bonaparte if we are not quick." Morton turned away from the carriage, looking about as though trying to find a place to begin. "Jimmy and I will ask about here and see what we might learn. Then we'll go down to the quay. They will need a boat if they are to assassinate the emperor."

Westcott took out his pocket watch and flicked open the silver cover. "Let us meet in three hours' time. There is a public house on the quay called the Blue Pillars. Anyone can direct you."

As the navy man strode off into the grey obscurity, Morton and Presley began with the ostler.

"They arrived early this morn," the man said. He reached up a finger and stretched the skin taut at the corner of his twitching eye.

"How many of them?"

"Three coves; Frenchmen, every one."

"And what did they look like, these Frenchmen?" Morton wondered.

The man closed his eyes tightly and then opened them both, blinking three or four times, the spasm apparently over. "A young French nobleman, all in fancy embroidered clothes. A short little cove who looked after everything—paid the bills and made arrangements. T'other one didn't say anything but to his traveling companions. He was sullen looking—had one of those claret spills on his head." The man turned back to the harness he was repairing. "Oh, and there was a driver." He shrugged. "Looked like anyone else, really. Nothing to mark him."

Morton thought it would be hard to find a better description of Eustache d'Auvraye, Rolles, and Jean Boulot. "To whom did they speak?" he asked the man.

"Myself. Mr. Tooley, the manager."

Morton tipped the man, and they went into the big old inn.

Mr. Tooley was, not surprisingly, an Irishman—a gentleman of some fifty years and enormous energies. He did everything at a pace that would leave a younger man breathless, and never did one thing when he could be doing two. He was curly haired and handsome and not, it seemed, particularly fond of the law.

"I only spoke to one gentleman," he said, his soft Irish accent almost worn away by what Morton suspected was most of a lifetime in England. "Don't know about any others."

"And what speech passed between you?"

The man glanced up from the sums he was doing rapidly on long sheets of paper. He glared at Morton with undisguised hostility. "Disputed some charges on his bill a little." His gaze went back to his paperwork, spread out over a large standing desk that took up the greater part of the narrow, low-ceilinged room.

"Mr. Tooley," Morton said, his own anger rising, "we believe these men travelled to Plymouth to commit a murder. If you do not help us, I shall have you on trial for aiding and abetting them."

The man looked up. "These gentlemen? Murderers?"

"By day's end, sir. Now, what passed between you and these Frenchmen?"

The man set down his pen and thought a moment. "They asked to leave their carriage here for two days," he said, "and then wanted to know if it was far to the quayside." He paused. "And they enquired after a men's clothier. I directed them to Lawley and Sons. I can think of nothing else."

Lawley and Sons was but a few short blocks away. It was not, as Morton expected, a gentlemen's shop, at least not such as you'd find in London. No, Lawley's catered to the less well-to-do. Law clerks and other such functionaries. Working men with clean nails, as his mother put it. Not the kind of shop where you'd expect Eustache d'Auvraye to find his wardrobe—though Boulot's dress would have been improved by a visit.

Mr. Lawley himself was not present, but one of his sons was.

"Yes, three French gentlemen, just as we opened for business," the younger Lawley said. He was an overly serious young man and would have made a perfect priest, Morton thought. "Two of them made purchases. Very tasteful."

"One had a raspberry mark on his head?"

"That's right." Lawley the younger gestured. "He sat on the stair there the whole time. Never said a word. I thought he might be ill."

"And what did they purchase, these French gentlemen?"

"A complete suit of clothes for the young nobleman. He was dressed for the French court, it seemed—you've never seen such embroidery! When I enquired, he said that he did not wish to stand out so but to travel quietly among the English people."

"Did they say anything more?"

"Very little. They seemed in a hurry. They asked about Bonaparte, but of course all visitors do, these days."

"What did they ask, specifically? Do you remember?"

"Only if Bonaparte was still here, and how you'd recognise the ship he's on. I told them there'd be no trouble—there must be a thousand small boats surrounding the *Bellerophon*." The young man considered a moment. "I can't think of anything else."

"Do you know where they went from here?"

The young man shrugged. "They went down the hill. Likely to find a boat to take them out into the sound, as everyone does. I hope you've rooms arranged. You might have trouble finding lodgings otherwise."

Morton and Presley went out onto the street, where tendrils of fog wafted gently up from the harbour below. The sun tried to break through, silvering the foggy sky.

"Where do we go now?" Presley said. "Down to the quay to look for three Frenchies trying to pass quietly among the English?"

"I think we can do a little better than that," Morton said, and Jimmy looked at him, raising an eyebrow. "We'll go down to the quay and ask for Berman."

Presley stopped. "You mean Berman wasn't a London waterman after all?"

"If he was, the River Police could never find him. All along we've thought the assassination was of d'Auvraye and that Boulot said *bâtiment*—ship—when he meant to say *bachot,* or wherry, for it was a wherry that took the count's murderers away. But what if he did mean ship? Now I wonder if the assassination will not instead be Bonaparte, and if Berman might be found on the Plymouth quay."

They were soon down the hill, searching along the stone quay where the fishermen and costermongers jostled among the throngs of holidayers there hoping to catch a glimpse of the fallen Emperor of the French. The scene itself was strange, dreamlike. Upon the narrow quay people swam through the thick fog, men and women in their bright holiday clothes, the dark-faced fishermen working among them, big-knuckled hands mending nets, flinging fish to the costermongers by their carts. Morton had a sense that there were not many engaged in the fishing trade that day—fishermen had gone over to the more lucrative trade of ferrying people out to view Bonaparte.

Of the ships beyond, nothing could be seen, for the fog was dense, impenetrable. Boats appeared, presaged by the knuckle knock of oars working against thole pins. The people aboard were oddly silent, perhaps disappointed, though Morton had a sense that it was the uncanny and impenetrable fog that had stolen people's words away, or had them whispering. At least there was no cry upon the quay that aught was amiss, that Bonaparte had been cut down as he strolled the deck.

Morton and Presley began asking among the fishermen and people who found their employment along the waterfront. After half an hour Jimmy came hurrying out of the fog.

"A net mender says we should find our man down the way," the young Runner said.

"Then we're not wrong," Morton said, both relieved

and suddenly more uneasy. He checked his pocket watch, mindful of the hour.

"Have we time before we meet Westcott?" Presley asked.

"A little. Let us go see what we can learn of Berman."

They strode along the damp stone, the reek of fish strong in their nostrils. Morton hunted among the passing faces, searching for the raspberry-stained pate, the secretive little Rolles, the dark-eyed young count. An unlikely trio of assassins—and one of them had left London in their company only reluctantly. Had Boulot changed his allegiance on the journey? Had the young count offered him what his father had not—a return to his beloved France? Morton thought that Boulot would be disappointed by his return. His old life was gone, swept away by two decades of revolution and Bonaparte's failed empire. There would be no crowds waiting now to hear him sing, no one, perhaps, who even remembered his name. Boulot's France was gone, as was the young man Boulot had been, however promising. He was an *ivrogne* now, a drunkard and a near derelict, a man who would sell his friends for a bottle, or for a thirty-mile passage across the Channel.

Across from the anchorage they found a little knot of older fishermen, sitting around on barrels and nets.

Morton put a hand on his young companion's shoulder, slowing him, then said quietly, "It would seem almost certain that good Mr. Berman is a smuggler or involved with the smugglers in some way. I don't think he will feel too kindly toward constables from Bow Street. We might try to keep our real profession to ourselves for a while."

Presley nodded.

Morton approached the lounging fishermen respectfully. "Is Mr. Berman about?"

The half-dozen faces turned toward him. Morton had an immediate sense that these men were guarded, though they did much to hide it.

"Come to view the Corsican, have you?" one of the men said.

It occurred to Morton that one of these men might be Berman but wouldn't reveal himself until he was satisfied that Morton was not some member of the Customs Service.

"I've a bit of business with Mr. Berman," Morton said, keeping his tone pleasant.

The men looked about at one another.

"He might be back by and by," one of them said, and they went back to their conversation.

Morton looked at his young companion, and the two retreated a little. "Let's see who else here might know Berman."

The two Runners went in opposite directions. Morton waited until he was hidden from Berman's friends by the fog, then began a quiet enquiry. Half an hour later he stood talking to a costerwoman who was filling her barrow with shellfish. She was a few years older than Morton, broad and strong. But from within this unlikely shape came the most melodious voice. Her very speech was song.

"Berman? He's off to the *Bellerophon*. Saw him set out not an hour ago."

"And who had he for passengers, did you see?"

The woman shrugged as she arranged her merchandise. "Half a dozen men—down from Bath, I think."

"French gentlemen?"

The woman shook her head. "English all," she said.

"None with a raspberry stain on the head?"

"The gentlemen wore hats, as you'd expect," she answered.

"This man you'd know. His mark stretches down onto his forehead."

"Didn't see such," she said, picking up mussels by the double-handful and shovelling them into her barrel with a clatter.

"But did you hear them speak? Are you certain they were English?"

The woman stopped, hunched over her barrow, turned her head, and looked up at Morton suspiciously. "I can tell you no more," she said, and went back to her work.

Morton continued to canvass the quay without much luck until it came time to meet Westcott. He arrived at the Blue Pillars to find Westcott and Presley waiting for him, the young Runner shovelling down some of the proprietor's best John Dory in cream sauce. It was a Devon delicacy, but the way Jimmy approached it was anything but delicate.

"Berman is said to have carried a group of men out to view the Corsican," Morton reported as he took a seat. "How long they'll stay is dependent upon the depth of their purses."

Westcott looked exhausted and worried. "I managed to see Keith's secretary, who promised to pass my message to the lord admiral, but I was unable to impress the gravity of the situation upon the man. Our lack of actual evidence was telling. Though corpses are appearing at an alarming rate—five, by my last count—we do not have a single witness who can tell us, in plain truth, what these men are planning. Until we have that or some other form of evidence, I think the lords of the Admiralty will stay their course."

Morton nodded. Westcott was right. He had only his hunch, his intuition, that these royalists were going to try to murder Bonaparte. So who had those men been the night Morton had listened outside Boulot's door? Royalists? He was sure that Eustache d'Auvraye and Rolles had not been among them. Lafond and his followers?

Westcott's own meal arrived, and Morton called for a plate of Presley's fish.

"And where was Admiral Lord Keith?" Westcott went on. "He was off in a barge, running from some barrister with a writ of habeas corpus that a kindly judge has issued for the person of one Napoleon Bonaparte. It seems the man wants Bonaparte to appear in court as a *witness* in some financial matter to do with the sinking of an English ship—a transparent ploy to get the Corsican ashore! But the admiral is bound by the laws of England. If the writ is delivered to him in person, he will have no choice but to produce Napoleon Bonaparte; so he is doing everything within his power to avoid this lawyer and his writ!" Westcott snorted. "I have only one bit of good news to report. I've managed to secure us a gig for a few hours. If nothing else, we can row out to Maitland's ship and look for our assassins. Perhaps we'll find Keith fleeing his barrister."

The two Runners and the navy man devoured their meals and were back on the quay in half an hour. It was a good walk to the navy docks, and then it took time to assemble their promised crew.

The Runners clambered aboard, their boots echoing hollowly in the dank, cloudy air. The stern seat, the place traditionally taken by the superior officer, was given to Westcott. Morton sat in the bow with Presley just behind him. The coxswain gave his quiet orders, and the boat was away, oars settling into place. They were soon out in the sound, ghosting past anchored ships that loomed darkly out of the fog. A low ground swell lifted the smooth waters of the sound in a slow undulating rhythm. Visibility was not twenty yards, Morton thought. How would they even find the *Bellerophon*?—for Plymouth Sound was not small.

Suddenly ships' bells rang out from all around.

"Six bells," announced the coxswain.

"Seven of an evening," Westcott said for the benefit of Presley and Morton.

The two Runners shared a glance. Neither of them needed to say it: The day was slipping away.

A small boat rowed past carrying a silent cargo of holidayers.

"Know you Berman?" Morton called to the man at the oars.

"Aye," the man answered.

"Is he out here, at the *Bellerophon*?"

"Mayhap he is. There's a mite of fog, if you hadn't noticed."

Morton settled back onto his damp thwart, the cool wood of the gunwale beneath his fingers. A gull circled, crying sadly, then made off into the mist, wondering, perhaps, where all the fishermen had gone.

Out of the shroud of silence a lady's face appeared, and Morton was reminded of the woman beneath the snows in Skelton's surgery. This lady, however, rode in a small boat and was very much alive. Somewhere nearby, Bonaparte, too, was buried beneath this bank of fog, this damp, cold shroud.

A few more strokes of the oars, and a host of other craft were revealed, their people talking solemnly, as though a funeral procession passed. Morton stood to search among the sea of faces. Above this clinging mass of small craft the *Bellerophon* rose up, half-obscured in the sea's cumulus. Morton could just make out men moving along the rail. As he searched the quarterdeck he held his breath, but the cockaded hat was not to be seen.

"Has he been sighted this day?" Morton asked as they passed close by the stern of a small punt.

A man shook his head in answer.

"Morton?" Westcott said from the stern. "We'll circle slowly round. There's not much else we can do. If we get into this mass, we might be an hour extricating ourselves."

"Can you go aboard and warn Captain Maitland?"

Westcott shook his head, his look sour. "No one is to approach the ship without Keith's written orders. They would turn me back."

Morton cursed at this foolishness. The coxswain began to steer around the fleet of gathered craft, keeping them so close that the oar blades all but struck the boats nearest. The Runner searched among the faces, though most were turned away, watching the *Bellerophon*.

"Berman!" Morton called out, and in the near silence heads turned, a look of surprised offence upon the faces. But Morton kept it up, calling out every so often and searching among those present for the raspberry pate, the little secretary, and his young master.

Inside the circle of craft a navy cutter passed, enforcing a ring of clear water round the great ship. "Be wary, there!" Morton called to the officer in the cutter. "I'm from Bow Street, and we've reason to believe there is an assassin waiting for Bonaparte to appear."

"I'm from Bristol," a young buck called, "and I'd pay

double to see Bonaparte shot." The waiting audience thereabout laughed, but everyone turned to see who had made such a claim, and the rumour washed down the ranks of lingering men and women.

Every ten yards Morton called out again, "Berman?" but no one answered.

As they circled to larboard, Presley stood on the thwart. "Morton..." he said, raising an arm to point. There among a crowd of men he caught a glimpse of red-stained skin, and then ranks closed and it was lost.

Westcott ordered the coxswain to nudge the gig up to the nearest boat.

Morton went over the side onto the stern of the first boat, pushing his way through the crowd. "Bow Street," he said as he went, trying to make as little fuss as he could. "We must pass." Presley was behind him, and the two large men clambered from one boat to the next until they came to a lugger in the thick of the crowd. Morton pulled himself up the side, for it was a larger craft than most of the others. It was also the type of craft favored by smugglers, for they were said to be fast and weatherly.

Morton immediately marked the man Presley had spotted, but as he pushed his way through the crowd on deck, the man turned. He had a raspberry birthmark on his head, but he was not Jean Boulot.

"What is it you want, sir?" asked a gentleman standing nearby. "We've hired this ship, not you, and your presence is not wanted."

Morton made a bow to the gentleman. "My apologies, sir," he said. "We're constables from Bow Street, seeking criminals."

The man looked at Morton a moment, and then his look of anger was replaced by a sly smile. "Well, only

Spencer over there is a criminal—a barrister, to be sure."
The people collected on the deck laughed.

Morton backed away, climbing down the side and
making his way across the flotilla to the gig. Presley
stepped over the side after him and smiled at Morton,
embarrassed.

"Not to worry, Jimmy," Morton said. "Better to make
a dozen mistakes than let a murderer slip away."

The sides of the great ship loomed over the surrounding boats in the mist. Sounds from near at hand were
strangely loud and sharply defined: the creaking of the
Bellerophon's cordage as the ship rolled ponderously in
the low swell, the knocking of gunwales as the hundreds
of boats thudded against each other, the cries of circling
gulls.

Morton continued to call Berman's name as they
passed down the larboard side. A young gentleman
standing in a boat turned as he heard Morton call.

"Berman?" the young buck echoed. "He's here." He
gestured toward a square-built man in a fisherman's
garb and cap. The fisherman gave the young man a sour
look and then eyed Morton suspiciously.

"Bow Street!" Jimmy called out. "We want a word
with you!"

And Berman was off, scrambling across the raft of
boats, jumping from gunwale to stem, his boots clattering on the wood. Boatmen made way for him, even offered hands for balance. The coxswain nudged the bow
up to the stern of a larger craft, and Morton grabbed the
rail and scrambled over, Jimmy right behind. The men
and women in the little ship made no effort to ease his
passing, and around about men began to jeer and curse
the "bloody horneys!"

Morton pushed through the crowd and climbed

quickly down the side, his foot finding the gunwale of a
small boat that rocked dangerously beneath his weight.
He could see Berman, fifty feet ahead now and moving
nimbly over the boats. If he opened the gap to a hundred
feet, he'd be lost in the fog, and then one of his fisherman friends might carry him ashore.

Presley came clumsily down the side, almost pitching
Morton into the water as he landed heavily on the boat.
The occupants were all thrown to one side and squealed
with fright. Unlike Morton, most people could not swim
and had a terrible fear of drowning.

Morton leapt to the next boat and was about to step
over a small gap of water when someone grabbed his
coattail, throwing off his already precarious balance.
One foot went into the water, and Morton fell forward
into the next boat, which was packed with gawkers.

"I'll break your bleeding pate for that!" Presley
roared, and the sheer volume and passion of his cry
opened a path for Morton. He scrambled up and, pushing off men's shoulders, was across this boat and into
the next. Leaping, he put one foot on a narrow stem and
vaulted up the steep side of the lugger.

He pounded across the deck, the onlookers muttering
imprecations. The Runner realised now that passing
among the people was what slowed him, and he skirted
the edges of boats so that he could step off the stern or
the stem. He used the crowds of bodies as handholds,
grabbing shoulders and heads, ignoring the curses and
threats. Even so, Berman was almost lost in the fog. If
he ducked down somewhere and no one gave him away,
he'd be gone.

Vaulting over the heads of two small children,
Morton landed on the stern of a boat, his foot slipping
down onto the floorboards, his calf smarting from a long

gouge. In an instant he was up, balancing along the stern, stepping awkwardly onto the next boat. Men tried to close ranks enough to slow him, forcing Morton to shove two men roughly aside.

"Drown the bastard!" someone called, and Morton was sure they didn't mean Berman.

He leapt onto the gunwale of an open boat. Only at the last second did he see the sweating faces of the men, the glazed eyes. As he tried to step across the boat, the smell of liquor engulfed him. The men to either side grabbed his legs, and Morton struggled to keep his balance, trying to fumble his baton out of its pocket.

Tumbling forward, Morton struck hard wood, and men piled on him, shouting drunkenly. He was struggling against unfair odds, in no position to strike out or even to push himself up.

A spatter of blood sprayed across the planks and frames by Morton's face, and the man who had taken to thumping him on the back fell limply away. Another was jerked roughly into the air, and Morton heard Jimmy Presley cursing loudly. The drunken men were falling back, trying to stay out of range of the young Runner's truncheon.

"I'll spill all your brains!" Presley was shouting. He threw another man bodily aside and pulled Morton up by his shoulder.

Not pausing to even look at his partner, Morton leapt into the next boat, his baton out now and his choler high. People took one look at him and shrank away.

Morton could just see Berman's dark blue jacket as he climbed over a crowd on the far edge of the circle of visibility. Morton's anger propelled him on, and he leapt and thrust his way forward, heedless of his own safety.

Berman's turn of luck came then. As he scrambled up

the side of a big trawler, he managed to lose his hand-hold and fall into an opening between the boats. The sea washed out as he hit the surface, then rolled back over him. He was gone like a stone. People on the nearby boats stared down into the translucent green, dumb-founded, waiting, perhaps, for him to reappear—but he did not.

Morton peeled off his coat and boots as he came up to the water's edge. He dove into the cold water between the boats, hoping that there would still be an opening when he surfaced. The sea was shadowy from the boats overhead and the mist that blotted the sky. He could see the hapless Berman sinking slowly a few yards away. The man waved his arms ineffectively, but his boots were dragging him down.

Morton struck out and in a moment had hold of the man's collar. He broke for the surface, dragging the dead weight of the fisherman, kicking furiously as he felt the need for air overwhelm him. He broke the sur-face and pulled in a lungful of air. Jimmy Presley reached out a hand to him, and they soon had Berman laid out in a crowded boat. The man choked and coughed, spewing seawater like a ship's pump.

Jimmy helped Morton over the side, where he sat catching his breath, water running from his hair and clothing.

"Morton? Are you whole?"

"Aye, Jimmy," Morton gasped. "Just need a minute to catch my breath."

Westcott hailed them then, having brought the gig as close as he could. Morton raised a hand in response, ig-noring the horrified stares of the people around him. Presley held Morton's still-dry coat, boots, and baton in one hand, their captive in the other.

"Have I still pistols in my pockets, Jimmy?" Morton asked.

Presley quickly felt the pockets of Morton's coat. "You have them yet."

Morton turned to Berman. "Innocent men don't run," he said, his breath rapidly returning.

"Here on the Devon coast we've lived in fear of the press gangs for twenty years and more."

Morton stood, dripping, and took his boots, coat, and baton from Presley. "We're not the press gang, Berman. We're from Bow Street, and well you knew it. Bring him on, Jimmy."

To much muttering and cursing from the crowd, they dragged the fisherman over the boats to the waiting gig and deposited him in the bow.

"You've no cause to be—" But Morton cut him off with a glare. The Runner was still angry at his treatment by the mob, and this fisherman had a healthy respect for angry men.

"Gervais is dead," Morton said as the oarsmen set out into the fog and gathering dusk.

A startled Berman rocked back a little in his seat. "What's that?"

Morton was glad to see his guess was not wrong. "Gervais is dead. He was murdered by the men Boulot travels with—three royalists trying to pass themselves off as common Frenchmen. Where have you taken them?"

This unsettled the man, Morton could see. "And who are you, sir?" he asked.

"Henry Morton of Bow Street. But I'm not here to enquire into your activities, however illegal they might be. I'm chasing murderers. These Frenchmen with Boulot—did they carry firearms?"

The man did not answer.

"Demmit, man, those men are royalists and travelled here to kill a man. They likely intend to kill Jean Boulot, though he doesn't know it. You were seen taking Boulot and these others out in your boat. I have sworn witnesses. If they commit a murder, you will be tried for aiding them. A capital crime, man!"

Berman crossed his arms and stared at Morton a moment. "How do you know those men are royalists?"

"The young one is Eustache d'Auvraye, son of the late count. The small man was the old count's secretary, a man named Rolles. They brought Boulot with them against his will—at least so it was to begin. There is a fourth man, I believe, but of him I know nothing." Morton could see the man was not swayed by Morton's claims. "I saw the body of Gervais last night. As terrible a scene as I have ever witnessed. He had been shot, and another hacked to death with an axe. The other dead man was unknown to me, but he had a wound on his arm, all bound up, that makes me believe he was one of the men who murdered the Count d'Auvraye."

The fisherman had gone pale as a wave crest. "I—I know nothing of these men."

Already they were lost in the fog. Morton knew they would get nothing from this man if they delivered him to the local magistrate—nothing in time, anyway—but his anger had not yet ebbed.

"Take hold of him, Jimmy. We'll see how well he floats."

Presley did not hesitate but grabbed Berman by the arm and the seat of his pants.

"I've broken no law!" Berman struggled against the two larger men. "You can charge me with no crime!"

They hefted him half over the gunwale, but paused there, his hair dangling in the water.

"Aiding and abetting murderers will gain you the same penalty as the killers themselves," Morton said. "Have you ever seen a man hang before Newgate Prison, Berman? It's a lonely sight. A man's last moment on earth comforted only by the hangman and a minister who'll publish your 'last confession' for a few pounds.

"But if you aid us now, I will see you are no more than a witness, if such is needed. You can choose which side of the courtroom fence you'll stand on, Berman. Only tell us where you've taken Jean Boulot and these others. If you have any friendship for Boulot, you will tell us where they have gone, for these men are ruthless and are as like to kill him as not."

Berman had stopped struggling, his face a few inches above the passing sea. Morton could sense that his words were sinking in—with the help of a little persuasion. Morton nodded to Jimmy, and they pulled the man back aboard, red-faced, and set him on the thwart.

"I give you my word this is no deception, Berman. I am not paid to chase down smugglers, as you must know. There will be a murder this night if we cannot stop it."

"Whose murder?" the man asked softly.

"Boulot's, almost certainly," Morton said. "Perhaps another."

Berman's gaze turned out toward the sound, obscured still in fog. "Him?" he said quietly.

Morton did not answer but only stared at the man. Perhaps it was imagination, but he felt understanding passed between them.

The fisherman nodded. "I'll take you where I took Boulot."

Morton looked up at Westcott, who'd been listening from the stern. The officer had a watch in his hand and thumbed open the cover.

"This gig must be returned," Westcott said. "I've placed an officer in a bad situation, borrowing it as I have against all regulations."

"I'll get us a boat," Berman said, "if they'll take us to the quay. Boulot is a drunk, but once he was a worthy man—a friend." Berman looked around as though he were afraid of being seen with the Runners. " 'Tis almost night," he said.

"Yes. Pray we are in time," Morton answered.

The coxswain soon deposited them on the stone quay, and Berman led them quickly through the gathering gloom to a small open boat. They clambered down into it, the landsmen rocking it overly. Westcott surprised Morton by taking up the second set of oars—the blades hovered an instant in the air while he caught the smuggler's rhythm, and then they dipped into the calm waters, propelling the vessel forward. Distant bells chimed the hour of ten. Night would wash out of the fog momentarily, like another layer of obscurity—like this whole matter, the truth hidden by layers of deceit and misapprehension.

The dark stain of night bled into the fog around them, enclosing them in silence and stillness. Only the metronome of oars dipping measured their movement, the breathing sea beneath them lifting and falling and lifting. How Berman could even guess their direction was beyond Morton's comprehension, but the smuggler carried them on without hesitation. They passed a few boats at anchor, and then they saw no more.

Wherever he took them, it was not near, for some time passed. Morton felt the press of it as he wondered how the assassination would be accomplished. Perhaps this was what he'd missed. They would shoot Bonaparte at night, through the stern gallery windows. How easy it would be to slip off into the darkness then, no fleet of gawkers to get in the way, no one to identify them in the dark.

A small wind rippled the sea, stirring the dark fog around them. A star appeared overhead and, as though it were a sign, a voice lifted in song not far distant.

As the fog tore to ribbons and fluttered away in the growing breeze, a long, sleek hull appeared before them. Starlight illuminated spars thrust up toward the sky.

"Who is that singing?" Westcott asked quietly.

"That," Morton said, "is Jean Boulot."

Chapter 31

W hat, not drunk?"

Henry Morton adjusted the wick of the lamp swinging from a deck beam in the lugger's cramped cabin. In the brighter glow Jean Boulot's face was very white, and the stain on his bald head very red. He was stretched out on a narrow berth, his arms folded behind him, watching the Runner. Overhead the hatch was open, through which he had been singing to the night sky.

"No, Bow Street. On this night of nights, you find me in a very philosophical state. Welcome aboard the *Nancy*."

"They left you nothing to drink, I expect."

Boulot shifted to reach behind himself, and as he did the chain that held his ankle clanked quietly. He produced a bottle, open but almost full. *"Voici,"* he said. "Have it."

Morton released a short, humourless laugh. "You have reformed?"

Boulot pointed to the low deck above him. "There are

others besides your fat young colleague. Who? Even more police? Why do they not come to see me, too?"

"I want privacy. It is time for you and I to have some serious talk, Boulot. No more lies, no more obfuscation. Time to speak up."

"I wonder how you found me, Bow Street."

"It seems one of your smuggling friends likes you enough to have saved your life."

"Why you think my life *en danger*?"

"We saw what was done to the man Gervais and his companion in a barn on Dartmoor. These royalists will not need you after tonight. Are you ready to tell the truth?"

"*In vino veritas*. So said the Romans, Bow Street. Though I think in French wine there are more lies than truths. Give me a drink, and we will see."

Morton slid the bottle back across the tiny table, and Boulot pulled the cork. He put it up to his lips and was about to tip it back but then set it down, his look haunted and infinitely sad.

"Where have the rest of them gone, Boulot? Have they gone to kill Bonaparte?"

"Bonaparte is already dead—the dream is dead." He looked up and saw Morton's reaction. "No, Bow Street. The man who made himself emperor still breathes and speaks—you should ask *him* to tell you the truth." He rubbed a hand back over his sweaty neck, grimacing as he did so. "I tell you *la vérité,* the truth—what little truth I know. I tell you because you are an honest man and, although this surprise you, so am I. Yes, I, Jean Boulot, of Malmaison, *votre serviteur*. Honest, mainly. But first you must tell me something. Did you like my song? I sing it well, I think. Now, it is not *une chanson d'opéra,* not an opera song, but a love song, very sad, from the Auvergne. The lyric is in *langue d'oc,* but I translate. The man sings to the woman he has betrayed, to the woman he has betrayed with another. But he does not ask for forgiveness, no. He tells her only that he loves her. *I have betrayed you; I love you.* Is that not strange? He never love her, not truly, till he has betrayed her. This is sad, *bien sûr.*"

Morton scowled in impatience. "Five people have been slain now, Boulot. Make your choice. I told you before, you can help us find the guilty, or you can hang by their sides."

Boulot grunted. "I am glad you do not assume I am one of these guilty, Bow Street. That is sympathetic. That is *gentil.* And you know, you 'ave reason. It is true, I never kill"—but he hesitated—"I was going to say *no one.* But perhaps that is not so true. I kill *la belle* Desmarches, perhaps. *La belle* Angelique. Not with my hands. But perhaps I did. And perhaps I will kill the emperor, too. But that does not matter so much, I think."

"How did you kill Madame Desmarches?"

Someone stepped across the deck above their heads, distracting the Frenchman, and he stared upward for a moment. Then he said flatly, "I betray her. Like the man in the song. She was passing intelligence from her royalist lover to the friends of Bonaparte in London. They tell me, to gain my aid, and I tell *le comte.* He do not believe me, at first, but I prove to him by showing the letter he had receive from Fouché, that she copied. It was really very simple thing. And now, yes, just as in the song, I love her, I sing to the stars about her. You know, I did tell an untruth to you, before. I *was* once her lover, and I am not *fou,* not mad, as I say this. Just one night, two year ago in a room in the Pulteney Hotel. *Mon Dieu,* I never forget this night. I weep to think. But I tell you truthfully, Bow Street, I think I *she* forget. I was nothing to her. A mistake. *Une bagatelle*."

"Who killed her?"

Boulot mused. "But no, I am something to her now. Her betrayer, her destroyer. That is something very intimate. Do not mistake me, Bow Street, I did not do it for revenge, not at all. I had no idea it would happen this way. Perhaps I 'ad some fool's idea that *le comte* would throw her aside and then ... who would she go to?" He shook his head sadly. "I treasured her, she was *mon beau idéal*. My dream. It is the most terrible thing, that I have destroyed her, the most terrible thing that I can imagine." And his voice did almost crack as he said it. "And yet, also, there is something ... glorious. You should know this sensation, *monsieur la police*. A great, great betrayal. It feel like nothing else. You should know it. It help you in your work."

"How did it happen? Who killed her, dem you!"

But Boulot's head had sunk to his breast now, and Morton could see that his shoulders were shaking. He waited. Then when it seemed to have subsided, he repeated more quietly.

"Who killed her?"

"*Le comte* d'Auvraye and his shadow, Rolles."

"And then your friends, the supporters of Bonaparte, killed the count in revenge."

Boulot looked at him in dull surprise, wiping at his tear-stained cheeks with his sleeve. "No, no, Bow Street. *Le petit comte*—the son. Eustache. He killed her."

"Eustache d'Auvraye? He and Rolles? How do you know this?"

"Because they tell me. They tell me to frighten me, but I believe them. They say the old man, the father, 'e write a note to Bow Street telling you to come to 'is 'ouse in Barnes. He will tell you that Angelique Desmarches was a Bonapartist—a spy. The old man he would tell you she must have been killed by people who wanted to know about her friends, the other Bonapartists. How long would it 'ave taken you then to find your way to Rolles? Not long."

"Eustache killed the count?"

" 'E had 'im killed," Boulot said, as though this were unimportant. His gaze lost focus. "Do you know the irony, Bow Street? They did not mean to kill her. Just to find out the things they need to know, but she throw herself out the window so that she would not tell. That's why they needed me, Jean Boulot. I am not so brave. Not so...*engagé*—committed. I would tell them what they wanted. But they could not find me, Bow Street. You had to do it for them.

"I tell you something. Gervais was also my friend. And I also betray him, *par* accident. I lead Monsieur Eustache there, to his hiding place, his *grange* out in the moors. I lead them there, these *monstres,* this parricide and his little lackey, to the home of my friend. I had not betrayed enough people yet. For money I hoped this old friend of mine would help us, provide the boat we needed, arrange our escape to France. But Gervais is like me, he once was a supporter of Bonaparte, who lost his faith when the man he worshipped—the champion of *égalité*—put a crown on his head. He ran in trouble of the secret police and escaped 'ere. He did not like these royalists and took up an axe to send them away. But he did not know Pierre. Pierre is *fou,* a killer, a man who take pleasure from it. Pierre attacked 'im, and Gervais was forced to kill 'im with his axe. Rolles and d'Auvraye, they carried pistols and..." He rubbed his trembling hands over his face, head bowed. Reaching out, he snatched up the uncorked bottle, but again he stopped. He merely cradled it in his hand, almost tenderly.

Morton took out his own pistols and laid them on the table.

"What is it you do, Bow Street?"

"What every constable has been trained to do: assure himself of his weapons at such times. Where are d'Auvraye and Rolles? Do they really think they can shoot Bonaparte on the deck of His Majesty's ship? They will never escape!"

Boulot closed his eyes and shook his head slowly. "You do not see it yet, Bow Street. You come all this way doing your duty, but you do not understand. My betrayal is more complete than that. It is almost glorious in its scale. You remember that night outside my rooms, the men you met? You know that Bonaparte 'as agents in England, yes?"

"They were spies?"

"Well, once they were, now they are nothing. Men with no country, no leader, no cause. They are like Jean Boulot, but they don't yet know it. I tell them I will do anything if they will get me a pardon from Fouché, but they never do. They tell me Fouché always need a little more proof of my loyalty. Fouché, who is loyal to no one and nothing." The Frenchman sat back, slumping against the wooden slats, the 'ceiling,' that ran across the frames. He stared up at nothing. "Imagine that a little constable from the Magistrate's Court, a constable who never give up, would arrive here this night."

"I'm growing impatient, Boulot. So far your story is nothing but a long denial that you are guilty of these crimes."

Boulot fixed him with a bleary-eyed stare. " 'Ave you

not been listening? I am guilty of a hundred crimes. This
is my confession—and you are my priest, Bow Street."

"How will they kill Bonaparte?"

"Kill him? They plan to save him first."

"You are mad," Morton said in disgust.

"No, I tell you the truth, Bow Street." He leaned forward again, planting his elbows on the table, hands
pressed against his cheeks, distorting his sweating face.
"What is the hour?"

Morton took out his brass repeater. "It is past eleven."

"Then per'aps there is time. Per'aps."

"Start speaking, Boulot. The simple truth!"

"As if anyone could! You say five persons have died?
But what is that, Bow Street? What is that? Millions
have died. You know this. But don't look so impatient. I
tell you."

Boulot breathed deeply and looked down at his chest
again a moment, thinking. Somehow he was different, it
seemed to Morton. More a man and less a clown.

"The smugglers here on the *Nancy*, they think Rolles
and d'Auvraye are my friends, friends of the Bonaparte
loyalists who 'ave come here to 'elp. They tell them the
exact hour, the exact location...that they bring him
ashore."

Morton and Boulot stared at each other a long moment.

"It is not possible, Boulot. It can't be managed."

"Eh, *oui,* they think they can do it. The others, that
is, my old friends. They are desperate, they gather
up lovers of the emperor from everywhere, from the
strangest places. This *bâtiment*, this *Nancy* that we are
in, it belong to an English, a smuggling-man, name
Rattenbury, from somewhere there on the Devon coast.
I know him from before, from the wartime. They have

some soldiers also, as 'ave escape from the prison on the moor, and they have some other men, brave and mad, who have pistols and swords."

"The Royal Navy will take the most absolute care. We are in a harbour full of warships. You are talking nonsense."

"They don't plan to sail away with him. No, no. They need only to get him ashore. They have a lawyer there, an *écossais,* with *papiers,* court documents, there will be a *procès,* a trial. The very moment he put one boot on English sand, then he is saved."

"They cannot get him off a ship of seventy-four guns with over two hundred men aboard!"

"They say to do it by stealth. They have two boat, about a dozen men. One boat create *la diversion, la ruse de guerre,* and talk to the cutter that patrol. Then slip in the other and bring him out rapidly through the window of the great cabin, in the stern of *le navire.* They are prepared there, Bertrand and the others. They know, and expect. They will lower him on a rope, and Bertrand will impersonate him. Then all the others need do is row so fast as they possibly can to the beach and arrive there before the Britishes. On the beach they light a fire, to show the way."

"It cannot prosper," breathed Morton.

"*Bien,* Bow Street, then there is no difficulty, is there?" Boulot was sardonic. "You may sit here the evening and agree with yourself that it cannot succeed, God bless the Navy Royale. And I may spare myself *la crise de conscience.* I will 'ave my reward, and all will be well."

"If these royalists now know about this plot, they will be able to prevent it, they will warn the navy."

"Oh no, Bow Street, *pas de tout,* not at all! That is

why I say you do not see. They do not *want* to prevent it. They *want* it to succeed. So they can be there, waiting. They want him dead. No more prison. No more Elba. *La mort.*"

Morton uttered a heartfelt curse. "Where, Boulot? Where will they bring him ashore? Is that where Eustache and Rolles will wait?"

Boulot placed his palms together and tapped his fingers thoughtfully against his lips for a moment.

"I remember. The smuggler left here to watch the ship, he say he take them to the beach at the place called Bovisan' Bay. Maybe someone know where that is. You will find who you want there."

"The hour! Tell me the hour this is to happen!"

"An hour past midnight, Bow Street."

Morton stared at the enigmatic little man a moment, then climbed up the ladder to the deck. The sky was bright with stars, the fog washed away by a small breeze.

"Bow Street!" Boulot called.

Morton turned and looked back down into the tiny cabin.

"Can you not release me? They will kill me when they find out what I have done."

"Can you swim?" Morton asked.

"No."

"Then best stay as you are."

He turned away. "Did you hear all that?" he asked Presley and Westcott.

They nodded.

"Is it possible? Can they do it?"

Westcott considered. "Yes, perhaps."

"Then we must strike out for the ship and see if we can stop them."

"The ship is distant," Berman said. The smuggler perched on the rail, his feet dangling over the side. "You will not reach it in time. Bovisand Bay is near."

Morton dropped down into the boat that rocked alongside. "Then it is Bovisand Bay." He reached into his coat and took out one of his Parker pistols, handing it, butt first, to Westcott. "I expect Sir Nathaniel will forgive me."

Westcott smiled.

They pushed off from the *Nancy*, Westcott and Berman at the oars.

"The beach at Bovisand Bay is narrow and meagre," Berman said. "These Frenchmen will certainly see us approaching."

"We will have to take our chances," Morton said.

"Well, that is fine for you, but I'd be glad to keep living a few years yet. There is another small beach over a rise. A narrow track connects the two. I could land you there, and you could come upon them by stealth."

"How much farther is it? Our time is short."

"Not far. You will see."

Chapter 32

Bovisand Bay was far on the other side of Mount Batten, out toward the open Channel. The *Nancy* had been anchored in the sound near the eastern shore, but the bay was still some distance off.

Far ahead and to the left the dark coastline was featureless, lightless, empty, and Morton began for the first time to feel a low grumble of anxiety stirring within. He was in the bow, staring out into the night. Presley sat in the stern, a shadowy form clinging to the gunwales, none too comfortable about setting off into the dark Channel in such a small boat.

Smooth, elongated clouds began to drift across the stars, and the risen moon, three-quarters full, cast a pale light over the ocean. Its glow also lit for a few moments a dim whiteness in the face of the headland, before it passed again behind a cloud, illuminating it from within.

"They's Ram Cliff Point, the cliffs there," Berman said quietly. "Statten's next. Bovisand Bay's beyond."

They altered course and worked their way parallel to

the invisible shore below the cliffs, surrounded entirely now by pitchy blackness. They looked constantly from larboard to starboard, on the one hand for signs of the beach, and on the other for any motion or sound coming from the direction of the *Bellerophon*, which had to be somewhere off in the obscurity to the west.

After some minutes, from that direction, they began to hear a steady, quiet splashing sound. Morton asked the others to put up their oars, and they all sat still, straining to hear. The sound continued low and steady, neither strengthening nor receding.

Finally Berman whispered, "Ah! That be the new breakwater."

Morton drew breath, and they set off again. Twenty minutes later Berman muttered that they should come about now and head in.

Then it went more quickly, as they surged along with the low swell, all of them keeping very quiet. Out of the dark they soon saw emerging a horizontal ribbon of pale grey, and began to hear the surf. A minute later their keel grated on the shore. Morton and Berman silently leapt into the shallows and pulled the boat briskly up into the shelter of black, weed-slick rocks.

For a moment the four men stood on the strand, listening. But they heard only the breeze whistling softly around them and the low, hollow crash of each new wave on the beach, the slow moan as it retreated. A wavering line of foam stretched off both ways into the dimness.

"You have no part in this," Morton said to Berman. "But I would be obliged if you would wait by the boat, which we might need to return."

Berman nodded quickly and turned back to his boat, coiling the painter with quick, smooth motions. Morton thought he had the man's measure. The smugglers along this coast could be dangerous folk and were not averse to violence or even murder when their interests were at stake—as some of the customs officers had discovered to their woe. But Berman didn't want to be party to a murder that failed to serve his own advantage. These Bow Street men had not pressed him on his role in these doings, and as long as they didn't threaten his freedom, he would stay quiet. And ferry any man left standing to the destination of his choice—for a price.

Morton turned to Westcott and Presley. "There should be only three men here for us to contend with: d'Auvraye, Rolles, and the third who accompanies them."

"But didn't Boulot say there are a dozen men out to fetch the Corsican? Three royalists against twelve, Morton."

"Three armed men who have the element of surprise. And we don't know how fanatical these three might be. They might not care if they are killed themselves." Morton could hardly make out the others' faces in the deep darkness, but Westcott was shifting from foot to foot.

"Morton," the navy man said, "if they somehow manage to get Bonaparte off the ship, I think stopping him from coming ashore will be paramount. These royalists, we can pick them up at our leisure—or they can escape. It hardly matters. But Bonaparte..."

Morton shook his head. "I am here to arrest men who are suspected in five murders. Bonaparte is nothing to me. I'm a Bow Street constable, and my duties are clear."

"But what of your duties as an Englishman?"

"If Bonaparte comes ashore, Captain, it will be a matter for my government to deal with."

"Well," Westcott said angrily, "our duties are not the same here."

"Then you must do yours, Captain Westcott."

With these cold words hanging in the air, the three men set out along the slippery stone beach.

Berman had promised that Bovisand beach was less than a mile to the north. After a few hundred yards Morton led the way up from the water and started to skirt the base of the bluffs, where rocks and projections of various sizes provided shadows and concealment. Their progress slowed as they peered cautiously ahead.

Several times black forms looked like men but turned out to be still, silent mounds of rock or the strange shapes of weathered wood cast up from the sea. Straining to look into the darkness, they moved forward with ever more hesitation. There was an unearthly silence and emptiness here, a world occupied with spectral forms, the uncanny shapes of imagination seeming to flit across the distant sands each time the lightening veils of cloud shifted briefly away from the face of the moon.

They were forced up a narrow path where the cliff met the sea, but the rise was small, and they were soon almost at the crest. Morton held them up with a gesture of his hand; he did not want the silhouettes of their figures to appear along the skyline, their motion detectable in the moonlight. Leaving the path, he scouted along the slope until he found a small depression that provided them a place to lie on their bellies and peer through the tufts of grass that grew raggedly along the ridge. Cautiously all three brought themselves into position, working their way just far enough forward on their elbows, and looked over. Below them, still and quiet, lay a dark curving beach, the pale line of surf just visible in the dim light.

For a long moment they all gazed.

"Bovisand Bay," Westcott said.

"But no one's home," Presley said.

But then halfway along the curve of the bay, a flame lifted up, wavered in the black, and began to spread outward. A shadow passed before the orange glow, and then another. The shapes of men, gathered near. Three men. And close.

The three watchers above studied the scene for another long minute, without speaking.

"Smugglers light signal fires for their friends out at sea," Westcott cautioned.

"I'd be very surprised if those weren't our men," Morton answered quietly. He drew himself back below the top, and the others followed suit. In a moment they were crouching together in the lee.

"How should we proceed, Morton?" Presley took out his pistol and nervously checked the priming. Morton and Westcott left their own weapons pocketed.

"It is dark, and their night vision will be spoiled by the firelight," said Morton. "If we stay near the base of the cliff and go quietly, we can surprise them from behind."

"We might be detected the moment we cross that ridge." Westcott gestured upward with a nod of his head.

"A risk we must take, I think."

"Let's at them," Jimmy Presley muttered.

The two Runners started upward again. Morton was looking for someplace where they could easily slip over the space of greatest visibility and conceal themselves again against the darkness of the far hillside. As they hesitated just below the ridge-top, Westcott's voice, calm but somehow changed, spoke from behind.

"Morton?" The familiar sound of a pistol being cocked came to their ears. "Hold where you are, both of you."

Neither Morton nor Presley moved nor turned around.

"I shall have your pistols, if you please," Westcott said calmly.

"You can only shoot one of us, Captain," Morton said. "But I doubt you are that much of a traitor."

"I'm not a traitor at all," Westcott said, a cold edge in his voice. "I will not see Bonaparte come ashore and make a mockery of England because of our own foolish laws! The man cannot be allowed to simply go free. Can you not see that? He will wait until the Bourbons have antagonized the people of France, and then he will cross the Channel one night, and it will all begin again. And you would allow that? Who is the traitor here?"

"You are, Westcott. And the Admiralty will hang you for it. Did you not hear what Boulot said of these royalists? They've killed five people. Eustache d'Auvraye allowed his own father to be murdered."

"Boulot is a drunkard and a liar."

"A drunkard, yes, but about these murders I believe he tells the truth." Morton went to step forward.

"Do not force me to fire, Morton!"

"No one is forcing you to do this, Captain. Let us see how deep your treachery runs." Morton began to move slowly up the slope in the darkness.

In the quiet night the cock struck the steel, sending out a little fountain of sparks. No shot fired.

Morton turned around to find a pistol aimed at his chest. "I had hoped you would not do that, Captain." He nodded to the pistol. "I emptied the pan and plugged the touch hole."

Westcott looked at the pistol in his hand as though it had betrayed him. Presley raised his own weapon to cover him.

"Boulot said that I led the royalists to him, but we went directly from the Golden Apple to the White Bear, to Boulot's refuge. How could I have led them to him? And then I remembered—you sent your driver off with a message for dinner companions. But it was to Eustache d'Auvraye this man went. While we were at Bow Street finding arms, d'Auvraye and Rolles went after Boulot, whom they'd been searching for anyway. I should have suspected you earlier when Lafond, thinking I was some other, asked which ship I would sail on, but I thought that was meant for Boulot. Now you will give me your word as a gentleman that you will stay quiet and not interfere in this matter, or I will truss you up and gag you."

Westcott drew himself up. "You will do no such thing."

"Indeed I will. Jimmy and I have dealt with stronger men than you, and our pistols are primed and loaded, unlike yours. And I've the feeling that Jimmy's in no gentle mood toward you either. Your word, Captain. I shall trust that it is still worth something, though your own service will doubt it after tonight."

A long silence in which, no doubt, Westcott had time to consider what these few moments meant to the remainder of his life. "You have my word," he muttered.

"Lay your pistol on that rock, then go back and wait with Berman."

Westcott stood a moment, staring at Morton. "When Bonaparte returns to France," the navy man said, "when the wars begin again and the nameless dead are heaped by the hundreds into pits, then you will know

which of us was the traitor, Morton. You are a little
man, with a small imagination. I had hoped for more
from you. Do your duty, Constable, and not one thing
more. It is all you're capable of." Westcott set his pistol
down, turned, and walked back into the darkness.

Morton retrieved the pistol, cleared the touch hole,
and reprimed the pan, then passed it to Presley to aug-
ment his own. If Westcott's words had touched him at
all, Presley could see no hint of it.

In the end, it was not so hard to slither crab-wise
across the top of the ridge. After a few awkward moments knocking knees against the stones on the far side,
they were able to resume their feet and find the path
again. As they began to pick their way down the rocky
slope, they kept their eyes fixed on the little cluster of
shapes by the fire on the beach below.

Morton whispered back to Presley as they went.
"Steel yourself, Jimmy. We are about to enter battle
against ruthless men."

"Then what shall we do? Shoot them from the darkness? They've not been convicted yet."

"No, we'll have to hail them, but they are standing in
the light, and we will be in the dark."

"They will flee."

"Yes, almost certainly they will. Be ready. If they dis-
charge pistols, we will fire to preserve our lives, but wait
until we are near. Don't go wasting our shot."

It hardly seemed a moment more before the two Runners had reached the level beach, their boots crunching
troublingly loud on its pebbles. Now they must act.

But just as they paused, the men by the fire stirred,
one rising from where he had been crouched. Then all
three began to step away from the fire toward the small

surf slapping the gravel shore. Two hundred feet out in the Channel a lantern flashed twice, then was covered or extinguished.

"Dem!" Morton cursed. He drew both his pistols and began to run.

Chapter 33

Morton and Presley sprinted forward, beach stones sliding and grinding beneath their feet. The fire blazed up a little, and the light of its flames revealed the men standing on the water's edge, looking out, so far oblivious to the two Bow Street men. On the dark sound small white crests rolled and tumbled onto the shore, rattling the small stones. A dark shape rocked over the waves, not so far out.

"There, Morton! Do you see?" gasped Presley as they ran.

"I do. Save your breath, Jimmy."

It could only be the supporters of Bonaparte and with them perhaps the fallen emperor himself. Morton tried to make his legs pump faster. Only a few moments more, unless they intervened, and the situation would slip beyond all control. Beside him Presley slipped and stumbled, falling in a spray of smooth, slick stones. Morton drove on, hearing his young companion scramble up to follow.

The shorebound boat could be seen clearly now, black

hulled and bobbing among the small crests. Sweeps dipped and pulled in unison, lifting up into the air, then dipping again. Clearly the men in the boat suspected nothing amiss. Morton almost cried out to warn them, but over the waves and wind and distance he was sure they would not hear, and even if they did, they would not heed his warning.

The boat was barely thirty feet out, the oars backing now, controlling the craft as it slid toward the shore. He could see the men in her now: four at the oars, a man at the tiller, and in the bow a small man in a greatcoat, his collar up against the night.

Morton pushed himself harder, realising he would not reach them before the two parties converged. All he could hear was his own ragged breathing and the sound of his feet, hardly anything more.

A few yards out in the rising waves the boat ran aground, and as two of the oarsmen jumped out into the surf, the men from the shore waded out to meet them. One started to raise his arm.

Stumbling to a halt, Morton tried to call out, but his "Bow Street!" emerged more as a gasp than as a bellow. He raised a pistol and fired into the air, fearing at this distance that he would hit some other, perhaps Napoleon himself.

But he was ignored, or not even heard. The man from the beach levelled his pistol. A spurt of fire, the sound of a shot echoing off the cliff and out over the waves. The man seated in the bow tumbled back, the horrified faces of the oarsmen caught in the firelight.

"Dem!" panted Morton. Raising his other gun, he risked firing at them. But the distance was still too great, and his ball hissed wide. The closest man looked now toward Morton. Then he and his companions wheeled and ran, without glancing back, disappearing into the dark.

"Bow Street!" Morton bawled more audibly now, and Presley, coming up behind, added his great bellow.

But there was nothing to be done here. Whatever harm the attackers had inflicted could no longer be helped, and Morton's fury was up. He and Presley raced past the men milling about the boat, through the small island of flickering light, and then into near-total darkness. Morton cursed himself for glancing at the fire, which danced before his eyes now wherever he looked.

But then, from not far ahead, a pistol fired. Morton heard the ball cut through the air between them. Even without looking back, he realised the fire burned bright behind them. He reached out and pushed Presley toward the cliff.

"They can see us against the flame!" he shouted. "Into the shadows!"

Up against the cliff they found soft sand, which slowed them, their chests heaving. Ahead Morton could see cliffs lifting up and along their base a white fringe of waves. They looked anxiously about, searching, their eyes moment by moment adjusting.

"There, Morton! Do you see? Someone moving."

And Morton saw. A flickering shadow, skittering along the base of the cliff wall to their left. He instantly crouched, and Presley imitated him.

"Good man," Morton said, his breath coming easier now. "We'll have the bloody villains yet. But now we can go more cautiously. They'll not be able to climb up here. It appears too perilous."

Morton loaded his discharged pistols, and they crept forward. Along the cliff base the water swept in around their knees, the motion of it disorienting in the faint light. Shadows were everywhere. Rocks stood up from the surf, tall as men. Morton found his footing carefully. A fall here would drown his pistols, and then they would be helpless. They were already outnumbered three to two.

A muzzle-flash flared ten yards ahead, and a ball cracked against the cliff by Presley's knee. The young Runner raised a pistol and fired back—at what Morton wasn't sure. But perhaps it would keep their enemies from growing too brave.

Presley hurriedly reloaded while Morton peered hard into the obscurity. But then, to his amazement, he heard a small sound from *above*. Raising his eyes, he thought he saw some dark movement on the cliff ahead, not twenty feet up. So they were trying to climb after all. Be it on their own heads. He raised his pistol and fired. Someone scrabbled, arms flailing, and then half-slid, half-plummeted down the cliff face, landing with a splash at the bottom.

Silence. Morton wanted to reload, then decided against it. The Runners crept forward until suddenly another flash from above sent them reeling back against the cliff. So at least two of them had gone up there. A few feet away, in the sea-washed rocks, Morton could see the fallen man begin to move weakly. A wave raced in and rolled him hard against the cliff base, flinging his helpless body back and forth. Keeping close to the stone, Morton tucked his pistols into his belt and waded forward, the water splashing up and soaking him. He could hear the man choking now. Choking and trying to lift himself up out of the surging water.

As the sea retreated, Morton reached out quickly with one hand and caught hold of the man's jacket lest the Channel claim him. As he did, the man gasped and convulsively reached up to seize Morton's arm. But then there was the report of a pistol, a sharp snap half-carried away by the wind, and the struggling man went rigid. His fingers slipped from Morton's sleeve. After a moment Morton released his grip, knowing the feel of death, and the body slipped into the sea.

Another shot, but this time from behind. Presley came up beside him, tugging Morton back into the safety of the cliff. The dead man rolled limply against their legs as the sea surged in, then he was dragged out to sea, limp as kelp. In a moment gone.

Presley leaned close to his ear, as Morton pulled out his pistols again and they both bent to reload. "I think I hit the cully above. He's not moved since—neither up nor down. I thought he'd shot you."

"Nay; hit the man I was trying to rescue."

"Who was he?"

"Never saw him before," Morton said as he fished his powder flask out of the inner pocket of his coat. "I want to go on. I thought I saw something moving up ahead. Will you stay here and watch the man above? Try to convince him to climb down. Tell him you will shoot him if he tries to climb up."

Presley nodded, and Morton finished loading his pistols, the pan cover clicking into place. He prayed he could keep his powder dry. Starting out along the cliff face, he realised the seas were rising, and he had no notion of what the tide might be. It might rise some way yet, catching him here. He could likely swim to safety, but Presley, a born Londoner, couldn't manage a stroke.

Morton was still angry, and he was not about to let his prey go free. He went forward, wary but hurrying. The moon emerged from behind a cloud, its cold light washing over the sea and cliff. He kept himself low, pistols in hand. Every few beats the cold sea would wash in around his legs, then drag at him as it retreated. The water grew deeper as he went, the cliff curving out into the Channel. Above he could see shadows on the cliff face, long dark streaks that were fissures in the ancient stone.

Morton began to think that he had been wrong—all three must have gone up the escarpment—when he saw something move ahead. A pistol flashed, and Morton fired once in return.

The water was to his waist now, and when the waves came in, he was thrown about, holding his pistols high, praying that he could keep them dry.

A rocky headland jutted out raggedly, and beyond he found a tiny bay, perhaps twenty yards across but cut back into the cliff for some unknown distance. With the sea washing around his legs, Morton tried to load his discharged weapon, fumbling powder into the water, certain that the seawater splashed down the barrel. He rammed the wadding home, took a few long slow breaths, and went forward.

As a wave washed out, Morton reached a jutting edge, behind which he crouched to look around the corner. He could see no one and dodged out, finding some shelter behind another small projection of stone a few feet farther along. Exposing as little of himself as possible, he leaned out and examined the small bay at which he had arrived. Here the pebbled strand was above the water. Shadows were everywhere, pale stone faint in the moonlight. The cliffs, however, looked too steep to be climbed. If his royalist quarry had come in here, he was well hidden.

Morton stepped out from his hiding place into terrible darkness. He'd not gone three paces when he re-

alised he faced a man with a pistol levelled at his heart.
Eustache d'Auvraye. The young aristocrat was leaning
against the stone, his slight figure tucked into a hidden
niche in what had appeared to be smooth wall, a perfect
natural ambush. He stooped a little, his other hand
clutched to his abdomen. Morton observed that the
young Frenchman looked somehow amiss in his plain
English clothing, whose dark hues had helped conceal
him in the shadows of his hiding place.

"I think you have enough blood on your hands,
Count," Morton said evenly. But he was horribly con-
scious of the racing of his heart, the sickening prospect
of that small black hole barely an arm's length away.
And his own weapon useless by his side.

"And most of it is mine." Eustache took the hand
from his abdomen and revealed a wound. "You shot me,
you filth!"

"You are a murderer, several times over—"

"I am a servant to my king!" the young man hissed.

Morton could just make out his face now, the dark
deep-set eyes. The bitter mouth. His face unnaturally
pale and haunted.

"I am a servant," he repeated softly, and sagged
against the stone. "Bonaparte had to die. It does not
matter what happens to me. Bonaparte had to die." A
fleeting look of triumph passed over his face, then a
spasm of agony convulsed him.

"And what about all the others? Did it not matter
what happened to them, either?"

"It is a war, monsieur. In wars people die." The young
man's arm wavered, as though he weakened. The pistol
wandered in a slow circle, the black eye within the muzzle ring searching for Morton's heart.

"People do die in wars, but not many kill their own father, or have him killed."

D'Auvraye blinked several times, shaking his head. "It is a tradition of war that fathers sacrifice their sons," he said quietly, as though he were instructing an idiot. "I sacrificed my father. But not without cause. Not without reason. No, monsieur, I hoped to kill the father of us all. The father of this terrible age, this time of revolt, and Madame Guillotine, of blood, and the loss of all that was once good and glorious." He looked down at the blood running between his fingers. "This age of horrors—that is what sired me, monsieur. Kill my father? It is a pity someone did not kill him before I was born. Now I die in any case—the true son of this glorious age. I go to whatever darkness will have such a child, but I will take my murderer with me." He steadied his pistol with effort and pulled the trigger.

There was a sharp *tick* as flint struck steel; a feeble white spark flared and fell. But the gun did not go off. Eustache d'Auvraye's arm drooped, and the muzzle swayed away from its target, as if the effort to hold it up were beyond his power. An instant later the pistol fired. Pebbles scattered about Morton's boots, and they were encircled in a cloud of smoke, which then rolled off on the breeze. As it cleared, Morton saw the young count sliding down the stone, the weapon dropping from his fingers, clattering onto the gravel.

The gun had hung fire. Had d'Auvraye been able to hold it up a moment longer, Morton would be dead.

D'Auvraye crumpled onto the wet beach, limp, unseeing, gone into the darkness.

Rolles, too, was gone—wedged into the crevice he had been climbing—slain by Jimmy Presley's first shot. The young Runner climbed up into the dark and pulled the little secretary free, letting him tumble into the water below. The Runners dragged the bodies of the two Frenchmen round the small headland back to Bovisand Bay, where they laid them out above the high-tide line.

Along the beach the fire still burned, and Morton could see figures moving there.

"Shall we load our pistols, Morton?" Presley asked as they set off toward the firelight.

"I don't think we'll need them now, but perhaps prudence dictates we should take no chances. Here, take one of mine." Morton handed the young Runner a pistol. "I won't promise that it will fire, but just waving it in the air might be enough. I think the murderers are all dead."

But when they reached the fire, the boat was gone, and they found only Berman, feeding wood onto the blaze, and nearby a small man wrapped in a blanket.

"Ah, 'Enri," that man said. "I thought it would be you."

"Marcel?" Morton would have been less surprised to find Bonaparte himself. It was Houde, the chef from Boodle's.

"*Oui, c'est moi.* It is I, your old friend."

Morton stood looking down at the chef, who seemed very small there in the flickering light. "Where is Bonaparte? And where has everyone gone?"

Houde was cradling an arm, Morton realised.

"Bonaparte?" the little chef said. He shook his head sadly and hunched over his injury. "Gone. Taken out to sea this very night by the Navy Royale. Who knows what they have done with 'im. Transported 'im, perhaps, as they said they would."

"Then..." And then Morton realised: "That was you in the boat!"

"Yes, it was Houde, unluckily. That royalist fool shot me before I could point out the small differences between myself and Napoleon Bonaparte."

"Are you badly wounded?"

"My arm. Not so bad, I think. His hand was shaking with excitement, and 'e missed *mon cœur*. Not by much. *Le bon Dieu* like 'is little joke and keep me alive."

Morton whistled softly as he bent to look. Houde was right. He too had been fortunate, and Morton remembered well the deliberate shot, before the three had fled.

"Now at least I have a wound from the wars. Not many chefs can say that. What of those royalists?"

"All dead, I'm afraid."

Houde shrugged, a splendidly expressive Gallic gesture, despite his hurt. "*Tant pis*. But no great loss. Royalist scum. Who were they?"

"Count Eustache d'Auvraye. His secretary, Rolles. A third man I did not know."

"And how did you find us?"

"Boulot."

"Ah, but how did the royalists find us?"

"Boulot."

"How helpful he has been to everyone."

Morton sat down on the gravel, letting the fire warm his sodden legs. All at once he was deeply weary. "Where is Westcott?" he asked.

"Went off in my boat," Berman said.

"You let him take your boat?"

"He told me to come over here and be what help I could. He'd be back with marines."

Presley laughed. "Marines! 'Tis Westcott they'll be chasing."

"And who was this?" Houde asked.

"A navy captain who fell under the influence of Lafond. A disappointed man, passed over too many times. So he thought he saw a chance for glory. Glory to spite the service, who would condemn him for it. Maybe hang him, even. But glory all the same. One of the men who killed Napoleon and saved England."

"Ah, but they only managed to wound a French chef-cook named Marcel Houde. How glorious was that, 'Enri?" Houde opened up his blanket and looked at his arm.

Morton knelt to examine it in the firelight. Houde's soft white skin was puckered and red where the ball had cut a trough in the outer arm below the shoulder muscles. Not serious unless it became septic.

"How could a man like Westcott ally himself with such a pack of murderers?" Presley wondered. "Or did he not believe Eustache and Rolles had dished up Madame Desmarches and the others?"

Morton sat back on his heels and shrugged. "He did not want to believe. After all, it looked very much like they had been killed by the supporters of Bonaparte." He glanced up at the sky. "It will be light in two hours." He turned to Berman. "Is it far back to Plymouth-town?"

"A goodly stroll."

Morton turned back to Houde. "Are you up to it, Marcel?"

"Ah, *oui*. A little discomfort, it is the least price to pay for folly like mine."

Morton frowned. But Houde had brought it up. "I

must say I am sorry to see you here, Marcel. I thought you had given up politics."

"I had, but politics 'ave not given up me, *évidemment*."

"Breaking the peace of the land that harbours you. Trying to bring their bitterest enemy into that land. Not to mention betraying the trust of your friend. To what end, Marcel? More *crimes in the name of liberty*?"

Houde scowled and looked down, unhappy. "I am sorry for these things. Especially I am sorry to deceive you, not to tell you more, when you were in *ma cuisine*. But you cannot know what it was, 'Enri, to be *un français,* when 'e led us to glory. You can never know. Such 'opes, such dreams as ours. *Oui,* in the end, there was no liberty. *Oui,* 'e was a tyrant. But I joost could not see such a man as 'im murdered by those *canaille,* those vile scum. That is why I help. Let 'im die in exile, but save 'im from the revenge of those arrogant *poseurs* who should, each night, lick clean 'is boots!"

"I see there is much to tell. Where should we begin, I wonder?"

"Every story begin the same way," Houde said. "A man or a woman is born. It is 'ow they travel through life after that make the story. How they get to this beach 'ere in England one night when they are almost old, but still young enough to make the fool."

"And you, Marcel, where were you born?"

"In Chartres. 'Ave you been there?"

"No, but I understand there is a great cathedral in that city."

Houde blew air through his lips. "The cathedral is nothing. You must taste my father's *pâtisseries*!"

Chapter 34

It was indeed a "goodly stroll" to town. They found a farmer with a cart who bore the bodies. Marcel Houde rode, too, though he continued to be ready to do penance by walking the whole way. Berman, having put them on the road, slipped away, no doubt to make his way back eastward along the coast to the smuggling dens. Morton and Presley were left to ride shank's mare. He was not sure if it was the excitement of the night, but Morton felt oddly light-headed as they trudged into Plymouth. It was as though the events of the night had not been real. As though he had wakened from a strange dream and found himself far from the bed in which he had fallen asleep.

Perhaps having a pistol hang fire when aimed at his heart could be expected to leave a man in such a state. Perhaps that was all it was. He didn't know.

He did know that the morning seemed especially fine, the sky a vivid blue, clouds chalked across the azure in thin wavering lines. The grass was living green, and the hills looked like the most perfect land on earth. No doubt this euphoria would pass in a few days.

The farmer took them to the local magistrate's, where to Morton's surprise, they found Arabella and Lord Arthur Darley.

"What are you doing here?" Morton asked.

It was agreed they should repair to a hotel to discuss it—as soon as Morton had told all that had happened to the magistrate and written a letter to Sir Nathaniel Conant in London.

Some hours later Henry Morton found Arabella and Darley seated at a table in a private dining room in the Royal Hotel on George Street. It was, of course, supposed to be Plymouth's finest: Darley had chosen. Their window gave them a fine view out over the sound.

"You look positively..." Arabella did not finish, but Morton could tell by the look of concern that his present appearance was not what he might hope. He'd not seen a mirror—or for that matter a razor or a clothes brush—for quite some time.

Morton dropped into a chair and gazed at his two friends. Well, he was properly tired now. Darley and Arabella looked like man and wife sitting there. A handsome, pleasant-looking aristocrat and his beautiful, much younger bride. Arabella could play this part to perfection when she chose to. There with the white linen and delicate bone china, the gleaming, monogrammed silver.

"What brings you to Plymouth?" Morton repeated, as soon as he had sent an offended waiter off to bring him bangers and mash—hardly a specialty of the Royal's renowned kitchens.

Arabella still looked at him as though he'd been discovered in a hospital, badly injured. She reached out and squeezed his hand for a moment. "I had the most extraordinary visit—when? Three nights past? A young woman called on me at the theatre after our performance. She claimed to be Honoria d'Auvraye. In her possession was a letter that she wanted me to deliver to a certain Mr. Henry Morton—why she thought I would have amongst my acquaintances someone so vulgar as a Bow Street Runner, I don't understand. She said a man had brought the letter to her father a few nights before his death and that the letter had caused a great deal of distress in her household. I took the liberty of reading this missive."

Darley produced a folded sheet of paper from a pocket and handed it across the table to Morton, who skimmed it quickly. "It is from Fouché," he said, feeling rather obtuse. "What does this mean? 'Final arrangements have been made for the little general. But he must be sent away to some remote place with his suite of followers'?"

Darley made an odd shrugging motion. "I think it means that Fouché has found some way to have Bonaparte murdered."

"Assassiner!"

Darley and Arabella looked at him oddly.

"That is what the men I overheard from outside Boulot's door said: 'they will assassinate him.' I thought they were talking about their own confederates planning a murder, and later I thought it was the count they murdered, but I was wrong. They were talking about this." He struck the letter with the backs of his fingers. "Boulot had this letter somehow."

"It is not difficult to guess how," Arabella said. "It is a copy made, I am certain, by Madame Angelique Desmarches. She passed it to her friends the De le Coeurs, who either gave it to Boulot or to others who gave it to Boulot."

"The latter, I think," said Morton. He stared down at the letter, at the elegant hand. "So this is what set it all in motion. This and Boulot's betrayal. He told Gerrard d'Auvraye about this—gave him the letter apparently—and the count cast off his mistress. Boulot must also have told the count that the supporters of Bonaparte in England planned to rescue their hero: this was the coin he would trade for his return to France. The son, Eustache, and Rolles were followers of this man Lafond, or admirers of him. They tortured Madame Desmarches to find out who was planning this rescue of Bonaparte and where they could find them." He looked up at his companions. "But do you know what Boulot told me? That Madame Desmarches leapt to her death rather than betray her compatriots." Morton glanced at the letter again, then set it carefully on the brilliantly white tablecloth. His tired mind was racing, connecting up the chain of events. "They were then in trouble. The old count wrote me from his house in Barnes to come visit him, for he had decided, no doubt, to tell me that Madame Desmarches was a spy for the Corsican, as deeply embarrassing as this admission would be. Rolles knew the contents of the count's letter and perhaps his master's intentions as well. Once I learned about it, I would want to know why Rolles had given me a list of Bonapartists as the probable murderers of Madame Desmarches, when he knew perfectly well that she was a Bonapartist herself. The count had to be stopped then. And so it went. The count's servant had to be killed because he recognised Rolles or whoever it was that accompanied Pierre to murder the count."

Morton's meal arrived, and he took a moment to fortify himself, apologising to his companions.

When he had done, Morton pushed away his plate and stared out over the harbour, filled with warships returning now from their duties blockading the coasts of France. Small boats plied among the great ships, like skimmers on a pond. The fishing boats wandered out into the Channel on this bright day, returning to the immemorial rituals of their peaceful trade, now that Bonaparte was gone.

"What will we do with this letter?" Morton said.

"I sent a copy to certain members of the government," Darley answered. "I don't know what they shall do. Perhaps try to find out who amongst Bonaparte's followers might be inclined to murder his master." Lord Arthur reached down for his teacup. "Perhaps they will do nothing."

Morton told the rest of the story, the chase out to Plymouth, the encounter in Bovisand Bay. The pistol that hung fire.

"What became of Westcott?" Darley asked.

Morton shrugged. "He's not been seen. Nor can anyone find Berman's boat. Admiral Lord Keith thinks he set out across the Channel, which he assured me could be done given the weather and Westcott's abilities. He can pass for a Frenchman, so perhaps he will find a place to hide there."

"Oh, he'll be found out eventually."

"A nobleman who came to the aid of those trying to kill Bonaparte?" Morton mused. "I rather doubt King Louis's police will be much interested in flushing him out. And we mustn't forget Lafond and the other royalists. Westcott knew them well. He was the liaison with these men for many years. They will protect him if they can." Morton closed his eyes for a moment, the dancing glitter of sun on water still visible. "Even Boulot is gone, it seems. The smugglers have whisked him away. Perhaps back to France at last. I hope Fouché does not find him. But then, perhaps he will not care. Who is Boulot, after all? A drunkard. A man whose wretched loneliness led him to . . . these insignificantly small acts of betrayal, that brought about the deaths of eight people."

As the little party lapsed into thoughtful silence, sipping their coffee, Morton's eye wandered again to the window, the sound, the blue Channel beyond. A ship of the line loosed her sails as he watched, the wind filling them. The great dark ship gathered way and shaped her course for the southwest. It passed across the glittering path of the reflected sun, like a shadow, and was off, in few minutes rounding the headland, heading for the open sea.

Chapter 35

Morton brought two members of the Foot Patrole as well as Vickery. He left them all before the house, standing by the hackney-coach, its door yawning open. A servant answered, pretended not to know Morton, and went looking for the master of the house. In the vestibule the Runner waited impatiently, leaving the door conspicuously agape.

It was some moments before the young master of the house appeared, blurry eyed and yawning but discomfited all the same.

"Mr. Wilfred Stokes?" Morton demanded.

"Yes.... Am I correctly informed?" he said as he reached the foot of the stair. "You are from Bow Street?"

"That is correct, sir. Henry Morton." He held up a folded sheet of paper. "And I have here a writ to allow the search of your domicile and the seizure of stolen property."

The man, all six foot five of him, stared at Morton in mute surprise. "What in the world—!" But the sentence

was lost in outrage and fear. He was not, the Runner realised, a man of dazzling intellect.

Morton stepped aside to afford the young man a view
of the Patrole men and the waiting coach. "I shall call
my fellows in to roust your home...." Morton let the
pause linger. "Or you can return the painting I seek: a
seascape by Claude-Joseph Vernet. You know of what I
speak."

"I have no knowledge of such a—"

Morton waved to the men standing by the coach, who
all started forward.

"Wait! Wait!" the young man said. "A Vernet, you
say? Perhaps I do know of such a painting. I purchased
it recently."

"I'm well aware of the circumstances under which
you acquired it," Morton said. "If I can't convince a
magistrate that you conspired with Lord Robert
Richardson to steal it, then I'm sure I can convince him
that you knowingly received stolen goods in return for
paying Lord Robert's gambling debt at White's. Theft
of goods valued at excess of forty pounds is a hanging offence. I will have the painting this instant, or I shall
have both you and the painting. The choice is yours."

Stokes hardly considered this a moment before motioning to his servant, who followed him up the stairs.

"There are," Morton called up the stairs, "a number
of my associates watching the back of this house. Do not
even consider sneaking the painting out that way."

Stokes paused on the stair, half-turned toward
Morton, and then continued his ascent. A few moments
later Stokes and his servant reappeared, carrying between them the painting in its heavy gilt frame. Morton
waved to the Patroles, who came and took the painting
toward the waiting coach.

"What more will you have of me?" the young man asked disdainfully.

"Nothing more," Morton said with a slight bow of his head. He turned and stepped back out into the sunlight.

"What will you do with the painting?" the young man called from behind.

"Return it to its owner," Morton replied, not looking round.

But the young man had not done. "When you appeared at my door, you deceived me, for you dress like a gentleman. But you're nothing but a bloody horney."

"And despite all appearances, you're nothing but a thief." Morton mounted the steps to the carriage, its springs rocking and squeaking as he did. He took a seat and gazed out. The young nobleman still stood in the doorway, staring after him as though trying to think of a final line, but failing utterly.

Lincoln's Inn Fields was quiet, respectable. A family strolled beneath the trees in the park. Two elderly gentlemen sat upon a bench, saying nothing, staring contentedly to the south.

Morton sent his calling card in with a servant and waited. A few moments later Caroline Richardson appeared, hanging back slightly from the door. Morton had the driver help him with the painting, which they set down inside the entry.

Caroline gazed for a moment at the canvas, then turned to Morton, a smile of pleasure and relief on her face.

"How in the world did you find it?"

"Ah, secrets of my trade can't be revealed to the lay public."

She laughed. She wore a day dress of printed muslin in the fashionable Turkish red, a gauzy chemisette filling in the low neckline. Morton thought that today she did not bear such a resemblance to him, but she was a lovely young woman, dark-eyed and gracious of manner. A keen and curious intelligence shone from those eyes, and she missed very little. Morton found himself feeling suddenly awkward, as though not sure what was expected of him.

"And what is the price of such a miracle?" Caroline asked.

"One cannot put a price on a miracle," Morton answered. "It is my pleasure to have been of service."

"But did you not have to pay the rogue who took it?"

"I offered him a stay of execution in return for the painting. He thought it a rather good bargain."

"Well, Mr. Morton, I thank you." She curtsied.

Morton made his good-byes and turned to go.

"Mr. Morton?" she said as he stepped over the threshold.

He turned back. For a moment their eyes met—like staring into a mirror, Morton thought, though not quite.

"Paintings do not get stolen here often enough. I should hate to think we'd have to wait for such an occasion to meet again."

"And how would we meet?" Morton wondered. "We both of us detest Almack's." It was a jest: Morton would never have been allowed through the doors of Almack's.

"Perhaps I might have myself invited to Darley's. I understand the company is varied, and the conversation among the best in London."

Morton found himself oddly affected by this remark, and when he spoke, his voice was somewhat strained.

"I'm sure Lord Arthur would be delighted to have your company." Morton bowed again.

He was about to turn to go when she spoke again. "We shall be . . . *friends,* Mr. Morton. Mark my words. I am seldom wrong."

Morton could not help it. He smiled. He doffed his hat to her once more and set out onto the street. Something caused him to look back. In a high window he could see the slouched shape of his half-brother, Robert. The young man stared down at Morton for a moment, his face almost entirely obscured by reflections on the glass. Then he turned away and disappeared into the depths of the house.

"Robbie" would bear watching, Morton thought, and set off down the quiet street toward the teeming, vital thoroughfares of London.

About the Author

T. F. Banks is the pseudonym for Sean Russell and Ian Dennis, two Canadian writers who collaborate on the *Memoirs of a Bow Street Runner* series. Their previous Henry Morton novel was *The Thief-Taker,* also published by Bantam Dell.